I0891557

I LEFT YOU BEHIND

stories

NAZNEEN SHEIKH

MAWENZI HOUSE

Copyright ©2024 Nazneen Sheikh

Except for purposes of review, no part of this book may be reproduced in any form without prior permission of the publisher.

We acknowledge the support of the Canada Council for the Arts for our publishing program. We also acknowledge support from the Government of Ontario through the Ontario Arts Council, and the support of the Government of Canada through the Canada Book Fund.

ONTARIO ARTS COUNCIL
CONSEIL DES ARTS DE L'ONTARIO
an Ontario government agency
un organisme du gouvernement de l'Ontario

Canada Council for the Arts Conseil des arts du Canada

Canada

Cover design by Jonathan Heffelfinger and Sabrina Pignataro

Library and Archives Canada Cataloguing in Publication

Title: I left you behind : stories / Nazneen Sheikh.

Names: Sheikh, Nazneen, 1944- author

Identifiers: Canadiana (print) 20240448812 | Canadiana (ebook) 20240448820 | ISBN 9781774151808 (softcover) | ISBN 9781774151815 (EPUB) | ISBN 9781774151822 (PDF)

Subjects: LCGFT: Short stories.

Classification: LCC PS8587.H379 I25 2024 | DDC C813/.54—dc23

Printed and bound in Canada by Coach House Printing

Mawenzi House Publishers Ltd.
39 Woburn Avenue (B)
Toronto, Ontario M5M 1K5
Canada

www.mawenzihouse.com

For my Grandson Ciaran and Granddaughter Lotus,
so they can solve mysteries

"You gather things to you like an old road. You are peopled with echoes and nostalgic voices. I awoke and at times birds fled and migrated that had been sleeping in your soul."

PABLO NERUDA

Twenty Love Poems and a Song of Despair

CONTENTS

The Girl on the Rock

Rose Villa, Pindi Point, Murree, 1949

She sits on the large boulder at the head of the gravel driveway. The boulder has a mystery: it could have come from the set of a Tarzan film. Her brother had shown her a book where a near-naked man swings from tree to tree to jump off a boulder and land in a blue river. She is captivated by the notion of living in jungles wearing very few clothes, surrounded by trees and splendid animals. She often rebels against how her mother dresses, which depends on the season and an unbreakable formality. The surface of the boulder where she sits is a flat, wide circle. Sometimes she lies on it gazing at the blue sky and feels as though the clouds are the shapes of Tarzan's animals. Her mother permits her this indulgence once every two weeks, knowing that she will not leave her perch until the person she waits for appears.

She is five years old and wears a cotton dress, ankle socks, and sturdy leather shoes. Underneath this dress are a pair of soft cotton knickers and a muslin camisole. Her head is capped by glossy auburn hair with a line of bangs trimmed by her mother. The face is high cheek-boned with a small nose and eyes which are soft brown, the iris ringed in blue. The ring of blue signals rebellion that will mark her all her life. At five she displays a resolute air. She goes to school and is a precocious reader.

Her bare legs press lightly into the rough surface of the rock and she shifts them often. Around her is the dance of daisies on the long grass. Tall pine trees of varying lengths ring the property, some of them standing on the green slope that heading towards a cloaked ravine. With a child's fear, she worries about them, with the thought that they could crash down, but this never happens. The mountain air is cool and pure. The mountains in the distance are watchful sentinels, though sometimes they hide their peaks in the clouds. The house behind her is long, with shuttered windows and verandas. Outside the windows are the flower beds. Crimson roses grow here, guarded by sharp thorns. They are like a fairy tale gone wrong. She is always drawn to them but learns that this has to be love from a distance. Their scent is sweet and heady and beckoning, but any attempt to pluck one will result in bloody fingers. It is her first introduction to beauty's double-edged sword.

Her brother, who is a year older, often climbs on the rock after her and a small game of pushing begins. The centre of the circular top is the command post and he challenges her half-heartedly, surprised at the fury with which she defends it. He laughs, slides down, and taunts her that she is waiting on the wrong day. She never believes him and keeps her eyes on the driveway. He often redeems himself by bringing her a slice of buttered bread spread with plum jam. The little offering is crushed and misshapen as he has carried it in his pocket for some time. She takes it from his fingers and flashes him a perfect smile of gratitude. He grins and saunters off. This smile between them will last forever.

The first sound comes from a distance. Closer, it is unmistakable—pebbles and small stones spitting under the tires of the jeep. Her heart pounds and the palms of her small hands begin to sweat. Over the crest of the winding road, the top of the jeep appears. The driver is wearing a beret which reveals his dark wavy hair fanning the collar of his jacket. He blows the horn merrily. She rises from the rock and waves at him frantically. He drives right up to the rock and parks. His perfect smile mirrors hers as he pulls out a small shiny brown leather attaché case and kneeling, puts it on the ground next to him. He does not rise but holds out his arms and calls her name.

She slides down the rock oblivious to the scratching on the backs of her thighs. Like a torpedo, she flings herself forward into the circle of his arms. He throws his head back, laughs as he holds her, crooning her name. His grip is strong but the kisses raining on her forehead and cheeks are light as feather. Even the voices behind them, of the others, cannot dislodge the moment.

"Look, look," he says freeing both hands now to open the attaché case.

She watches how he snaps open both metal clasps together with a click. He leans back and lifts the lid backward, like a magician with a trick. His eyes pin her gaze and his lips are already parted to respond to her reaction. She looks down and loses her breath. She blinks once, thinking when she reopens her eyes the contents of the case will disappear.

They don't.

She sees a riot of imported chocolates in the case. Rows of Smarties, Mars bars, Cadbury fruit-and-nut bars. He has found every chocolate bar in Rawalpindi and crammed it into the case.

He lifts a small brown paper bag and shakes it open in the palm of her hand. The multi-coloured cascade of chocolate-dipped pellets drop like gems from a treasure chest for her.

"What is your favourite colour?" he asks.

"Purple," she says.

"Mine also." He finds two purple smarties and pops one into her mouth and the other into his.

She bites down hard, and her mouth is flooded with chocolate. He laughs again, a low soft chuckle. It is their moment. It is cement more powerful than life itself that fuses them. This is the birth of her.

Her lifelong passion for chocolate, and with it the association of love that flows between them.

"Chocolate is your father," says the brilliant psychiatrist she marries later in her life.

"No, the universe is my father, everything that I love is him," she would protest and finally dissolve into laughter herself.

"Do you want to carry it," her father closes the lid and holds out the case. "Yes," she puts her fingers around the handle and realizes it is heavy.

He laughs and hoists her up in one arm, holds the case in the other, and marches towards the house where her mother stands on the front veranda. He drops the case on the wooden floor of the veranda when he reaches her mother. He lowers her gently down and removes his beret and places it on her head. She feels the warmth he has left behind in the rim of the beret and looks up at her mother for approval.

Her mother stands there leaning forward to receive her father's embrace. Her garments are silken and traditional. The long chiffon dupatta draped around her neck and shoulders is the colour of cherries and above it rises a beautiful face. Her mother's beauty is quite unbearable, as everything is perfect. The features are aquiline and the complexion is fair and the natural blush rising on her cheeks is due to the mountain air and not a cosmetic. The fine hair is gathered in a chignon and smudged lipstick outlines her perfect lips. Her eyes are hazel and always soft. She stays for only a few seconds in the circle of her father's arms and then looks down at the little girl and raises both eyebrows comically at the beret on her head.

"The chocolates are to be shared and eaten after dinner. But you get to choose yourself," she kneels and lifts the attaché case.

When her mother catches her father's wink aimed only at the girl, she intercepts it. "You are spoiling her." A small line appears between her mother's two eyebrows.

The little girl is familiar with this line, which sometimes also appears around her mother's lips when she purses them. Like the thorns on the roses, lines on faces spell hazard. In soft even tones, her mother can announce a draconian consequence of misbehaviour. Her brother is the resident naughty child and his fearless penchant for following his dictates and not their mother's wins the girl's secret admiration. Her elder sister is the model child. She is docile and obedient and generally ignores her younger siblings.

When her father returns from his out-of-town duties both parents retire to their room for a while. It is a large room with two beds joined together. Two night tables with single pullout drawers flank the beds. The lamps have camel-skin shades that glow with a mellow yellowing light. There are also huge armoires which hold their clothes. Each armoire also has a secret drawer; and her mother places something in hers. She has never seen that something and often wonders about it. In the summer her mother places metal water jugs filled with daisies on the window ledge of this room. The girl likes to twirl around on the rough carpet in this room, thrilled by the flowers at the window. She is in awe of her mother's ability to change the universe with one jug of flowers.

The discussion between the adults on this day is about the Rock. The little girl has no inkling about this. It happens at the dinner table. This is also where the little girl finds out who her father is.

The dining room at Rose Villa is large, with a beamed ceiling. The dining table is of shiny wood and always covered with a tablecloth embroidered with flowers and curling vines. The platters of food are passed around. The children are expected to serve themselves without spilling. Their mother watches them while their father serves himself enthusiastically. As he chews the food he beams repeatedly at their mother. Although she has a helper in the kitchen, she herself is a very good cook. She habitually includes their favourite dishes but everything is expected to be eaten. The little girl does not like meat and hides it under other food on her plate. The mother knows and all she says is, "You have to have one piece as you must taste everything on the table. It is good manners."

The little girl feels the power of this exalted creature, her mother, and swallows a scrap of chicken. She desires this invisible commodity called "good manners," which would bring her closer to her mother.

Her brother once refused and his plate was not cleared. Then followed a battle of wills. While others left the table, he sat before his plate. Their mother sat by him with an engaging smile on her face. The contest lasted about nine minutes until he swallowed the vegetable with a gulp of water. His plate was removed.

On this day the father announces that there will be some changes they would see. The rock will be removed and something built in its place. He looks at the little girl when he says this.

The little girl feels he has thrown a spear at her heart. She cries out loudly.

"No! No! It's my rock and nobody can move it!" Her face is white with anger.

He has stopped eating and lays his fork and knife on one side of his plate. Then he lifts his head and takes a deep breath and faces her. But she has turned her face away from him, looking down towards her shoulder. He has become the bad person in the story. The person who betrays and has become a villain. It's as if she thinks that if she does not see his face he will disappear.

"We are leaving to go to a big city and there are plans to change the house for the people who will live here next. There will be a guard hut where the rock sits. But it doesn't matter, as you will not be living here anymore." He says this briskly.

"No," she says in a rough voice that is not her own. Her mother's silvery laugh floats around the table.

"Your darling is not going to forgive you," she says to the father.

The little girl hates them both at this moment. The rock is more than her command post; it elevates her and is where unusual thoughts enter her mind. These thoughts separate her from the more mundane aspects of the life of a child who is ruled by adults. She is certain that her mother is aware of this.

"What do you do on your rock?" she's often asked with a smile. "Are you making stories in your head?"

"It's my rock and I like to be higher than everyone else."

"What happens when you come down?"

"I become your little girl," comes the quick answer.

Then he tells her, the great betrayer and no longer her best friend, that they would live in a city by the sea. She has seen the pictures of waves and blue water in a book of photographs her elder sister guards in a drawer in her room. She will not make it easier for him and keeps her face turned away as the tears gather behind her eyelids. He is quick and has seen them and gets up to come by her chair. She tries to rise from the chair, but he is faster and holds her on the seat with both his hands. "Come with me please, and I will tell you a secret." He has already lifted her from the chair and holds her hand.

They are outside now, and he has walked to the rock and placed her on it and stands in front of her legs, which dangle down.

"Now, when I go away for many days and come back to see you, I have been doing something which was supposed to get back something we lost."

The expression on his face has changed, so she knows this is serious. "Did you find it," she asks.

"No. It is lost forever, we have to be different people now."

"The rock will never move or go away. We can't leave it here," she wails.

"We have to settle in Karachi. There will be another house. You will go to a big school. It is a city by a beautiful ocean and we can find another rock for you." He tweaks her nose.

"Why couldn't you find what you lost?" She tries to sound angry.

"It's a battle and you have to be secretive but strong. I wasn't that strong." He looks far into the horizon over the mountain.

"Tell me where you lost it. I can try to find it for you," she wants to help him.

"You will. Perhaps one day when you grow up. Do you want to write your name on the rock?"

"No. I want you to tell me more about what you lost. If we both get together and look for it, we could find it."

"Your birthplace, Srinagar, and the glorious province of Kashmir have been lost." He sighs deeply.

"Did someone take it?" she has never seen him look so sad.

"Yes. Although I am working for our brand-new government, I have been working with people who send messages to Kashmiris. They do this through a radio station. So the ones we left behind in Kashmir know that we have not forgotten them and will try and come back."

She is excited. "We should go back and make them feel happy."

"There is a border. We cannot go back. They have blocked the transmission of our Free Kashmir program. I wrote the messages on the program and announced them. Sometimes a beautiful dream ends when you wake up," he ruffles her hair but looks towards the mountains.

"You have to try harder." She remembers what her mother often tells her.

"Now I have a big and responsible job with the new government. My family has to come first, I have to take care of all of you," he says firmly, looking like someone different now.

"I don't need the chocolates. I can say goodbye to the rock, but I don't want you to be sad." She starts crying.

He knows that she has sensed his despair. It is the despair he has always hidden from her. He pulls out a crumpled handkerchief from his pocket and dries her cheeks and dabs at her eyes.

"I will teach you a new word but it must be our secret." He looks at her seriously.

"From everyone?" she gestures at the house.

"Yes. *Resistance*."

She says the word, stumbling over the two s's.

"When something happens and you don't like it, you don't have to accept it. But you have to organize yourself into a proper resistance movement to say you don't like it." He is still a serious person and not like the father she knows.

"I can make this resistance with my brother. He is very strong and runs as fast as me." She wants to make his sadness go away.

He throws back his head and laughs and lifts her off the rock and places her firmly on the ground. He is back now, her familiar merry father. The sadness has sailed away like a cloud. She repeats the strange new word in her mind. It is a grownup word but she likes it. It is an important word, she thinks. Now all she has to do is use it so she does not have to go away to a city by the sea and leave her rock behind.

"When you go away do you do this resistance," she asks him.

"Yes. But now we are stopping and building a new country. This country was made for you. It will be your home forever and no one will take it away from you." He takes her hand and leads her towards the steps to the house.

She races ahead of him and almost collides with her mother.

"I am going to do resistance! I am going to do resistance!" she yells at the top of her lungs. "About what?" Her mother is smiling.

"About moving and leaving my rock," she stops and scowls at her mother.

"We were always going to go. You will love the city and your new school. Everything will be all right," her mother says and smiles at her, but her eyes go past her head to her father, who has entered behind her.

"What do you expect? She is the daughter of a revolutionary," her father says jauntily.

"Please don't fill her head with this nonsense. She has to do her reading now. The nuns are very strict."

"I don't want to read. I want to write a story for my rock," she dodges her mother and races to her room.

In her room, her brother is lying across her bed, rifling through his Tarzan book. She flops beside him and looks at him excitedly.

"Do you want to be in my resistance?" she asks him seriously.

"What is that? Is it a game?" He narrows his eyes and looks at her derisively.

"This is what our father does when he goes away. But he has ended it and I want to do it just like him. Let's both do it together for him."

He ignores her. He does that often. But she leans towards his ear and whispers about the conversation outside. He pushes her away and sits up.

"It's rubbish. You can't do anything. Mother will not let you make a fuss."

"You are scared. You are not brave," she tells him angrily.

"Ha ha. Let's see who gets scared!"

"I will do it alone then. Go away," she pushes him back, but she is also afraid that tears might roll out of her eyes again.

She is awakened the next morning by the loud sounds of machines. She races out of her bedroom still in her nightgown and bare feet. There is a large truck with a shovel near the rock and three men standing by it. Then she sees her father headed for his parked jeep. Her mother appears and says sharply. "Where are your slippers?"

She dodges her mother and runs towards the rock, shouting, "Resistance! Resistance!" at the top of her lungs. The men are startled and stare at her. Her father turns back towards her and her mother has come out holding her slippers. Even her brother has come out.

"You are crazy. Crazy," he bellows at her.

They have surrounded her now in a tight circle, both her parents and her brother. Her mother is kneeling, placing her bare feet inside her slippers. Her father is standing in front of her. She looks up at him and knows he has once again changed into a serious person.

"Little girls do not run out in their nightgowns," he says. His tone is cool.

"Make them stop!" she shouts at him.

"Take her inside, please," he says to her mother. "I don't want a scene in front of the workmen."

She turns around, pushes her mother and brother aside, and races back to the house herself. One of her slippers falls off. Her father picks it up. She dashes back to her room, shuts the door, and draws the latch to lock it. Then she goes to the window, which looks to the front lawn, kneels and looks out, her chin on the ledge. From here she will be able to see how the rock will be moved. She can see her father and mother talking. She sees her father looking back at the house as though searching for her goodbye wave. For the first time, she is not there to make it. She watches his jeep drive away and does not care. The truck brings the gigantic shovel close to the rock and starts digging under it. All of a sudden she feels she has become smaller. As though a giant from a fairy tale has stepped on her and she cannot breathe. She does not cry. Instead, she watches the rock being lifted by the shovel. She watches the truck drive away, carrying the rock. Within minutes the truck vanishes and with it her best friend and the object that gave her a place for her imagination to roam.

She hears her mother's voice outside the door.

"We are going to fry chips and make your favourite chicken sandwiches for lunch. Please open the door."

She does not reply.

"Do you know your father came back with your slipper and left a message for you?" her mother cajoles.

She opens the door only because she is tired of the thoughts running through her head. Her mother kneels and holds her. The girl finds comfort, folded into her mother's body.

"Everything will be all right. Do you know, in three days after packing we will all take a train to Karachi, you don't even know what a train is. You will love it."

She suspects the warbling happy lilt in her mother's voice.

"Your father said to tell you that you are his brave daughter and he is proud of you." That is the moment she asks her mother her first adult question.

"Do you miss the place you left behind?"

"Yes. Like the way you will miss your rock, but you will find other things to love."

"You should have done that Resistance," she accuses her mother.

Six months later she walks with her father on the shore of a beach. She loves the deep blue ocean and the foam-flecked waves. Most of all she loves the wet sand which could be used to build sandcastles.

But this afternoon they walk behind a small dune that truncates the beach. He leads her on a narrow path behind it and suddenly it appears right in their path. She stops. It's there—her rock. She runs towards it as her rubber sandals sink into the wet sand. He is right behind her. They climb it together, holding the crevices on the surface to get a firm grip.

"When the tide is high, half of the rock is in the water, but when the tide recedes, it rises again. It will be here forever."

She looks at his wind-swept hair and bare shoulders, red from the fierce sun, and the horizonless ocean ahead of them, and wonders how he knew about this rock.

"We can only come here on the weekends, but what will you do on this rock?"

"I am going to be a mermaid and write stories about the rock."

"It's a good plan," he strokes her hair, which is now below her shoulders.

"Maybe someone will write about your resistance," her heart bursts with love for him.

"Perhaps it will be you when you grow up."

Four decades later she does, but he has already died. She does this after she visits Kashmir, the country he had lost, only to discover that a resistance movement flourishes there that will never die.

The Storyteller

Karachi, 1955

Her mother had gone away. Yet her presence was everywhere, because she was talked about constantly. The dressing room where armoires housed her clothes, shoes, and handbags remained shut. The large bottle of French perfume on the dressing table was also missing. The house was now run by three live-in staff members and her father. Although nothing had changed in the routine of the ten-year-old girl's life, it was as though its sheen had gone off. Also, the hazard was missing. Her mother had maintained order like a general. Breaking that order had been an exciting hazard. Both she and her brother, who was a year older, were habitual and reckless rule-breakers. With a missing mother, nobody was caught and no daunting consequences followed. Also missing were the delightful surprises only their mother could orchestrate.

She had gone to a place called America to study at a university and would return at the end of the year. This is what she and her siblings were told by their father. Their mother instantly became a heroine of sorts. More so because she wrote letters on blue paper which was folded over to become an envelope. Oddly enough, when she wrote, the postage stamp was printed on the letter. The envelope was called an Aerogram. The letters indicated that she seemed to know what was happening in their lives all the time. There were also great descriptions of her life. Occasionally an actual envelope with colourful stamps would arrive. There would be photographs of her with her American friends. In the photographs, her beauty had a different quality from before. She had a new sophisticated and fashionable appearance. Would she be the same mother when she returned, wondered the girl.

Their father pampered them as though they had suddenly been orphaned. They were allowed to see one movie a month at the Rex Cinema, but when he asked them whether it was a new month they would lie like troopers and fool him. They did not know that he only pretended to be fooled. He taught them how to play cards and after a rambunctious game he simply announced, "All right, cheating is allowed for five minutes only." He would then remove his wristwatch and place it in the centre of the table. Nobody cheated after that. He invited female relatives to visit and stay with them. It was something to do with "the mother's touch" theory.

The aunt arrived one early evening, creating a flurry of excitement. She had taken a train from the northern city of Rawalpindi to the southern city of Karachi. Their father had gone to receive her and drove her home. She was his sister and seemed to be from a different planet. Before he left he told them he was bringing a surprise for them and the little girl thought it would be a meringue cake from their favourite bakery. Instead, it was this bulky, formidable creature. She was dressed in an austere white cotton shalwar kameez suit. Her broad feet rested in black leather crisscross sandals that looked so sturdy that it seemed she could walk for miles in them. She patted their heads and held their hands but there were no other physical gestures. Her features could only faintly resemble their father's if one stared hard at her. She wore black-rimmed glasses and a sliver of grey hair peeked out from the top of her dupatta. She wore no jewelry. She looked at the girl and announced that she would sleep in her bedroom, where a separate bed had already been made up for her.

"She is not going to let you read all night in the armoire with your flashlight," her brother whispered in her ear.

"I will, after she goes to sleep. She is an old lady," she hissed back at him.

She noticed the formality between her father and his sister. If the girl were older she would have called that relationship one of tension. Conversation between them at the dining table did not have the light-hearted flavour associated with the mother. The girl thought that the aunt made her miss her mother more than before. She also noted how all the domestics in the house deferred to her as though she had taken her mother's place. She thought her father was responsible for this act of treachery. The aunt also engaged in culinary projects. She made pickles. Although the pickles contained fascinating things marinated in spices, everything had to sit out in the sun for days. The lids on the jars could never be left open or the pickles would go bad. The girl much preferred her mother's homemade pistachio ice cream and marmalade.

The aunt asked to see the girl's English exercise book one day. It was the one she wrote her essays in. She always got top marks in her class. The aunt sat in a chair and leafed through the book. She removed her glasses and rubbed them clean with a little handkerchief and read with a serious expression on her face. The girl wondered if she understood English because she only spoke Urdu. Also, a couple of times a day she unfurled a little carpet and said her prayers. The girl ran away at those times. Her mother did not say prayers and neither did her father.

"Do you want me to teach you?" the aunt asked one day when she had finished her prayer and was folding the little carpet up.

"No, thank you. I prefer to read my books," the girl gestured to her little glass-fronted wood cabinet which housed her collection of books.

"What do you like to read?" the aunt's eyes had a strange glint.

"Enid Blyton's stories but *Alice in Wonderland* is still my favourite book."

"Ah," suddenly a smile wreathed the aunt's face. "I will tell you a story tonight before you go to sleep."

"You have a special book to read from?"

"No. Everyone knows this story by heart. I don't think you do. I will tell you the story."

"Like a storyteller?"

"Yes."

After dinner some nights the girl delayed her bedtime by visiting her brother in his room, which was at the other end of the house. The most interesting space in his room was under his bed, where he kept a cardboard shoebox on the floor. The shoebox was lined with cotton wool and an egg nestled in the cotton. A lamp was positioned above the shoebox and they both knew that the heat would make the egg hatch and a chick would appear. They would stare at the egg, willing a crack to appear and the chick to break out. Of course, this contraption was a secret and her brother made sure that when his room was cleaned nobody looked under the bed.

Tonight her brother refused to let her in, so she trudged back to her room miserably. She was convinced she would miss the moment. The aunt was reclining on her bed reading from a little booklet. The girl got ready for bed. Their two beds were close, just a small space between them. She brushed her teeth vigorously because she had promised her mother she would. She knew there was no way she could dodge the promised storytelling session and a small part of her was also curious.

The aunt was now sitting cross-legged on her bed. A light coverlet was draped across her shoulders and her hair had been loosened for the night. It flowed over her shoulders and had altered her appearance, the sheen on the salt-and-pepper giving her the majestic look of an elderly queen.

"You can sit on your bed and face me please."

Her voice was low-pitched but melodic. The story began with a man who was called Hussain. He had many important relatives. They were not kings and queens but were known to be good people.

"You mean they did not do anything bad?" asked the girl.

"Never! They followed a way of thinking and living which became a religion."

The girl thought this could become a boring story. Perhaps she could pretend to fall asleep in a little while.

"The story of Hussain is about a battle that he fought."

"Was he a brave warrior? Did he win?"

"He was not a soldier but the leader of a community. He lost the battle and won something important instead. He created a legend and it is alive till today."

Then the story began formally. It was terrifying. Hussain believed in peace and unity. But there was an evil King who had stolen Hussain's place as the leader and did not like the ideas that Hussain was spreading. Hussain thought that this man could harm him and his family, so he decided to move to a safer country. He had about seventy people with him, of whom many were his family members and others were his friends. But they were pursued by the evil man with a large army of soldiers and trapped by the banks of a river. They had run out of food and water. They had mothers and sisters and babies among them. In vain they begged for water for the children. They were refused. If anyone tried to get water to drink the soldiers let loose a hail of arrows upon them. But they fought and they were all killed.

The story did two remarkable things. It transformed the storyteller and the listener. Suddenly, the stuffy aunt became magical. This magic was the ability to captivate an audience that did not want the story to end. The girl experienced fear and wonder. If she closed her eyes she could see the story unfurl in pictures before her eyes. Hussain's white horse, goatskins strapped on his saddle to collect water, arrows piercing his body. The goatskins leaked and the water never gathered.

Hussain was killed and beheaded. The people on the bank who watched in terror somehow transported their agony to the girl. She could feel every fragment of their sadness. It made her feel like summoning her army of hundreds of soldiers and stopping the arrows. It also made her want to cry, but she kept telling herself it was just a story.

The girl did not fall asleep easily that night. She felt her entire body was a storyboard. Images and sounds entered her mind from all sorts of places. More than anything she wanted to see the white horse and be on that riverbank shouting at everyone, "Please stop!" Outside her bedroom window the wind was blowing hard and the branches shook, casting shadows on her wall. The leaves rustled and the shadows became frightening. Tonight, as the aunt lay fast asleep, the girl lay rigidly in her bed unable to take her eyes off the wall. Her mother's comfort was no longer there for her but her fear now was different. She raised herself on her elbows and stared hard ahead. She saw a horse rising out of water. Arrows stuck out of his body. The horse rose and water cascaded down its body. She closed her eyes and thought she heard the people shouting his name, "Zuljanah!" as though they were cheering a champion on a sports field.

She sat up in bed. She looked at the aunt, a mound beneath her sheet. The sheet rose and fell with the gentle snoring. The girl tiptoed to her desk and collected a blank copybook, pen, and flashlight. She came to bed and covered herself completely with the light cotton bed cover; she made a desk out of her pillow and switched on the flashlight. She was going to write a story.

The pen moved fast over the pages, writing an adventure story about a magical white horse that people wanted to catch. The horse flew to many places and always managed to escape. The copybook had nine pages and she covered them easily but did not end the story. She let the last page dangle without an ending. Finally she placed the book under her pillow and switched off the flashlight and fell asleep.

The next morning the first thing she did was make sure her copybook was placed safely in her school bag. She greeted her aunt cheerfully and knew that she now saw her in a different light. It was like opening a parcel wrapped in dull brown paper and finding butterflies in a box inside. At recess she took the copybook out and wandered off to a quiet place far from her friends.

"Where are you going?" her best friend called after her.

"To a quiet place, I have written a story and I want to read it," she replied.

"There is no homework to write a story."

"This is for me. I may let you read it when I have finished."

Two days later the aunt received a letter and the father announced that a relative was ill so the aunt was shortening her stay and going back the next morning. The girl had been too shy to show her the story, but she hid the rough copy in a shawl in her suitcase. She felt sad when she said goodbye to the aunt because she wanted to tell her many things and there was no time.

"You should ask your father to recite for you poetry that is written in Urdu," was her parting comment as though she had looked inside the girl's head and found just what she should have.

"Poetry?" the girl was interested.

"Yes. Sometimes great stories are written as poems. There are many about Hussain, you know. They are called marsias and are sung beautifully."

Then it happened one day at the school assembly. The announcement of a short story competition, for which a prize would be awarded. Her English teacher Mrs Potts chose three girls from the class. The girl was one of them. She read the instructions for writing, which were typed neatly on lined paper. The girl was nervous, because a girl called Romana Rodrigues, who was quite a whiz, had also been selected. They were given a week to prepare their stories. When the girl was handing in her story, she saw an ink smudge on one of her pages, but she handed it in anyway. She did not tell her father but wrote to her mother about it. She and her siblings wrote a one-page letter once a month to their mother and their father would mail it to her in America. That is how the mother knew what was happening in their lives. The girl wrote a very short letter; it covered half a page. "I have written a story and given it to my teacher for the competition but I don't think I will win the prize but I liked writing it."

She was asked to stay behind at the end of the English class one day.

"How did you get the idea for this story?" Mrs Potts asked, a puzzled look on her face.

"I heard the story and I loved the horse the most. It was a sad story but I wanted to change the sadness. Did you like the horse?"

"You know this is a religious story don't you?"

"I think so. My aunt told me about the story of Hussain and his battle. It is just a story and anyone should be able to write it as they wish. I just imagined different things."

"It is a good story, but you could upset people who think it is sacred." Mrs Potts had a strange look on her face.

"What is sacred?" asked the girl.

"Belief. Tradition. History. These things are absolute and not meant to change."

The girl felt her heart sinking. "Can't I enter the competition with the story?"

"You have a good imagination, so I shall enter your story. Let's hope the judges think that as well."

The day the announcement was made, her name was not called out. The girl wondered if it was the ink smudge on the page. Or was it for the reasons Mrs Potts had mentioned? Romana had won the competition with her story, and she flashed a triumphant smile at the girl as she climbed the podium to collect her prize, which was a collection of Charles Dickens's novels.

She told her brother about her story when she got home. He wanted to read it and she gave him the rough copy she had in her exercise book. When he finished it, he gave her a wide smile and said, "I bet you could write one of the Hardy Boy books when you grow up." He seemed to be proud of her. Her heart melted.

"I got the idea from the story Aunt recited to me one night."

"I know the story. It is about Hussain the Martyr. It is a religious story. Your story is far more interesting." He punched her playfully on the arm.

"Yes, but the school did not think so," she let her disappointment spill out.

"It is just a stupid school. You keep writing your stories. This one makes me want to find out more about the horse. But you have kept the end a mystery . . . Do you want to see the egg?"

"Yes."

The following week, Mrs Potts asked her to stay behind in class. The girl waited until everyone else had filed out. Mrs Potts pulled out a few sheets of typed paper and showed them to the girl.

"This is your story and I have typed it out. See how easy it is to read it. Would you like to read it again and see if you would like to make any changes?"

"Changes?" the girl, asked, admiring the neat and clean script on the pages.

"Yes. I think you will write more stories."

"I have made another up. But I never want to show it to anyone," the girl said.

"Why?"

"Because when you write a story, you put yourself into it."

"I know."

"So when someone does not like it, they don't like you."

The teacher smiled and told her that criticism was also a good way to learn and improve. The writer had to always separate herself from what she was writing. The girl did not agree with her but did not say anything. She felt that her stories were a part of her. They were her thoughts and her imagination. She loved the horse and instead of a horrible fate, she as a writer could change that fate, so readers could get joy out of the story. Sadness was like a stone that weighed you down. Everything was not easy all the time, as she had found that out in her math class. Yet to solve a problem was an adventure and it made her think harder about many solutions. Finding the right one at the end was a moment of great pleasure. It had nothing to do with winning a prize. You would be recognized for the way you handled the problem.

There was a phone call one evening and her father told her that the aunt wanted to speak to her. He held out the black heavy plastic receiver for her and smiled.

"I have just read the story you placed in my shawl in the suitcase."

"Oh. Did you read it?"

"Yes. It is untidy and two of the pages are incorrectly numbered but I liked it very much."

The girl was so surprised that she almost dropped the receiver but then tightened her grip on it.

"Did you like the ending?" she asked hesitantly.

"I liked all of it. You describe things very well. They become real. Your teachers at school must tell you that," continued the aunt.

"They did not like it and I did not win the competition."

"That does not matter. Show it to your father please, he reads a lot. Please send me other stories you write."

That is when a thought entered the girl's mind. She would write a story and call it the Storyteller and describe what had happened between them.

"Are you coming back for another visit?" she asked.

"Only when you write another story that you can read out to me," the aunt said and chuckled.

"We have second-term exams so it will take a while."

"There is no rush, I can wait."

She got the summons from her brother one Saturday afternoon and ran to his room. He stood in front of his door, which was open just a crack.

"Very quietly. The egg has a big crack—all we have to do is wait."

She crawled under the bed with him and saw that the egg had a crack in two places.

"Settle down. Don't make a noise. We don't want the chick to be scared in a new world. Watch . . . watch," he whispered.

The egg moved a little as though there was something inside it. For the girl the excitement was unbearable. Then before her eyes, a small beak poked through the eggshell and then after a few tremors, the chick broke free, the egg cracked, releasing fragments of eggshells. The chick had a downy yellow coat and it tried to walk.

"I am going to let you hold it. Give me your hand," her brother commanded.

He lifted the chick and brushed the broken eggshells away; he then extended it toward her. The girl cupped both her palms and extended them. The little webbed feet scratched her palms and she stroked the down with her fingertips. She was holding the newborn chick and its soft yellow down looked exactly as it did in books. It was a moment of perfection. A brand-new life now hopped out of her palms and scampered away from under the bed. They both crawled after it, watching how the chick darted here and there and made tiny chirping sounds. The moment when she had finished her story was just like this one. When something is born, seen, and, shared, it has broken through the state which had confined it. The shells rested within the storyteller but it was her imagination that had brought the story out.

"Is it looking for the mother?" asked the girl.

"Yes. But it will adjust very quickly. We have to find something soft to feed it and some water."

"Won't the chick be lonely or even sad wandering alone?"

"No. Let's go to the kitchen and get some water."

That Saturday morning she went to her parents' bedroom. Her father was in bed surrounded by newspapers. His morning tea sat on a tray on the table next to the bed. He looked up and patted a place by his side.

"Do you want to see the cartoon section in this newspaper?"

"Do you know any poems?" she asked.

He took off his glasses and gave her an amused smile. "Poems?"

"Yes. Aunt said you know how to recite poems, and I would like to listen." He was quiet and there was a thoughtful expression on his face.

"When I was in university I was on the debating team and I even won a big prize. That was long ago. I love poetry but don't normally recite it."

"We are learning one poem in the English class at school. It's about daffodils."

"I wandered lonely as a cloud, by William Wordsworth. A big English poet."

"My teacher recites it so well. Just like Aunt recited the story." The girl felt she was having a grownup conversation with her father.

"There are storytellers who compose long poems about wars and love and philosophy. You will study them all. Storytelling is a lost art. Would you like to tell stories?"

"I would like to write them," said the girl.

Master Sahib

Karachi, 1957

The announcement was made by the mother with odd gravity. "Master Sahib will come once a week and teach you and your brother to read the Quran."

The girl, who was thirteen, had seen this book. It was wrapped in a green velvet cloth and sat on the top shelf of a bookcase. It sat apart always. The girl had no idea that it was written in a language she had no exposure to.

"I can read it myself," she replied to her mother.

The mother ignored her comment. "He will arrive at four and both of you will be waiting for him punctually," she said. "You also have to cover your head—one of your scarves will do."

"Why do I have to wear a scarf just to read a book?"

"It is a sign of respect," the mother used her steely voice. "It is a holy book. Also, make sure you have washed your hands and they are clean before your lesson."

The girl knew that when the mother used that voice there could never be any further discussion. She glanced at her brother, who gave her a wicked smile.

When the day arrived, which was Thursday, she waited with her brother. On her head was her Eiffel Tower scarf from Paris, which her father had brought for her as a gift. She felt utterly foolish—normally she wore this scarf at the beach, or on long drives in the car. Often she would knot it around her throat, feeling very fashionable. It was a white square with a print of the Eiffel Tower in a deep blue and it was made of real silk. It felt wrong to wear it to read a book.

They were seated at a table and across from them was an armchair for the teacher. As soon as he came in, she took an instant dislike to him, because he patted her on the head and shook hands with her brother. She felt the pat on the head demeaned her status. It also made the scarf slide backward. He was a stout man stuffed into a knee-length coat with a high collar. The coat was worn over grey trousers and his shoes were black and tightly laced. He wore steel-rimmed spectacles on his broad face, which had a sprinkling of a beard. On his head was a black cap that could not conceal the scent of some hair oil. It was pungent and unpleasant. He sank heavily into his chair and placed a thin book in front of each of them and one in front of himself. The mother made a brief appearance and beamed, announcing that tea for Master Sahib would arrive momentarily. The children of course had already had their after-school snacks. The man with the strange name of Master Sahib gave a broad smile at their mother and his eyes behind his glasses gleamed.

He told them to open the book on the first page.

"This is the first chapter and we will read all 114," he announced.

Her brother groaned softly under his breath and her heart sank as she realized that this would go on for months. A big book written in a foreign language dispelled any notion of whipping through it with speed. When she opened the book, she was surprised. The writing was ornate and unfamiliar. All the words were joined together with dots and slanting little lines over some of them. It was a foreign language which was called Arabic but the alphabet was also used for the Urdu language. The girl did poorly in Urdu at school, where the entire medium of instruction was English. English was her first language. It was spoken in the home and in school. Master Sahib had a strange method where he would recite a line at a time from his book and they had to repeat it while tracing the line with the index finger of the right hand. This was different from her French classes.

"What do the words mean?" she said, perplexed.

"That will come much later. It is not important right now. You will simply repeat what I say." He gave her a stern look.

She wanted to scream but she kept quiet. She was pitted against her powerful mother and this odious man whom she had already decided to dislike. To add insult to injury they were informed that the lines would be read from right to left, which was the complete opposite of English and French.

All of a sudden, the cook's assistant staggered in with a tea tray, which he placed near the teacher's elbow on the broad table. The contents were a pot of tea, a plate with two large samosas, and a plate of local sweets. There was enough tea for four people. They watched the man instantly pour a cup of tea and wolf down both the samosas. He belched at the end, and the girl knew that if it was up to her she would pour some poison into the teapot. The teacher then lifted one of the heavy sweet pieces of barfi and ate that as well. He did not close his mouth when he chewed which was rather shocking for the girl. She felt her mother had gone mad to send such a sumptuous tea to such a gluttonous tormentor.

The first lesson contradicted every learning experience they had ever had both at school and at home. The foreign language had unusual guttural, throaty, and sing-song sounds. Master Sahib recited and they were supposed to imitate him. Her brother took great license and exaggerated the sounds. The girl refused to mimic the guttural sounds on principle. The teacher's eyes narrowed with displeasure until they became tiny slits of glittering malevolence. Oddly enough, the first chapter was just a page long. They began the second one, which was much longer. This chapter had a name and it was "The Cow."

"If you do not listen properly you will keep repeating the lines until you do it right," he wagged a finger at her brother but glared at her.

A sharp kick landed at her ankle under the table and she drew a quick breath but did not exhale to make a moan. She lost her place on the page. She glanced at the culprit, her brother, but he was slowly tracing lines on the page and mispronouncing them. The girl decided to use another tactic. She folded her hands under her armpits and leaned away from the table. Here she sat like a stone statuette that would never move. She even closed her eyes. She knew she could hold this pose for a long time. It was a game called Statue, which they played in the garden where the players had to freeze in a pose and whoever held out the longest was the winner. She was good at this game and often won.

Suddenly she heard a chair being dragged and furious exhortation in the foreign language called Arabic, and then there was silence. The girl kept her eyes shut and did not move. A familiar fragrance wafted over her. Her brother muttered something hurriedly. Then she heard the voice.

"Please apologize to Master Sahib immediately and tell him this will not happen again."

The girl opened her eyes and saw her mother standing beside Master Sahib's chair. On his face, a triumphant smile.

Her mother's show of authority the girl resented for the first time in her thirteen-year-old existence. Her mother was wrong, and so was the plan of reading 114 chapters of a book in a foreign language. She was tongue-tied but her mind told her she needed some ingenious plan.

The lesson continued and the girl did exactly what she was told. She switched off a part of her mind and became mechanical. Some of the words would repeat themselves with a frequency which formed a pattern. The entire exercise was one of deceptive mimicry. She managed to fool the Master Sahib and even helped her brother along. The index finger of her right hand flew across the meaningless words with speed—until at one stage Master Sahib reached forward and gripped her finger with two of his to slow her down. His touch turned her veins to ice. She felt violated. A thoroughly unwanted intimacy had been created by him which was only reserved for a family member, a relative, or a very close friend. This contact was alien and repulsive. It was as though her small finger had transformed into her entire body and had been held captive.

She approached her father later that evening as he strolled in the long front lawn with the large black German Shepherd called Duke. Her mother was not with him. She ran up to him and he stopped and held out his hand to her. She held his hand and relief coursed through her. This was the touch she was familiar with.

"Why are we learning to read this book in Arabic?"

"Book?" his eyebrows shot up with alarm.

"Yes, this Quran," she faced him resolutely.

"Not this Quran but the Holy Quran," he corrected her firmly.

"Yes, but the Master Sahib is horrible. I hate this lesson. I don't want to just repeat words like a parrot and not know what they mean."

"I see. Let's sit and talk about this," he led her towards the lawn chairs.

His grip on her hand seemed to tighten a little as though he felt she would run away. They reached the heavy wooden lawn chairs with sloping backs. She did not like them as she always felt she would slip backward, so she would sit on the edge and lean forward. The wooden slats on the seat pinched the backs of her legs. Duke flopped by her side on the grass. She stroked his neck where the fur was soft and silky and he licked her hand. It felt wonderful to be with her father whom she loved and the faithful dog who was supposed to be a guard dog but was just a bundle of calm black fur who would play with them and never barked. Basking in this feeling, she mistakenly felt her father would set everything right.

"Parents have to make certain their children have read the Holy Quran in the original text. There will be a big party when you finish and I think your mother has ordered a special gift for you as well," he winked at her.

"Is this about religion?" she struggled with her response.

"Of course it is."

"How can you like something which you do not understand?" she sounded shocked.

"Most people believe in a religion and they follow it. It's a good thing, it teaches you how to behave, and you have someone to pray to," he was looking down the length of the lawn and not at her.

"Do you?" she almost squeaked in surprise.

"Sometimes."

"So there are rules?"

"Don't you have them at school? Your mother has rules for how you live at home as well? Order is a good thing," he leaned forward and tweaked her nose.

She drew back from his hand. He was not taking her seriously.

She could not count on him, and a coil of anger unfurled inside her.

"My brother can do this. I don't want to. Please?"

"It is quite a beautiful language. Arabic. Give it a chance, you will understand the meaning of some of the words as they are repeated. There are English translations as well. I will try and find one for you later on."

"Why don't you give us the classes?" She was desperate.

"Master Sahib is more of an expert and he is teaching a few other children of your age."

"I don't like him. He smells, eats all the tea snacks, and then hurts my finger," her litany of complaints burst from her like a geyser.

"How does he hurt your finger?" his expression changed.

It felt as though she had scored the bullseye on the dartboard. Then he asked her to describe accurately when and how the finger was hurt during the lesson. She told him and his response was to laugh uproariously. Even Duke gave a few yelps as though he understood whatever amused her father.

"That's a tradition. You were reading too fast or making mistakes and he was slowing you down." He chuckled.

She leaped up from her chair.

"I don't want him to touch my finger!"

"That is not a problem. We will tell him not to touch your finger. But you will have to follow his instructions. He is the teacher." He was trying to stifle laughter.

"Thank you," she said carefully from a distance.

"You just have to read it. You do so well at school. This should be very easy for you."

She ignored her father and looked at Duke.

"Come on, Duke. Let's go." She turned to Duke who suddenly barked.

The next lesson on the dreaded Thursday introduced a new tension. Master Sahib ignored her and looked only at her brother as he gave his instructions. When they paused after reciting for twenty minutes, his tea arrived.

"What is this long chapter about?" she looked at him directly. He was pouring his tea but he glanced at her.

"It is about people who believe in God and those who do not, and how they will be punished." He took a loud sip of tea from the cup and then arranged his face into a stern look.

The room became transformed into a war room of sorts.

Her brother had warned her that Master Sahib was like a villain in a bad story. He may have fooled their parents but they had to be very crafty and pretend to be following him. After a few more lessons, he let them read by themselves, since they had mastered how to join the alphabet characters together, and he simply listened.

Two pages, said her brother, could be turned together, shortening the chapter considerably. He was finally caught. The teacher sat up straight in his chair. He removed her brother's finger from the page he was reading and turned it back, and then the one before that.

"God sees everything."

"Sorry, Master Sahib, I think the pages were stuck together," her brother said hurriedly. "And you?" he glanced at the girl, "what mischief are you up to in the middle of reading the Holy Quran?"

"Nothing," she said truculently, knowing she had turned two pages together much earlier and not got caught.

"If I tell your mother, she will be very unhappy. Do you want that?"

"I think she will be very pleased that we are reading better and faster because you have taught us so well," the girl said blandly.

"Move your chairs further apart. I don't want you sitting so close to each other," he said irritably.

The girl was being educated in a Catholic school. It had a convent attached to it where young postulants took their vows. The Sisters of St Joseph had come from Austria and built a school, convent house, and chapel in Karachi. The principal was an Austrian nun, as were some other teachers. The school curriculum was based on the Cambridge School Leaving Certificate at both Ordinary and Advanced Levels. It was a famous school where the results were always good. The convent was run like a military bootcamp. The nuns enforced ironclad discipline to mold the students' character and behaviour. The students, a large majority of whom belonged to Muslim homes, were free to wander into the chapel and attend a service if they chose to. There was no religious instruction, but one subject called Moral Science was mandatory. It was based on universal principles of virtue and respect. The girl and her two friends had ducked into the chapel often and even recited the Lord's Prayer, which they regarded as quite poetic. There was an undeniable fascination for the nuns in their long habits, their rosaries clicking as they walked. They all indulged in endless schoolgirlish speculations about their hair, which was never seen, and the fact that they were all married to Jesus. This religious aspect of the school made them feel they were on some exotic trip to a foreign culture. However, it was kept hidden and never discussed. There was a book called the Bible, but no one was ever required to read even though it was written in English.

Her brother went to a school called St Patrick's, run by Jesuit fathers who did not shy away from corporal punishment. Caning was their favourite method of disciplining unruly boys, sometimes accompanied by letters to the parents by the principal, Father Raymond.

In contrast, the lessons with Master Sahib, which were also concerned with religion, became a wretched experience for the girl.

Despite her brother's high-octane level of delinquency, the Master grimly made them read aloud and the pages turned rapidly.

"My tongue has become crooked. Show me you yours?" her brother said before a lesson one day as they waited for the teacher, who was uncharacteristically late.

Laughing, she stuck her tongue out to him for inspection. At this point Master Sahib walked in and flung himself into the armchair.

"You have to be respectful and not laugh ever," he said dourly.

"Ever, Master Sahib?" the brother said with feigned innocence.

"Never here. Never when you have the Holy Quran in front of you and you have still to complete reading it all. Your mother is coming today to see how you are reading." It was a warning that he knew would settle them.

The mother made an appearance with the manner of an inspector doing a spot check. Master Sahib's reputation rested on how well they did. The girl felt revenge could be exacted. She kicked her brother under the table, and he guessed what was on her mind. If they read badly, then perhaps the mother would consider this project to be a failure and stop it. Master Sahib had a tense expression on his face. His pupils could not let him down. He had become very partial to the elaborate tea and his fees.

In his mind, the girl was the real problem. She was bright and had learned to read very well indeed, but had a built-in resistance to the exercise. Often she would stop and demand a translation. He did not care for that at all. He generally ignored her request and simply forced her to continue reading.

"Why is it called a Surah. What does this word mean?" she asked once.

"This is Arabic. It's a holy language." He replied shortly.

"So everyone in this country called Arabia is a holy person because they use a holy language?"

"You are going to the wrong school. It is run by Christian nuns and they have taught you to be rude," he said.

"Why don't you tell my mother that and see what happens," the brother suggested caustically.

The mother glided into the room like a ship of state. She greeted Master Sahib graciously and smiled at the kids. It was an encouraging smile that said you are my bright children and you will never let me down. It was that secret language a parent has with a child. The Master Sahib put a dent into it by first commenting on their general lack of discipline.

"Is it a behaviour problem Master Sahib?" she fixed a pair of very cool eyes on him.

"Well," he struggled, "Your daughter is always busy with questions, and then her brother who is much slower gets distracted."

Soft laughter arose from her mother's beautiful lips like the tinkling of bells. She glanced at the girl and widened her eyes. Then she turned to Master Sahib.

"She is a top student in her class at the Convent. She loves reading and has a library of books in her room which are quite mature for her age. Her curiosity, Master Sahib, is part of how she learns. Restrict her questions, perhaps to three per class?" She smiled at Master Sahib.

The girl wanted to leap out of her chair and hug her mother. Her mother had defended her and at the same time placated Master Sahib. Even though she was solely responsible for inflicting this torture on them of reading in a language they did not understand, she would protect them against anyone who would try to denigrate them.

"Well, well," Master Sahib backed off instantly in the face of this unwavering maternal spirit, "it's not that serious. I can handle it. I can handle both of them."

"Please do," said the mother diplomatically, "of course we are relying on your vast experience."

Various gauntlets had been thrown on the table where the lessons were conducted. A mother who sought success for her children and the Master who had a reputation to protect at any cost. For that spell, the girl realized that both she and her brother were the principal players. Both adults were demanding results that only the young ones were capable of delivering. It was apparent that the lessons would continue until the last chapter was reached. The girl at thirteen years of age made a decision wise beyond her years. It would be better to deliver good results than not, and the trick was to detach from the exercise emotionally.

The mother selected a section for them to read. It was a random one that they had already read before, and there was no possibility for the mother to conclude that Master Sahib had coached them in advance to impress her.

The brother read first. It was a laboured effort and he dispensed with using his index finger to trace the lines. He cut a valiant figure, using a sing-song imitation of Master Sahib's recitation style. When he finished, he was neither complimented nor criticized. However, the mother had pursed her lips. She quickly nodded and turned to the girl, suggesting the section to read could be her own choice.

The Master Sahib, thoroughly scandalized by the boy's performance, fixed his gaze on the girl. He removed his glasses, polished them with a square of cloth, and replaced them on his nose. The exercise was his response to the boy's incredible performance; he had read disjointed lines because he did not have his finger to guide him, and he had mimicked the teacher's style perfectly.

The girl was acutely aware of the suspense-laden air in the room. She saw the grim intensity of Master Sahib's fleeting glance. He was willing her to do much better than her brother. A spirit of competition rose in her. It came from an unfamiliar place within her. She knew that winning the approval of her mother meant everything to her despite Master Sahib's bullying. She sat up straight and even checked the sliding scarf by knotting it firmly under her chin. She then turned the pages of the new chapter which they had begun last week and placed her index finger at the beginning of the first line.

She did not produce the throaty sounds imitated by her brother but read in her own accent and voice, following line upon line as though there were a mechanical device inside controlling her. She read fast, hardly ever stumbling on a word, and turned one page after another calmly.

"This is very good," the mother leaned forward and stopped the girl's moving finger.

The test was over. A smile appeared on Master Sahib's face as did one on her mother's. Her brother gave her a wide smile.

A few days later her father visited her in her room after dinner. The girl was lying on her bed reading.

"I hear you are doing very well in your Quran-reading lessons," he said, sitting on the edge of her bed. The girl shut her book.

"It's easy once you get to know how to join the alphabet," she replied, resorting to the modesty which the nuns in her school always insisted upon.

"No, I hear you beat your brother." He winked at her.

"He was able to read as much as I was," she sprang to his defense.

"Are you feeling better about this exciting project now?" he asked.

"Why should it be exciting?"

"Well, the Holy Quran is a book of revelations and about Islam. Your religion, my religion, and that of generations of our family."

She remained silent. There was no way to tell him that she preferred reading her books, which were all written in English and had real adventures. This thing called religion had suddenly popped into her life.

The worst part was that she could not understand a thing it said. Privately, she thought both her parents had gone a little mad.

"I think Master Sahib has turned out to be a very good teacher," he continued.

"He answers the three questions I am allowed to ask him," she added in a fit of generosity.

"So you don't hate him anymore?"

She sat up and looked at him.

"I think he should have a blackboard and write out the words on it and then explain exactly what they mean."

"I don't think that's been done before," he had a line on his forehead now and his eyes were scrunched up.

"I need to finish my book, we have a test tomorrow," she lied to dismiss her father.

"We'll talk again," he leaned forward and kissed her on the forehead and walked out.

Months sped by and the girl was astonished at the number of chapters that were completed. Her stance about the lessons never changed; she read the lines like a robot. She knew that Master Sahib viewed her with different eyes now. She was his champion and her brother's abysmal results were ignored. Every now and then he would exclaim, "Subhan Allah" and beam at her.

She wondered if that was a compliment. But she found out from her father that the words meant "By the grace of God."

So it was God who had made her read so well? It was not a compliment for her but God. She was tempted to tell the teacher that God was nowhere in the room, but she did not give in to the temptation.

Years later when she left for Canada, her father brought a collection of books for her. They rested in a cabin trunk, which she called The Box of Books. A few years later she went through the box in the basement locker of her apartment building in Toronto. She found in it a dark green copy of the Quran, and the inscription on the title page read, "May this be a source of great consolation for you."

It was a copy of the Quran with an English translation on each page. It took another twenty years for her to open the book and discover that the footnotes on each page masterfully revealed different shades of meaning of the Arabic text. The theologian scholar who had compiled this Quran had done it for a Western readership. He had a great reputation, but he was considered to be a rebel. However, his Quran edition had become a collector's item. Her father had mentioned, much later, that it was her childhood nemesis, Master Sahib, who had chosen the Quran for her.

The Eyes of Texas . . .

Oak Cliff, Dallas, 1961

In precisely twenty-one hours her world was replaced by another. She was seventeen, had been prepared for this, but now lying in a strange bed grappling with jet lag, she continued to resist the lure of the vista of Manhattan's skyscrapers outside her window and the overwhelming notion that perhaps she had simply landed in a chapter of H G Wells's *The Time Machine.*

When she disembarked from the large PanAm plane that had brought her from Karachi to New York, she followed the other passengers to a hall where a man with her name written on a cardboard smiled and quickly moved up to her.

"Welcome to the United States of America. Call me Papa Galatti, everyone does," he said and beamed at her.

This man, who proceeded to carry her small airline bag, was a legend, according to all the promotional literature of the Scholarship Fund which was mailed to her parents in Karachi. He was an Italian American who—as he told it—had taken an ambulance and roamed through France and other European countries during WWII, helping sick and wounded people reach hospitals. The short stocky man now crammed into a blue suit had on his return to the US, in the early 60's created the biggest International Exchange Scholarship program. Students from different countries spent a year in the US, living with matched families, while attending their last year of high school. Papa Galatti believed that this was the way to create global harmony and mutual respect among nations. American families leaped up to support the program, enthralled by the prospect of having a foreign child in their homes for a year. Foundations and philanthropic groups came up with financial support. The foreign students became young ambassadors for their native countries and experienced American culture firsthand.

Her parents had encouraged her to apply and she had been selected. Although she had completed her International Baccalaureate from her Convent School in Karachi, she would now be exposed to the curriculum and culture of an American public school. Papa Galatti had driven her to the American Field Service building on First Avenue close to the UN Building, fed her her first cafeteria dinner and then taken her up to her room where she would spend the night. She would take a plane in the morning to Dallas, Texas to live with a family that had been carefully matched with her own in Pakistan. The hosts had sent welcoming letters with photographs of their home, where she would live, and her American siblings. It was as though the big glossy Life Magazine available in fashionable Karachi bookstores had come to life.

Now as she sat on the American Airlines flight to Dallas, where the glamour of the blonde stewardesses with bright red lipstick and the satiny shimmer of their stockinged legs she found dizzying, she noted the interest they displayed in her native shalwar kameez.

"You have stepped out of an Eastern fairy tale, honey," breathed a stewardess who had previously complimented her on her long auburn braid.

She was cocooned by all the warmth displayed to her and did not miss anyone she had left behind. Instead, she whipped out the little diary her mother had given her and scribbled her impressions of all the newness.

When she descended the steps of the aircraft at Dallas airport, a group of people standing on the tarmac waved enthusiastically at her. The encounter that followed, with multiple introductions, was the most seductive experience she had ever had.

The tall American father immediately won her heart.

"Well sugar, you are going to be my Pakistani daughter for a year and we are going to make you a Texan before you leave." He roared with laughter.

He was a tall man with a craggy face and twinkling eyes. She thought he looked like one of the faces she had seen in pictures of the famous Mount Rushmore sculptures. The mother was shorter, with wavy brown hair and a beautiful face studded with a pair of deep blue eyes. Her clothing was feminine and a cloud of floral fragrance enveloped her. Her accent was a soft drawl and the spontaneous embrace which she gave her was genuine.

The sibling who matched her age was a tall gangly girl with her father's face, though hers had a dusting of freckles and eyes which changed colour from hazel to mottled green. She also spoke in the Texan drawl and was shy and somewhat introverted.

"We are going to share a bedroom. I hope you don't mind, but it's very large and I have a record player in it. We are downstairs and everyone else is upstairs." She rolled her eyes mischievously.

When she was driven to school the next morning the sight she saw was unbelievable. Hundreds of students sat sprawled out on the long steps to the front entrance. Heads swung towards her.

Whistles, raucous cheers, and students circling her to be introduced was overwhelming. The profusion of blonde hair and purple and white school jackets with the word "Sunset" and the logo of an American bison on them denoted a tribe of sorts. The austere and monochromatic uniform of her convent school in Karachi was nudged aside by pure American freedom. It was the world of rock n' roll, the Beatles, Hollywood, and a film star called James Dean. She was transfixed. She felt that she was seated at a never-ending buffet table where she would eat everything.

She entered the school with her American sister through the sea of jostling students and was led to the big school auditorium.

"Is it the morning assembly?" she asked her sibling.

"This one is just for you!" came the reply.

When she was led to the stage by the school principal and introduced, eight hundred students jumped to their feet, clapped, cheered, and whistled. Somehow she had acquired star power and this was her first introduction to it. She had a role to play.

Weeks sped by; the little calendar she had been given by her Texan mother had an activity daily. American football, dating, sightseeing, meals at restaurants, social clubs at school, and her sudden friendships with students both in her class and outside. Theatre at a thrilling venue as well as musicals at the state fair park. There was also a wardrobe shift. Dresses and American teenage trendy outfits were created and gifted to her. She wore them with ease, she was not unfamiliar with them. Her long dark hair was always complimented upon although secretly she longed to cut it off.

Once a month the faint wavering voices of her parents in Karachi could be heard on the telephone on something called a trunk call. She babbled with excitement about her life and the American parents also chimed in and complimented her achievements enthusiastically. She was homesick for nothing. Her English classes introduced her to the works of great American writers. Tennessee Williams, John Steinbeck, J D Salinger, and Hemingway. She had been weaned on the English classics, Lawrence, Hardy, and Dickens, and recently the silvery sensuous prose of Lawrence Durrell.

The musicals *West Side Story* and *Porgy and Bess* revealed to her a different America. Oak Cliff, where her American family lived, was a segregated neighbourhood. It was White America but the maid who came to clean and do laundry once a week was a Black woman called Jhonny Lee. She was a slender wiry woman who vacuumed with ferocity, called her Missy and had a Camel cigarette permanently inserted in one side of her mouth. The ash on the cigarette grew alarmingly long but never dropped. Her manner of speech was lilting and throaty and she laughed when she heard her speak.

"You sure talk like the people in England. The ones in the movies, like the Queen."

Her position was that of maid and household pet. Ed Royse, the father, had inserted a toilet and washbasin in the West Dallas shack where she lived. Groceries and household items were given to her regularly apart from her wages. In no way did she resemble the domestic staff in her parents' home. Jhonny Lee had stepped out of the pages of an unwritten American history book and had sparked her curiosity to learn more about this invisible race in the country she was waltzing through.

A moment arrived like a bolt of lightning in her charmed life and left her guilt-ridden for decades.

She quickly became the star of the school debating team. It was the combination of her diction, writing skills, and ability to present a convincing argument extemporaneously. Trophies piled up for her school. The last tournament was out of town. Miss Rebecca Thayer, the drama and debate coach, accompanied them on the school bus. The tall bulky woman with a high beehive hairdo of ginger-coloured hair was a force to contend with. In her youth, she had performed at the famous Pasadena Playhouse in California and nobody was allowed to forget this. The exchange student was her favourite and she coached her like one would a racehorse.

The bus hit the town of Waco just before noon. They were led to the cafeteria to have lunch before the debate at 1:30. In the lineup, a tall boy was ahead of her. He sensed her presence and turned around and smiled. She was transfixed by his appearance. Although he was Black like Jhonny Lee, his complexion was fairer. The skin seemed velvety and she had an intense desire to touch him. He was tall and stunningly handsome. He drawled at her lazily.

"Here for the debate?"

"Yes," she stammered.

"Are you the Foreign Exchange student?" his eyes flickered over her clothes.

"Yes, from Pakistan."

"Ours is from Germany, but she is not as pretty as you. Do you want to sit with me for lunch?"

"Yes. I would love that," she exhaled and moved along the line.

She was mesmerized by him. This was her first exposure to a member of the invisible community and her curiosity was boundless. He was a teenager just like her, but he was exotic beyond belief. She looked behind her and saw her team members and Miss Thayer in the lineup, and fluttered her hands in a wave and pointed at the boy, signifying she would be sitting with him.

Lunch was a helping of southern fried chicken, potato salad, and corn on the cob, accompanied by a glass of Coke and a slice of chocolate cake.

"You can have my cake if you like chocolate. I am on the basketball team and the coach would have a fit." He turned to her, grinning widely.

She laughed in delight as American chocolate cake with its mile-high icing had become a favourite of hers. He moved towards a long table and she followed him and within seconds she heard a furious voice in her ear.

"Where do you think you are going?" Miss Thayer's flushed-angry face and her formidable bulk blocked her path.

"I am going to eat lunch with this boy. He has invited me," she replied.

"No, you are not. You are to return to the table where your teammates are sitting."

"Why? It's only lunch. When I finish I will return to the school team." She hoped he had not heard this exchange, but he had already reached the table and pointed to the chair next to him.

"I am not going to be rude. He is waiting for me," she said.

That was when the thespian from the famed Pasadena Playhouse inhaled deeply and raised her shoulders into a formidable stance before delivering a blistering statement.

"If you do that, I shall remove you from the team. Sunset will not win, as you are the best speaker. You will let your team down, and what is worse, you will have let your school down when we return without the trophy."

It seemed as though a wall had come down between them. This wall was also going to keep the guy from her. It was blackmail of the worst sort. This was segregation pure and simple but she had never witnessed it. Her American fantasia, where Dallas was the ultimate Disneyland, had not prepared her for this.

"You cannot force me. Please, he is going to think I am so rude," she fought back desperately.

"Do I have to escort you back to the school bus where you will have to sit for two hours alone? I would say it would be enough time to wonder why you have betrayed your teammates and your school."

The wall now exacted its penalty. Censure from her teammates, even if it was silent or disappointment, was something she wanted to avoid. The nuns at the convent school where she was educated had taught her about personal sacrifice. At that moment she lost all respect for the debate coach and drama teacher. She was primed for the challenge of a school competition but not for this. She had lost, and she walked like a robot to the table where her two schoolmates sat. She did not glance at the boy, but stared at the food on her tray. She didn't taste the food.

After the competition, where she won the prize again and brought the trophy for her school, the only thing she tasted was an overpowering and debilitating guilt. But she was young and she hid it.

She was seventeen and in the middle of a carnival and did not discuss the incident with her Texan sibling and parents. There were no Blacks in her school. She knew they lived in "other places." Jhonny Lee, if she had been a fat woman, could have appeared in the novel *Gone with the Wind*. The newspaper which came to the house was *The Dallas Morning News* and the son of the owner was a good friend of hers at school. He was a small wiry boy with a lively mind and often discussed American politics concerning the Vietnam War. He was in the school ROTC program and marched in parades and wished to go to the West Point Military Academy. The paper however never had either a photograph or a story about Blacks.

The conversation eventually took place in a sensational setting. Her American father, Edwin, announced he was taking her to see a real Texan ranch for the weekend with another school friend. He believed this was the authentic Texan culture that she must experience. She would see working cowboys, cattle being branded, and sleep in a cabin and eat the Texan ranch barbeque. His eyes sparkled when he mentioned the eating part. Mischievously, he added that after the weekend at the ranch she would be made an honorary Texan by him. "The eyes of Texas are on you and they already like what they see."

It was a three-hour drive to the ranch, her friend Gretchen bouncing happily in the back seat.

"I have brought two pairs of boots and we can ride as well. You do ride, I know. Also, the boots are your size. They are a gift from my parents to you."

The ranch was straight out of the set of a cowboy movie. The host owner and his wife came to greet them and immediately took both girls to show the cabin with bunks where they would sleep. Outside there were fences and men dressed in jeans and plaid shirts wearing Stetson hats.

Lunch was served in the large central room of the ranch house. Wooden beams crisscrossed the ceiling and the stucco walls were hung with horns and antlers and old maps of the area. The lady who served lunch was Mexican. She had a lined weather-beaten face and masses of dark hair tumbling down her shoulders.

"Say hello to Maria, she has been with our family most of her life; her two sons were born on the ranch and work on it," the host said, addressing her specifically.

She thought the Mexican woman with her tan complexion and features resembled people of her own country. Her status was that of a domestic and her manner was deferential. The meal was delicious Tex-Mex. She tasted enchiladas and rice-and-beans. A fresh pile of tortillas would appear at the table in a conical straw basket.

Her American father buttered numerous of them, using them to scoop up the beans.

But later, when she watched wiry men grab and brand young calves, she became nauseous. She felt she had never witnessed anything so barbaric. Her Texan dad then took her for a horse ride. A gentle chestnut mare called Ginger was saddled for her. The saddle had a horn in the front. She had only ridden on an English saddle. The cowboy boots were stiff and constricted her toes but she was told they would open up. The ranch was enormous and the trails opened into an enormous pasture. She wrapped the reins around the horn and nudged the sides of the horse to make it gallop. She could hear her dad's voice behind her, but she allowed the horse to move along the pasture until they reached a stream. Here they stopped and she slipped down from the saddle.

"You were riding like the wind, sugar. How do you like Texas now?" said her Dad, when he reached her.

"The Mexicans are all ranch hands?" she inquired.

"No, and some of this land belonged to them years ago. They are very good at ranching and are loyal and don't steal like the Blacks. They know who they are."

She gazed at him silently, unable to tell him that his comment shocked her. But he was an astute man and sensed her silence.

"My right-hand man at my business and the workshop where I come up with my inventions is a black fella called Isiah. I will introduce him to you one day."

"Like a business partner?" She was surprised.

"A valued employee and he gets a bonus every Christmas. I am Royse Manufacturing and the sole proprietor."

Within forty-eight hours knowledge of the other America had pricked her mind. She had been introduced to the status of

Hispanic and Black Americans in the great state of Texas. "The Eyes of Texas," which she assumed implied a state of vigilance, was a popular song and sung at her school; the humour was reserved for the whites. It was a racist stripe carefully concealed in the indolent grace of those she was exposed to.

She had been raised in a society where the only social demarcation was between the wealthy and the poor. It was not based on racial stereotypes. Destitutes would approach cars on the road and beg for money, and the response of most adults was to open their wallets. Her mother at the festival of the Eid of the Sacrifice distributed neat brown meal parcels in an area of the city where the destitute congregated.

At the barbeque the next day the sight was amazing. Chunks of meat sizzled on the grills. A long narrow table had been set up heaped with salads and bread. The servers were all Hispanic and one of the women at a rotisserie was Black. She had a jovial, smiling face and corkscrews of curls swept back in a scarf. People lined up before her, holding out their plates to receive the meat. Now and then she would come up with a comment and move her large apron-draped body in a little mime of a dance. When she saw her approach she stopped.

"Your first Texan barbeque, Miss?"

"Yes." She could not help smiling at this goddess of bounty.

"Then you sure need to see Hank at the grill and get you some of that good Texan steak. Tell him Josie said to fix you one medium rare."

"No, no, it does not have to be rare. Just the ordinary one which everyone else is eating," she said, making a monumental gaffe.

"Oh my, oh my." Josie slapped her ample thighs and laughter wheezed out of her,

"You talk as pretty as a robin redbird sing clearly, but you gotta be Texan now. Medium rare means the meat is very soft, juicy, and pink inside."

She went to see Hank. The square chunk of grilled meat she received was unforgettable in its taste.

"It's delicious, but it's too much, I cannot finish it," she said mournfully to Ed Royse, who had come to sit next to her on one of tables scattered over the grass.

"I will help you finish it off," he leaned over and spearing the meat on her plate, placed it on his own.

"They are fabulous cooks," she told him.

"Yes. Old Josie is a wonder and Maria fixes all these salads. What is left is packed for the ranch hands. Mexicans have large families and they love Barbeque Day."

"When we drive back to Dallas can we see where they live?"

"Some live on the ranch in cabins, but their nearest town is far from here. A truck goes there, but it's not a pretty place. There is a quaint little cowboy town on the way back and a tortilla press that I think you will like better."

The town was a block with one store. A gnarled man in a Stetson greeted them inside. She selected a leather belt with a horseshoe buckle and a leather handbag which had hearts and roses embossed on it.

"The Mexican wetbacks make this leather and work on it. Turns out they are good for something," he chuckled. "They come cheap as we pay them less and a tidy profit comes from their handicraft."

It took one more decade to discover the invisible America she had missed out as a teenager. Her husband had a glamorous posting in New York. They spent two months in a hotel in Manhattan while they looked for a place to stay. Her companion during the days was her four-year-old daughter. Central Park Zoo was their favourite outing, and her daughter was mesmerized by the gorilla cage with its newborn called Pattycake. A courteous elderly Black gentleman often shared a park bench with her and also kept an eye on her child. They each displayed an urbane acceptance of each other. He once asked her if she had visited Harlem. She shook her head. "That is where you will see a large number of my people and hear the best music."

That was where she decided she would go.

With babysitting arrangements in hand one afternoon, she asked the concierge to arrange a cab for her. "Where would you be going, Madam?"

"Harlem," she replied gaily.

A shadow descended on his face. "Oh no, Madam. That is not a good place for you."

"Just call me a, cab, please," she said, turning her face away from him.

It was a cold March day and she wore her white wool coat with a fox-fur trim. The taxi driver weaved in and out of traffic and finally deposited her on a busy street of mostly bars and small cafes. The people on the street were Black and dressed modestly, and she felt self-conscious about the opulence of her coat. She attracted attention. There was no one else like her around, so she slipped into a bar from which music seeped out into the street. It was the saxophone that drew her in. The winter afternoon light flooded the bar, which had a small stage with a dim light. A few people were sitting at little tables near the stage. She chose a seat at the bar for safety and to be able to gaze at the entire space. The men seated on either side smiled at her. She ordered a glass of wine and removed her coat but could not find a place to hang it.

"Keep it with you. Sit on it," came the comment from her side.

He was wearing a bow tie and a worn-out velvet jacket.

"First time in Harlem?" he grinned showing white teeth which gleamed from his dark face.

"Yes, does it show?"

He slapped his thigh and laughed raucously.

"Yeah, like a white swan in the middle of a whole mess of black people. Don't worry, nothing will happen to you. I can't vouch for the sax player though. Big flirt. If you are into sax he is the best player. Actually he is just practising. Here most afternoons before his show at night."

"Oh, I love the sax. It is an instrument which talks."

Another man sat at the piano and played, and there was one on the drums. This was jazz and she connected with it. The musicians all dressed in mismatched clothing played as though the music came from their veins. She could have spent hours just listening but it was time to return to the hotel and her husband.

Her return back to the hotel was met by an angry husband.

"How could you go to the crime-riddled slum of this city with such abandon?" he thundered.

"I have never heard music like this before," she told him. "They were sensational. I want to take you there as well. This is a vital part of American culture and it is Black."

"American culture is not found in Harlem. Don't be a bloody tourist and never leave my daughter with a stranger again."

Rebellion in the Mountains

Skardu, Northern Pakistan, 8200 ft, 1963

She had declared herself to be a misfit. She did not say this openly, but her parents, particularly her mother, were acutely aware of this. Her refusal to continue university was based on her deep antipathy towards people of her age in Pakistan. She missed America. The year spent there had changed so many aspects of her thinking. She had travelled back to her home and country with the excess baggage of the memories of her American experience. They had somehow become a part of herself. Clothes, jewelry, society weddings, and forbidden crushes seemed to be the only preoccupations of the new acquaintances that were arranged for her in her home city.

There was no talk of books, films, or world events. Furthermore, her father was posted to the city of Lahore which was foreign to her. In comparison to Karachi, where all her school friends continued to live, she found Lahore to be slow and provincial. She felt as though she had been plucked from everywhere and hurled nowhere. So she buried herself in the two volumes of *Either / Or* by the Danish philosopher Søren Kierkegaard and hovered between two versions of herself.

She was asked one morning by her mother if she would like to visit her favourite uncle, who now lived in a fabled mountain outpost called Skardu, for a week. She accepted this offer eagerly. Uncle Amir was the flower child of the family. It was not just his impossible physical beauty and complete disregard for convention that had won her heart, but his ability to relate to her as a peer. Little did she know that her mother had spoken to Amir and asked him to convince her to join Kinnaird College for Women and continue with her undergraduate degree. Where everyone else had failed, Amir succeeded.

The small plane from Rawalpindi to Skardu was full. The passengers were all men. Some army officers were in uniform. Others were big burly men wearing wool caps and carrying bundles of food parcels on board. She found them all to be disagreeable. Although she pressed herself into her window seat looking out at the clouds, she drew their attention by her western clothes. Wool trousers and a sweater and soft suede walking high-top shoes. She kept her dark glasses on so she could avoid everyone's gaze. The sole flight attendant was most solicitous of her and she suspected her father had something to do with that.

The view outside her window mesmerized her. Cutting through soft mounds of clouds and passing between snow-covered mountains where one felt that they could be touched on either side created a daredevil sort of thrill in her. The pilot announced the name of the mighty Karakoram range and said it was fair weather in Skardu. The only sight of this remote outpost would be when the plane descended. For the first time in weeks she felt a rush of excitement.

The attendant came to her and said she had been invited by the pilot to the cockpit to view the valley in which Skardu nestled. She was now convinced that her prominent civil servant father had organized this. She took her camera and followed the steward. Half a minute later she was seated behind the pilot on a little benchlike seat. The young pilot had smiled at her and she recognized him. He was the son of a family friend.

"How long have you been a pilot?" she squawked.

"Long enough to learn how to fly this plane between the mountains," he gave her a wicked grin and then turned his face back to his instrument panel.

"I have a treat for you. I am going to beat the valley for you. The scenery is pure magic even for a girl from Karachi," he continued.

"It's Lahore now," she said and then felt the sudden dive of the plane.

The vista which sprang before her eyes consisted of terraced fields and fruit trees in flower and a blue ribbon of water snaking along boulders and pastures. All this was ringed by enormous snow-covered mountains. It could have been painted by a watercolourist, and she leaned forward photographing as much as she could, until suddenly the plane rose again. This descent and ascent almost rhythmically was called "beating" in the strange aeronautical jargon.

Then it was time for her to go back to her seat as they would be making the final descent to land. She said goodbye to the pilot who had been a great dancer at Karachi parties. He was much older than her but she remembered his reputation; apparently he had transferred his physical agility to flying a small plane through the mountains.

"Give my salaams to your father when you go back, and remember to visit the lake in Skardu, which local legend says was created by fairies."

She let the noisy gaggle of men descend first and then walked down the narrow, shaky staircase. Her handbag was tucked into her elbow and she gripped the straps of her camera tight in the other hand. The structure she walked toward could not be called an airport, it was just a large square tent at a distance.

She saw him immediately. He wore a cape that reached his knees and on his head was a cap with a small feather in the centre. His mustache curled over his lips and the hands on the arms he extended to her were pale. The ring on one finger gave a silvery flash, before a large agate covered with a script caught her eye.

"Look at you. My beautiful niece!" He pressed her into an embrace.

She caught the scent of his hair pomade and tobacco and smiled up at his great height. Amir had such an undeniable glamour to his beauty that it was rumoured that movie directors in Bombay in pre-Partition India had been ready with offers. He had been sent to Bombay to study engineering and his autocratic father had summoned him back to Srinagar. Acting in films was the profession of a scoundrel or lay-about and not for the respectable son of a great father.

"For you, I have brought the official jeep," he said and marched her briskly along with him. Within seconds an assault of mountain air and the perfume of fruit trees filled her lungs.

"Breathe slowly, you will adjust to the elevation in a minute," Amir said and smiled at her.

The paved tarmac soon ended and soft earth sprang underfoot. A khaki-coloured jeep appeared ahead and he led her to it. He tossed her suitcase in the back and helped her to climb into the front passenger seat.

He drove on a rough unpaved road that registered every bump and her small squeals of discomfort made him laugh.

"This is an army jeep and the official transport of the civilian supply officer, although I do many of my tours on horseback. Your aunt has been cooking since the morning and your six little cousins asked so many questions about you that I had to escape."

She remembered his quiet wife, who had a graceful affectionate air to her and the little cousins, but that had been years ago. The drive to his home took them through terraced fields and orchards. The fruits and vegetables were dried and stored for the winter months. The local inhabitants were called Balti as was their language. They crossed a tiny bazaar with a barbeque food shop, a general store, and a chemist, and then it ended abruptly. People stared unabashedly at the jeep. Some of them waved to her uncle and lifted their hands in greeting. As the jeep began moving away, one tall burly man approached them. He clasped a brown paper parcel to his chest. The jeep stopped and he handed the parcel to her uncle, who handed him some money and then thrust the parcel at her.

"Fresh cakes. The only baker in Skardu. His business runs out of his home. My children love them."

She clasped the still-warm brown paper bundle to her chest. The aroma of vanilla and eggs and flour rose through the paper. The genial smile on the man, who had the typical Balti features of high cheekbones and narrow almond-shaped eyes was heart-warming for her. There arose in the distance the ring of colossal mountains set as sentinels around them. She felt alive and present and did not hover between two versions of herself.

"Ready?" he looked at her.

"Yes. I love all this," she smiled at him.

"Let's take you home then," he shifted gears and took the road at speed.

He drove into a small lane and finally reached a home of grey stone. Gathered in front of the wooden front door were his wife and six children ranging in age from two to twelve. They were her little cousins wearing wool sweaters and sturdy shoes. Her aunt embraced her, squeezing the toddler in her arms between them, the others clamored shyly around her. The warmth and delight of the entire family at her presence were overwhelming.

The house was built of mud bricks and whitewashed. It was a cocoon nestled among the mountains. Inside, there were carpets and cylindrical bolsters lying on them. The walls were hung with ibex antlers and a genuine tiger skin. Little glass windows looked out to the mountains. It was a place of enchantment. She followed her aunt to the tiny kitchen where cloth bags of dried vegetables dangled from the ceiling. She watched how a clump of red dried skins exploded into a fiery tomato sauce for a dish of meat. They had their midday meal, seated on cushions around a low wooden table. Then her little cousins scampered around her, leading the way to the garden where wild roses tangled in the bushes. The sky was blue and the mountain air crisp.

Later that night after dinner she was led to another tiny room, which was her uncle's sanctum. She sat on the floor with him and she watched him brew cocoa for her in a minuscule silver samovar. Then he picked up a stringed instrument and played it. The soft chords were hypnotic. He watched her expression and mused softly, "This is paradise, my dear. Here you will find yourself."

The first few days were filled with long chats with her aunt as she cooked, playing with the toddlers, and rambling outdoors. The figure of her uncle seated on an enormous white horse was pure theatre. He arranged for another horse and took her out riding. The trip to the lake of fairies, Satpara, turned out to be a hair-raising adventure. The lake had an island in the centre where a picnic was planned. They were ferried across in a wooden boat with a hamper containing vanilla cake and a carpet to lie on.

The lake was emerald green and ringed by mountains. The water was cold and deep. When they scrambled onto the ground the carpet was unfurled and the picnic laid out. The boat returned to the shore; it would return three hours later. Only four children accompanied them, including the youngest, who was two. Her uncle lit a pipe contentedly and gazed at the mountains. She lay on the carpet with the little cousin, who crawled over her making animal sounds. The older children sent little stones skimming along the lake surface. Within two hours of this idyllic picnic, the weather changed. A fierce mountain wind rose and the water churned. Everything that was serene before now became hazardous. Her uncle cupped his hand and called out to the boatman to come immediately. The man shouted back that it was too dangerous, he could not come. This shouted exchange continued, the boatsman refusing to move and her uncle's temper rising with the lake water.

There was some activity on the shore around the boat. Someone was seated in it now, though the boatman was still on the shore. The boat moved towards the little island. As it got closer to them they realized it was the lame young nephew of the boatman who was rowing. It was a slow and perilous journey towards them and when it reached the island her uncle discarded the picnic hamper and put the two-year-old in her arms.

"You are going to hold him. No matter what happens in the boat you are not to let him go."

The boatman's nephew, wearing wet clothes, sat at the helm. Her uncle helped her in. He then put the other two older children on the floor and climbed in himself, sitting behind the boy, and lifted one oar. It was a slow excruciating journey as the jade-green lake turned darker and more sinister. The two older children had stricken faces and the toddler in her arms pushed fretfully within her arms. Nobody spoke until they were close to the shore. She pressed the little boy to her chest and closed her eyes, terrified about what would happen if the boat tipped over.

"It's fine, we are almost there," her uncle's voice sounded faint in the howling wind.

The boat struck the beach and he leaped out helped the two older children out. The lame boy rose awkwardly and extended a hand to her. She rose and held his hand gratefully. It was a thin bony hand with callouses. It was when she climbed out that she noticed the large boulder in the boat, there to steady it, and thought about the cowardly boatman who had sent a handicapped teenager on this dangerous mission. He was nowhere in sight.

"It's all right. I know where he will be found. Later," her uncle said and led them all to the jeep.

"He is a coward. He should be told that," she was furious.

"Let's reward our hero first, that is more important."

He went to the jeep and returned with a roll of cash which he gave to their rescuer. The boy looked over at her and just smiled. His manner and ability to overcome his handicap were pure grace.

Halfway home another large vehicle approached them. It had a few army men and the boatman, who had gone to town and sounded the alarm to round up rescuers. He was shocked by their presence; apparently he had had no idea that his nephew was capable of rowing the boat or even placing the rock unassisted inside. He hung his head down shamefully as her uncle thundered at him. At home, they were greeted like returning heroes by her aunt, who had also got the unfortunate news that "supply sahib," the children, and his niece were all marooned and probably drowned. She distracted herself by cooking an excellent pulao. The little cousin

Shujat said it was probably the fairies who gave the boatman's nephew special powers.

She slept that night chased by a nightmare of water and howling winds and rose to the acceptance that nature amidst spectacular beauty always had the upper hand. What was fearful and insurmountable was often relegated to the supernatural by a semiliterate and isolated community.

The invitation to visit the tiny neighbouring kingdom of Khaplu was presented by her uncle two days before her departure.

"Is it an official tour for you?" she asked.

"The rajah's new wife is a convent girl like you who speaks fluent English and would love to meet you," he grinned mischievously at her.

"Gosh, a rani! Why not? Perhaps I can find out more about life in these little kingdoms."

"Two-thirds of the journey will be by jeep but the last few kilometres will be on horseback. What do you think?"

"I will be ready."

They travelled on the winding roads towards Khaplu by jeep. The palace in Khaplu had been built in 1840. This was the second largest kingdom in old Baltistan, ruled by the Yabgo dynasty, and it guarded the trade routes to Ladakh. The first stage of the journey from Skardu was covered easily, a clearing revealed horses and grooms. The medieval touch excited her and James Hilton's novel *Far Horizons* came to mind. She mounted a big chestnut mare called Rani and her uncle sat astride a black horse. The rajah had sent two riders to escort them. An hour later they reached the palace, which looked upon vistas of both the Himalaya and Karakoram ranges. The rajah himself stood with a small group of attendants to greet them. She dismounted and stretched her legs and walked behind her uncle to greet the rajah. He was a short plump man with a merry face, a twirling mustache, and features that were distinctly Balti.

She was ushered up the stairs to the rani's quarters and informed that she would later have lunch with the rajah in the main dining area. She was led through a series of doors through a wooden interior sprinkled with Tibetan and Kashmiri motifs and ushered into a room. What greeted her eyes was a young girl of perhaps fourteen or fifteen years, seated behind an elaborate tea table. The attendant withdrew after murmuring the word "rani." She advanced towards the table, smiling at the teenage girl whose face lit up.

"You have brought me some books in English?"

"I am sorry. I was not asked. If I had known I would have brought them for you," she said and sat down on a chair and moved closer. "Are you the daughter of the rajah?"

A shadow passed across the girl's face. Her hair was fastened in two long braids and tied with shiny satin ribbons behind her ears. She wore a garnet-coloured wool sweater over which a heavy necklace of gold sovereigns cascaded down, and her delicate features created the impression that she was a young girl who had invaded her mother's jewelry box.

In perfect English with convent enunciation she stated, "I am the Rani of Khaplu."

She had lifted the teapot and proceeded to pour tea into a delicate bone-china teacup.

She felt as though the outrage and revulsion which coursed through her would suffocate her. She accepted the cup of tea with a shaking hand, unable to face the teenage queen who now held up a plate of ginger biscuits.

"I am sorry we cannot get pastries here and our cook does not know how to make them."

"Are you married?" she could not believe she was asking this question.

"Yes. You met the rajah outside. My husband."

What she could not block from her mind were images of the corpulent middle-aged rajah entwined with this schoolgirl.

"Did you also study at a convent school? I like how you are dressed for riding. I can't wear trousers like this and anyway I am not allowed to go riding," the rani said ruefully.

"Do you live here alone? Where is your mother?"

"After the marriage, I live here with the rajah. There is no one else, just all the servants." She straightened up and adopted a pose that seemed to have been taught to her.

"Well thank you so much for inviting me to tea," she rose and walked to the large window.

"What shall we talk about? See, my English is good."

"Your English is perfect. Did you not want to continue to study?"

She resisted the impulse to simply hug the girl.

"A rani cannot do that. I have duties." Again a shadow ran across her face.

The door opened and the attendant asked her to come to the dining hall with her. "I would prefer to sit here. I am not hungry for lunch." She was unwilling to leave the girl yet.

"But you must go. You must not keep the rajah waiting," the rani said and stood up. "The lunch has been prepared specially for you." She held out her hand.

She held the limp hand with both of hers, wishing to convey some sort of fragmented solidarity. What she wanted to do desperately was to spirit the schoolgirl away from the force which had arrested her adolescence and made her a prisoner in a gilded cage guarded by impenetrable mountains. This was a direct experience with the shocking plight of women in the country she had returned to. It was as though a serpent had crept into this idyllic paradise, and her beloved freedom-loving unconventional uncle had exposed her to this.

It was with the burden of her rage that she walked along the long corridor into a large room, in which on the floor was a long tablecloth with cylindrical cushions, and seated were the rajah, her uncle, and a few other men. She was asked to sit between her uncle and the rajah, who beamed at her and patted the bolster next to him. She slipped off her shoes and sank to the floor, avoiding the cushion. Her uncle looked at her but she avoided his gaze. A large platter of rice pilaf was presented, and the rajah served her, adding little nuggets of fat to her plate. This was a delicacy that made her nauseous as well as the all-male lunch from which the teenage rani had been banned as she was to be in purdah. She furtively hid the nuggets of fat under the mound of rice on her plate. The rajah spoke to her in accented English.

"You like Khaplu?" He flashed a smile revealing yellowing teeth.

"Is there a school here?" she asked politely.

The rajah clapped both his hands and laughed uproariously. He then narrowed his eyes and studied her face as though suddenly an insect had crawled on it and he had to decide if it was harmless or not.

"First we have to repair the palace. It is very old. You can take a picture outside for a souvenir." He gave a broad smile as though he had conferred some honor on her and turned away to speak to a man seated across from him.

She felt her uncle move closer to her and he whispered a warning in her ear, "No more questions."

Departure for Skardu took place immediately after lunch. She kept her eyes averted from the rajah and let her uncle do the formal goodbye. It was only when they were alone in the jeep that he finally tackled her silence.

"What is it? I have never seen you so quiet. Did the young rani enjoy your company?"

"Have you ever seen her?" she shot back.

"No. Of course not, she is in purdah. It is the tradition." He spoke softly.

"How can you condone this? I am revolted and angry."

He was silent. The landscape sped by and she kept seeing the face of the young girl with her hair braided and tied in ribbons presiding over the fine tea set.

"These are the little mountain kingdoms of Baltistan. He rules one, so the marriage was considered an advantage by her parents. Probably by her as well. Learn to accept different traditions."

"There must be a legal age for marriage, and rajah or not he must be breaking a law. No I cannot let this go."

"So you are looking for a change? It will be the result of education. So go to college, complete your studies and then tackle this." He smiled at her.

"That is the only way?"

"Yes. Now if you were a journalist you could write about this."

"I did not know I cared so much."

"That is called passion. Good quality to explore and excellent university professors will teach you how to channel it," he replied deftly.

"I will think about it."

"Let these mountains quell the superficial rebellion. Complete your higher education and then rescue all the underage girls from marriages forced upon them. That will be a noble rebellion. I am on your side always."

It was when he drove her to the airstrip to catch the small plane back that she realized that somehow a mission had crept into her consciousness. She needed to talk about her experience and find her voice. She needed to read different books now and learn the history of places like Khaplu. She needed guidance and mentors. Above all she wanted to rescue girls from underage marriages.

A week later she packed five English novels into a parcel and addressed them to her uncle in Skardu. At the post office she hastily included a letter which was taped to the top of the package.

"Please have these delivered to the Khaplu palace for the rani. There is a letter for her in the package."

A year later, when she was a third-year student a letter arrived for her from her uncle in Skardu. It was a large brown envelope and inside was another much smaller envelope. There was one word written on the envelope: Madam. The single sheet of paper inside was lined as though it had been taken from a school exercise book. The handwriting was clear and well-formed.

"*Jane Eyre* is my favourite book. When I have a daughter I will raise her to be just as strong as Jane Eyre. I am writing little stories for her, so I can read to her when she is old enough. The rajah has said that I can make one of the rooms into a schoolroom for all the children I will have. Will you return to visit us? I cannot forget you."

The Philosophy Professor

Kinnaird College, Lahore, 1964

She was a tall slender woman with a pale complexion, grey eyes, and short cropped brown hair. Her erect stature and manner suggested prestige and privilege. She was the new foreign professor of a type never seen before at Kinnaird College for Women. Bearing the weight of the academic prestige of Oxford, where she had excelled and lectured, her decision to sign a four-year contract to teach in Lahore, Pakistan could have been a Kipling adventure of sorts. The liberal arts university founded by the Presbyterian Mission Church in 1913 had rapidly become a sought-after institution for young women all over Pakistan.

The professor met her class one by one, shaking hands and pronouncing their names as correctly as she could. At some mispronunciation, a faint smile would move across her face. With the handshake, she studied the student. It was piercing scrutiny, whose purpose was to gauge intelligence. So the daring girl of nineteen locked her eyes in a fixed gaze and did not allow a smile to cross her face. The professor withdrew her hand and turned to the next student abruptly. The student felt as though a snapshot had been taken of her, revealing her entire life history. She also felt that a current had passed between them. Intuitively, she knew the professor would play a significant role in her academic year.

She found the lectures enthralling, as was her easy style of lecturing. One was conscious at all times that a large brain dictated the lectures and often caught rare glimpses of self-deprecating humour. It was a philosophy course with snatches of literature and psychology thrown in. She made an astonishing statement one day. Discussions of any philosophical nature could also be held informally at a drop-in at her living space on campus. She also selected the duration of the visits. She received at between five to seven PM twice a week. It was part of her experience of familiarizing herself with her students, as well as practicing the tutorial system of her alma mater. On certain days she wore the local shalwar kameez, and on others, skirt and buttoned blouse. Her kameez was like a fitted tunic and she dispensed with the dupatta. Nevertheless, she still looked like an English woman. She never wore jewelry except for a Swiss wristwatch. She had long elegant fingers. A fine web of blue veins could sometimes be seen on the hands. She was a combination of delicacy and a ramrod martial disposition.

The student found her lectures challenging. The first semester course was Fundamentals of Formal Logic. Just as the night ended to herald dawn and the sun, critical thinking was applied to illuminate existing intelligence and open up surprising new vistas. While her companions furiously scribbled bits of the lecture in their notebooks, she simply listened in a daze, every statement uttered by the professor dislodging her fledging repository of thoughts. One could apply this type of thinking even to current issues of the world she lived in. Aristotle and Plato, Socrates, Kant and Rousseau, and Nietzsche were players at some elite club and she had found them more dazzling than film stars.

She read voraciously, using both the library and scanning the shelves of bookstores in Lahore. The assignment papers she handed in were returned with red lines through some sentences and "yes" in the margins of others. "Explore further" often appeared on top of the paper. Surprisingly, the marks given were decent although the judgment was stringent. These long essays were languidly returned to their desks by the professor, who often let an enigmatic smile play on her features. "Don't be lazy, go further," she would whisper into her ear, so she could not be sure if the remark was meant for her. When she looked up startled, the mischievous smile hovering at the edges of the professor's lips were enough to convince her that the challenge was directed at her.

Often during class, the professor would preface a section by saying, "This is my opinion—now let's see what Miss Anwar has to say about this?" and she would lean back in her chair with arms folded and the same infuriating half smile on her face.

The student took the bait only to see her commentary challenged or even mocked. On some rare occasion, astonishingly, praise was offered generously. It became a game of sorts. The professor and her star pupil. The rest of the class looked forward to this exercise, which was in fact an effective teaching device.

"I have been reading Sartre and Bertrand Russell as well," she said recklessly one day.

"Changing the curriculum, I see. Perhaps the reading list for this term has bored you? Or is it interfering with the varsity debate tournaments? I gather you are on the team. Silver cups and trophies nudging the luminous Monsieur Rousseau aside." Her grey eyes were like steely discs.

"I am just fascinated and reading ahead, that's all," she said apologetically.

"Excellent. Excellent. Would you care to deliver tomorrow's lecture on applying philosophic reasoning to moral issues, Miss Anwar?"

"I am sorry. I didn't mean to be rude," she faltered.

"Never be sorry, Miss Anwar. Just be right, that's all."

The reference to the debate tournaments sliced through her self-confidence like a blade. She and her teammate Mina had been lavishly complimented by the faculty and the principal for their performances. Her father was equally pleased, placing the silver trophies on the living-room mantelpiece. Yet in the hands of this professor, her ego received a bruising.

She decided to make a visit with Mina to the professor's rooms one early evening. It was a second-floor set of rooms. The door was opened by the professor, who welcomed them and ushered them to her living room. It had a long sofa, two chairs, and a gigantic wooden bookcase. They both sat perched on the edge of the chairs nervously.

The professor said, "I am offering sherry and cigarettes, ladies."

She picked up a tray from the table behind the sofa and approached them. Although both students came from homes where alcohol was not served, both were ready to take the plunge.

The professor gave a wide smile and held out the sherry glasses. Then she held out the open cigarette box. Armed with a glass of sherry in one hand and a Pall Mall cigarette in the other, the girl determined to move closer to the professor in some undetermined fashion.

"Well, Miss Anwar, does the sherry meet with your approval?"

She took a big gulp as though to prove her courage or sophistication. The sweetish alcohol cut a fiery track down her throat.

"Always sip sherry. Just sip. It's a mild relaxant and perhaps Miss Anwar will reveal that she is a good conversationalist after all." She said this to Mina.

The laughter broke out spontaneously. Perhaps it was the relief of being treated as an equal and one did not have to be a bathroom smoker. Or perhaps the alcohol had relaxed them.

"The sherry of course remains an undiscussed item ladies. I can assure you I do not offer it to everyone, but I just thought Miss Anwar needed to relax a little, and you, Tehmina, are foolish enough to try anything once." Again the mischievous half-smile came to hover around the professor's fine lips.

The bookshelf stretching across one wall caught the student's eyes. She got up and walked to it as the professor and Mina talked about Pakistani summer fabrics, which the professor seemed to be most interested in. The spines of the books revealed titles she had just heard of but never seen. The Russian author Solzhenitsyn and the German Thomas Mann, the French Anaïs Nin and Marguerite Yourcenar. She pushed the books back carefully and returned to her chair.

It was a room full of freedom and intellectual wonder and their hostess seemed to be transformed.

"What are your plans after this degree?" she probed the student.

"I don't know. At present I am very excited about philosophy, but my father suggests I study law."

"What about 'I have a BA so I'm ready for marriage'?"

"Not at all."

"Boyfriends lurking in the bushes then?"

Again she made both her visitors laugh and resisted all their attempts to rinse sherry glasses. The student got home that day and realized that she'd had the best time since her return home from America. Her admiration for the professor leaped by bounds. It was a luxurious feeling. She didn't realize the hazard around this feeling.

An exciting notice was posted in the college notice board declaring that the professor would direct the annual college play. The choice of the play was equally perplexing, A A Milne's *Toad of Toad Hall.* A morality play about four animals and one who had to learn a lesson. Having taken part in school plays and with debating prizes behind her, the student decided to audition. She did not audition for the lead role but chose a supporting one. Auditions were held in the large college auditorium, with the professor seated on a stool in front. Her choice of role was dismissed and she was told to read for the lead character of Toad. She disliked Toad, a vain animal who was both wealthy and reckless. Foolishly she felt that this disgraceful character would somehow taint her persona.

Finally the professor changed her mind.

"I have decided you are best suited for the part of Judge. It's a solid role and it will teach you a lot about theatre." She waved her hands airily.

But she held her ground. "I will think about it."

"I don't want to play Judge," she said to Mina. "I think she is bullying me. It's all right in philosophy class, but not here. I have the right to choose."

The next philosophy class she was held back by the professor.

"I am giving you a copy of the script. Read the part of Judge and then give me your decision tomorrow, Miss Anwar. I believe that the theatre will teach you as much as your philosophy classes."

She read it through the night and realized this was a moral tale in itself. Even though all the characters were animals, their conflicts and adventures could be easily found in the human realm. Her ensnarement took place at four AM when she finished reading.

The valuable lesson about striving for excellence came when she was cast as the Judge and subjected to evening and weekend rehearsals where the professor hammered and wrung a faultless performance out of the entire cast. As nerve-wracking as the experience was, the thunderous applause of the audience on the opening night made her realize that she had received a privilege it would take years to fully acknowledge. It had also tantalized the fledging dramatic culture of Lahore by launching a spell-binding actress, Nivers, who played the lead role. Upon graduation she chose the prosaic halls of academia; stage and television could come later.

From the professor herself came a short "well done," the enigmatic half-smile, and no more.

The following year she would be cast as Portia in *The Merchant of Venice.*

However, past the play, basking in this new glory where a theatre review even mentioned her role, she made a mistake. The final debating tournament was held at the Law College and if she won, the debating shield would come back to Kinnaird College after five years. There would also be a celebrated lawyer who would be the chief guest at the event. She spent many hours working on her speech and calculating the potential challenges to it and how she would respond.

The tournament took place midmorning at the time of a philosophy class. She would miss it but planned to make up for it later. When she stood at the podium, a paper airplane sailed lazily from the opponent's podium towards her; she simply flicked it aside as one would a mosquito, refusing to make eye contact with the petty assailant.

She and Mina won second and third. The top prize went to a student from the law college; however, the shield would go to Kinnaird. They had brought it on the strength of two prizes. After the prize-giving there was a stir in the front row as the celebrated lawyer stood up to make a short speech. He said that he disagreed with the decision about the first prize, he thought it was easily won by Miss Anwar of Kinnaird College and he felt compelled to offer a personal prize to her in the form of a cheque in the amount of Rs 300.

Apart from the honor bestowed upon her, it was gratifying to realize that the long-standing College snack shop bill she shared with Mina could be settled. They would no longer have to hide in shame and get their friends to buy snacks for them. Reputations were saved.

The next day she raced to her philosophy lecture.

"Miss Anwar. You are not permitted to attend this class," the cold voice halted her just inside the door.

"Excuse me?" She could not believe what was happening.

"You missed your ethics lecture without informing me. I do not tolerate such behaviour—kindly leave."

"But Professor Cassin, I was at the Debate Tournament and I brought the shield home for our college after five years." Indignation in her voice.

"You are not welcome to my lecture. Kindly shut the door after yourself."

She turned on her heels and raced out of the class, forgetting to shut the door. Racing down the long corridor she felt tears press on her eyelids. Horrified that her mortification would be seen, she sought refuge in the first-floor bathrooms. Here she tried to understand the situation. She did not have the power to take the professor on. Her punishment was outlandish. While everyone else celebrated her triumph, the professor exhibited contempt and dismissal. She had no solution on hand.

The following week twice she attempted to enter the class, only to be barred. The professor no longer resembled her former self. This was not the person who served sherry and cigarettes in her living room or handled every encounter with finesse; instead, she resembled a tall slender column of ice.

She tried to read lecture notes taken by others and it was frustrating. She stood outside the lecture hall to listen. Her mission was twofold. Perhaps the professor catching sight of her would relent, or she could listen to the proceedings from outside. Both missions failed as some student would always be directed to close the door.

For a week the stand-off continued and the student felt as though the heart had gone out of her life at the college. Her English literature classes were taught by an American, who told her that she had the makings of a novelist herself. She had handed in a truly morbid but faultless paper on James Joyce.

"You are not participating as you normally do? Are you well?" she inquired gently after a class.

"I am trying to devise a plan so I can get back to my philosophy class."

"Ah! The wrath of Professor Cassin. But I hear you are a student she takes a keen interest in."

"For all wrong reasons this time," she responded irately.

"No. She is British and quite a disciplinarian. Negotiate with her. I think she would like that."

She picked up courage and landed up the same evening in the professor's living quarters. Visits were allowed on this day and she hoped she would be the only one present. She rang the doorbell with quivering fingers and a pounding heartbeat, which she felt could be heard a mile away. There was a delay before the door was opened. The professor stood in front of her.

"Come in Miss Anwar. I have been expecting you," she led the way to the armchairs. "Sherry, perhaps?" she asked in a genial tone.

"No. Thank you," blurted out the student.

"I see. Then it is your Dutch courage which shall see you

through this visit. I would have taken the sherry, it is more bracing and reliable." Her habitual half-smile was missing.

"What can I do to return to your classes. I am worried I am missing things and there are end-of-semester exams coming up. It's not fair, professor." She hated the sound of her desperate voice.

"Do I detect a rare form of hubris here, Miss Anwar?"

"Perhaps you could explain what hubris has do with this?" the student fired back.

Dutch courage, always associated with rare forms of bravado, opened the path for another discussion that would linger in her mind for years.

"Your previous show of hubris detected in your imagining that because you have won a Varsity Debate competition, missing an important end-of-term lecture paled in importance. You could ride on your celebrity status and not display the courtesy to inform me in advance."

The warmth of the sitting room vanished. The student felt herself shrink in the armchair. Courtesy was entwined with respect. Her inability to inform the professor had become a slight which she could not imagine ever parcelling to the professor. There was no way out of this.

"I am very sorry."

"An apology is a fine thing, Miss Anwar, but its sincerity is gauged by intent and not by consequence. What do you think?"

"Yes . . . it should be sincere. I thought you would forgive this. Perhaps gauge this from my perspective—an excited oversight."

"Miss Anwar. You are simply my student and I do not have a personal relationship with you. However, as you have shown the courage to walk into the lion's den and talk of negotiation, then I shall accept this. I require an essay on ethics, and if it meets with my approval, you may rejoin the class."

"Yes. Yes of course." Relief flooded into her.

"One thousand words, typewritten. Double spaced. Handed in by ten AM at the staff room."

The student felt as though an exam had been announced, with no time for preparation. She could not get home fast enough. Her father had given her a typewriter when she returned to college. And she had taught herself to type. She could slowly peck out words, and seeing clean printed words appear on paper was a thrill. It felt as though she were preparing an important document. Armed with books for reference she arranged everything on a table her mother used for tea on one side of the dining room. When dinner was over and the lights of the room switched off, she re-entered and set up her writing desk.

She wrote her essay out first and then went over it again, cleaning up the duplications and spelling errors. She checked with her dictionary, another gift from her father years ago. Her breathing was shallow and her concentration was intense. She knew this had to be as perfect as she could make it. The finished result was an essay on ethics and its relationship to both personal and public integrity.

She felt she had got carried away by this opportunity. A thousand words were not enough for her, but she had to hand in what was required. The professor would know with one glance if she had exceeded the quota of words. She wiped her hands and inserted the clean sheets to type the copy. It was late and close to three AM and would go on to later at her typing speed. Although she could not believe that her minor folly had resulted in this prodigious labour, another emotion suffused her. It was a sense of pride in being able to execute the task.

Her mother appeared at one point with a glass of warm milk and a handful of almonds. "The almonds are brain food," she said softly, withdrawing into the night shadows.

It was almost dawn when she joined all three sheets of paper with a paper clip and stumbled to bed.

The essay was delivered to the staff room. The next day when it was time for the philosophy class she walked with some trepidation to the lecture hall. The professor was seated at the large table beside the lectern. The student looked at her habitual seat in the second row but did not move towards it.

"Come in, Miss Anwar. You have some notes to read which you may have missed." She held out a sheaf of papers.

The student walked to her seat as the class began to fill up. No other word was exchanged. In her mind the invitation to return meant that the essay had been acceptable. She had at that point no way of knowing what the level of acceptability was.

It was another four months before she discovered what this level was, under the most unsettling of circumstances. She had agreed to marry; her boyfriend was four years older than her and had planned to immigrate to Canada to further his professional education. They would leave two weeks after their marriage for a new-world adventure.

When she informed the professor of this, on the day before the summer break, her response was one of the legendary outrages she was known for.

"You cannot do this," she raged. "You are my prize philosophy student and I have made an application for you for a Rhodes Scholarship to continue at Oxford. Your essay on ethics has had more than a favourable response."

"I am getting married, Professor Cassin," she said. But she was also stunned by the response.

"Put it off for a couple of years. Finish your education first. If he loves you, he will wait."

"No. You don't understand. We have just managed to convince my father to allow us to get married. We will be together and our new life in a different country comes first."

Five years later on a brief visit from Toronto to London accompanied by her husband and her year-old baby daughter, she went looking for the professor. She took a train from Paddington to Oxford. She was alone, her husband was taking care of the baby. She was dressed fashionably in a knit maxi dress and knee-high Italian boots. She had also washed her long wavy hair, which remained damp through the entire train journey.

It was a rainy November day. When she reached Oxford she took a taxi to the College she had been directed to. She made sure the strap of her long hippy handbag with its suede fringe was secure. She had a gift for the professor. When she got out, a rotund man in a bowler hat opened the grilled gate and pointed to a doorway. The professor was standing there wearing a chunky sweater over a tweed wool skirt. She also wore boots, but hers were more sensible. She simply held out her arms.

"So, Miss Anwar, you have returned to my dangerous embrace."

The whisper and chuckle were like music to her ears.

"Oh, how are you. It is wonderful to see you, just wonderful. You have not changed a bit, professor."

"Well, let's look at you. Marriage and motherhood seem to have agreed with you, I must say you are looking smashing."

The student felt the warmth of these words chase away the chill of the damp hair and the grey light of the rainy day.

"Come, we have been invited by my old tutor for sherry. He heads the philosophy department at Christ Church."

"Fantastic. I have not been warm ever since we got to London."

First, she was led to a space where Cardinal Wolsey's hat was displayed on a wooden stand. The college was named after the Cardinal, whose personal coat-of-arms became the college insignia. Pages of English history turned in her mind. Then upon reaching the heavy carved wooden door, the professor knocked softly and opened the door. The sight bore no resemblance to the rooms in Kinnaird College. An elderly man sat before a roaring log fire in a room filled with books and furniture, which seemed to also come out of history books.

He rose slowly and advanced towards them.

"So Christine, then this is your most intriguing visitor. Welcome to Christ Church my dear," he extended his hand.

"She has landed in Oxford with damp hair. We need to place her close to the fire." The professor smiled broadly and nudged her towards a chair closer to the fire.

"Well. Well. Then a hot brandy may be the answer and not sherry," the tutor peered at her with a twinkling set of blue eyes.

"Oh thank you so much, but it may be too strong for me?" She looked helplessly at the professor, who had seated herself on the small velvet couch in front of the fire.

Warmed by the crackling fireplace and sips of a cream sherry, the student then embarked on a conversation that taught her more about the professor than all her days as her student.

"It was really my ego which was hurt by your decision not to continue as a philosophy student. Your intelligence, which showed itself in your excellent academic material, made me shine as your teacher. You made me shine, which is gratifying for any teacher and you were stopping that."

"I made a life decision, professor," said the shocked student. "It was not your loss but simply that my destiny was in my own hands."

"Well," joined in the elderly tutor, "I was sent your remarkable essay by your professor, and I still wish to extend an invitation to you to come and continue studying at Oxford whenever you can arrange it."

"Oh, professor next you will ask me if I am using my mind. I have some proof with me"—the student smiled at her own professor and pulled out three typed pages from her hand bag.

As a busy young mother living in a large home, sharing the dizzying ascent of her young husband's career up the corporate ladder, she had taken a part-time course in journalism in Toronto. A class assignment was a profile on a visiting famous foreign correspondent who had attended a class. The student had many reservations about his opinions. Her profile was acerbic and demanded accountability. She knew she wanted to become a writer someday. She had brought that essay for the professor. The professor read the three pages and passed them to her own tutor. Then she threw back her head and laughed out boisterously.

"Yes, there is a mind here, no doubt about it. Is it journalism then? You are going to terrify people. Bravo."

"I hope you caught the defining term's premise. It is straight out of our first philosophy course with you," replied the student.

"Yes. I can see that. Perhaps I did not lose you entirely."

Death by Remote Control

Belleville, Ontario, 1976

It was a restless night. The large bed had become unfamiliar. Gone was the welcoming embrace of the familiar space on her left side. Gone was her husband, on a business trip to New York. He would return in a week.

She got up and walked out to the larger bedroom where her older daughter slept in her canopy bed. Her body was neatly arranged under the bedsheet. She bent over her and tucked the strand of curling hair away from the girl's cheeks and then gazed at the rows of dolls sitting on the shelf on the wall—exotic sentinels guarding her sleeping daughter. This was the daughter with the face of a lotus, her high cheekbones sculpting her face, complemented by a small graceful body trained in dance and gymnastics. Her report cards were festooned with A's and her personality even as a preteen was defined to make her sure-footed in all her endeavours. Moonlight flooded in from the gingham curtains on the large window. It was an interesting room bearing the stamp of the girl's personality. What was hidden from her, the mother, was always tucked away in invisible shadows. It was all camouflage anyway. Decades would reveal this. The designer wallpaper where matching lines had exacted painstaking labour from the mother. The antique wicker four-poster frame of the bed and the matching night table which had to be spray-painted white, another labour-intensive project undertaken by the mother. The study desk, which was just a large section of wood resting on a steel trestle, stretched across one smaller wall of the bedroom. The only false note was the mustard-coloured broadloom on the floor, which the father would not replace. He felt enough money had been already spent on the bedroom. So she never intruded on the privacy of the resident who dreamed of wild things in her canopy bed. Mother and daughter were bonded with a fierce glue of love, admiration, and humour. Often in the family dynamics they appeared as a team. They were like two peas in a pod.

She walked into the smaller, adjoining bedroom. Here the sleeping child, her younger daughter, had flung her arms and legs over the bedsheet and tucked her face into the cradle of her arms. Her wealth of midnight-coloured hair was half-trapped under the pillow. The face was different from her sister's. She had jet black eyes with long eyelashes and a broad face. Next to the small aquarium on top of the chest of drawers was a small nightlight. She had not completely lost her childish fear of the dark. The dim light could stay there forever, the mother felt.

The fish floated round lazily in their glass home. Next to the chest of drawers was the clothes closet. She had given her permission to draw and write with chalk on the door of the closet. Even though her husband had been displeased, she had supported this act of creative vandalism as it just took a damp sponge to wipe it clean. Plus the resident seemed to have a lot to say about her world. She was a spirited child, a chatterbox, and a scribbler of musical notes and images. The odd numerical diagram indicated that she also played make-believe teacher. It was her room and she could do whatever she pleased. Some of her stuffed toys lived in a plastic toy chest. The lid was always open. Books also wound up in this chest. The pièce de résistance, however, was the occupant of a little wicker pram. China baby lay here wearing a long purple velvet dress with a lace collar. The mother had made this doll herself. The head was of porcelain and the features were painted delicately at a doll-making class. The body was made of stuffed cloth with arms, legs, and torso. The mother had stitched the clothes and stressed how delicate she was. The little girl considered this a prize and kept her lying in state; she simply peeked at her or straightened the velvet dress. Nobody was allowed to lift her out or play with her. Out of habit the mother peeked at the China baby, remembering how taxing it was to paint the features, how she had raced to have it ready as a Christmas present. She arranged the toys and books neatly in the toy chest and withdrew without making a sound.

There was a bandbox perfection to her life. The life she lived in the three-bedroom split-level grey brick home with a deep garden. The community was family-friendly, with the school a two-minute walk away. It was a neighbourhood where children visited one another and the parents knew each other. Twenty minutes away from the city of Toronto, Thornhill was a suburban dream and chosen so her husband had just a twenty-minute drive to the corporate headquarters of the multinational where he worked. The Montessori school where the younger daughter studied was ten minutes away on Bayview Avenue. They had two cars, and a cleaning lady came twice a month. Her tennis club was a twenty-minute drive away. They took holidays in the Caribbean in the winter and overseas to visit the grandparents who still lived in the country they had left. His job took him to Europe and on one surprising occasion to Africa. There were trips to New York and to Texas to visit her extended American family. He worked at his job and she raised the daughters and tended to the daily needs of her family, with enough time for her own athletic and artistic pursuits.

In fifteen years the dream of settling in a new country had brought all the rewards of successful integration. There was a calm acceptance of how their life had been planned and lived. The flush of their adventurous romance had long disappeared as had the leaping flames of the new fire. It had settled down to glowing embers which often had to be released from the ashes. Shockingly, a new aspect of his temperament revealed itself. He was governed by a secret rage that would flare up two or three times a year. This would erupt in his shouting at her. She would back away in fear, keeping a safe distance from him. He became unrecognizable at those times but loathing and empathy for him grew silently in her heart. She knew the love that she had had for him was now being replaced by a haunting sense of danger. The friendship between them had altered. Silences invaded this union. He would brood for hours and she left him alone in their bedroom. Something was wrong with him but she could not put her finger on it. She protected her children from it, not letting his vocal eruptions contaminate the fierce love which she had for them. Nothing was allowed to disturb the order of their lives and mostly it did not.

Pressed like a rose in a book, the tragic event in their early life in Toronto had been tucked away. The subject had no part in the lives of their daughters or even their own now. Memory did not even bring the presence or reality of that pressed flower ever into their current lives. She had been twenty-one and he twenty-five. Now they were both in their early thirties brimming with vigor and the path ahead opened up to more seasons of living. Bad things happen to good people and both of them shied away from phrases like "unspeakable tragedy."

Something happened, but it had ended and life moved on. A normal but premature child suffered a haemorrhage and became severely brain damaged. This first born child who was now like a pressed flower living in exile unrecognizable and attended by the staff of a choice medical facility in a small town called Belleville. A battery of doctors and wise older people in their life had advised that this course be taken.

It had been a restless night. Sleep became a phantom and like a trickster could not land in her bedroom. Eventually at about 4:10 AM she fell asleep out of sheer exhaustion. The telephone on her night table rang at precisely 4:30. She woke up with a start and felt rested as though she had slept not just for twenty minutes but the whole night.

The voice on the phone established her identity and then made one short statement. "We have just lost him at 4:30 AM. It was very peaceful. He slipped away in his sleep."

She felt as though she had been lifted by an unseen typhoon and gently lowered into a meadow filled with wildflowers. A suction hose had just pumped memory and anguish out of her completely. It was an astonishing sensation. Yet she knew instinctively that a part of her body memory had perished in that hospital facility in a small town in Ontario. She had visited this place twice in her life. Once to deposit her child along with his history of damage, and the second time to indulge in thwarted maternal urges. This second visit, which she had made secretly without telling her husband had shocked her to the point that she felt dizzy. The ravaged near-skeletal face of her child clinging to his crib. Her physicians had warned her against ever doing this but she had gone anyway. Later, she was told she had fainted and there was some concern about her cardiac responses; her husband had been called and arrived in an hour to take her home.

Almost a decade ago words spoken by the physicians had become her enemies. She was aware they were experts in their fields, but the three wise women in her life had echoed them. Even long talks with her Western-educated mother back in Karachi were the same. She could not continue to give medical care to her severely brain-damaged son at home.

Also, there was a new child in her womb when this decision to institutionalize her first-born child was made. It was an accidental pregnancy; a bit of spotting had been discovered and her able gynecologist at Mount Sinai told her this was her chance at having joy in her life. This speck of a child had to be protected and given the best chance. There was hope and a different future that would bring her joy.

The same team of doctors surrounded her at the hospital. The first-born was the son who was ravaged by mysterious damage. This second child, a daughter, would be accident-free, normal, and staunch the pain and bewilderment.

After he was born, a month premature, shockingly underweight and manifesting the damage, he was not expected to survive. She had viewed him in a glass box called an incubator and whispered brave words to him. The young nurse who had wheeled her down had wet eyes.

"He can't hear you."

Tears rolled down her cheeks which she quickly wiped away. "He can hear me. I know it and I feel it. He is my son."

For three months she pumped her breasts and delivered the milk daily to the hospital. She had been encouraged to do this. It became the most important activity in her life. This jar of pale-coloured fluid which would be ingested by her child until he reached the weight where he could be brought home. She rode the Avenue Road bus daily to the hospital and was never allowed to see how they made him swallow it. The staff was gentle and kind to her, including the pediatrician who looked after him. However, no comments were made about a future recovery.

The diagnosis was severe brain damage, coupled with respiratory collapses that required urgent trips to the children's hospital. There were visits to institutes in Montreal and a radical one in the US. Her mother in Karachi visited holy shrines and prayed. But the prognosis would not change. For three and a half years she clasped him to her chest and took him everywhere. His physical beauty made people stop to admire him, his face in repose was perfect. He could not swallow, so it took her one hour to spoon a quarter cup of fluid into his throat. He simply looked ahead and could not move his arms and legs. Within months he became an appendage of her body until she placed him in his crib to sleep.

She read voraciously. She covered his diagnosis from various medical facilities. She learned about sensorial stimuli, she played soft music and sometimes Beethoven's Fifth for him. A wooden slide was built for him and volunteers from a local church came three times a day to exercise him. It was called patterning. The hope was that the dead brain cells could thus be retrained. It was false hope and the treatment eventually was abandoned. Everything died except her faith that there would be a cure. She tested this faith one evening. A legendary faith-healing evangelist from the US, Kathryn Kuhlman, came to Toronto and O'Keefe Centre was packed. She had got tickets for them and called the Belleville Children's Hospital to seek permission to withdraw the child for just one evening. The permission was not granted. The child was too delicate to withstand the rigors of any journey. They told her if her faith in the healer was so strong, she could just go and utter her prayer and it should be just as effective. The banner of hope made them both participate. They went to the large auditorium where they had gone to see magical theatre and hear symphonies. Now they watched the dramatic pageantry of people accompanied by family members in wheelchairs and on crutches all seeking a miracle from the American evangelist. The evangelist, dressed in a long white dress, with a mass of dark wavy hair, had the appearance of an angel. She walked up and down the aisles but mostly prayed from the stage podium where a few people were chosen to approach her. The auditorium was filled with collective expectations and they both felt for the first time that they were not alone.

Her husband held her hand, almost crushing it. She felt her palm and fingers curl up into a knot of tension over which his large hand had made a cage. Silently she repeated the child's name and prayed to the healer to help them. His eyes were red and tears escaped from them. Parenthood was like a canopy. It was the blue sky that always indicated protection for the child. Happiness and joy were the rainbows arching through this sky. They were not ready to dispense with the power of prayer. Neither of them was religious, they did not attend a house of worship, but here they were, supplicants seeking a universal God. People had been encouraged to write their requests, which would be collected by ushers and delivered to the healer after the service.

She had done this at home and put the paper in an envelope, which had their address and telephone number on the back. Her message was simple. "Please ask God to heal our child and return him to us. We beg you to do this for us." When the usher came to their row, she pulled the envelope out of her purse, she kissed it before handing it to him. Her husband watched her then shook his head and sighed deeply. She did not care. She would jump through a ring of fire if it was needed.

But the healer failed.

She was fully awake now and called her husband in his hotel in New York. He picked up the phone on the first ring. She wept when she heard his voice.

"Yes. I know. They called me as well. Thank God it is over. Bob Leach, our lawyer, is handling everything. The flights are booked. I will be home after the meeting tomorrow. It is over. Don't tell anyone."

She dropped the phone as though it were a piece of heated metal singeing her fingers. She found her dressing gown and walked down and out from the den to the back garden. Her feet were bare and pressed into the grass. She walked towards the Persian lilac hedge and plucked a branch and the fragrance flooded through this part of the garden. Her fingers connected with the blossoms and she tore them off the branch and crumpled them in her fist. She brought the fist up to her nose and inhaled deeply and repeatedly. She waited for tears but none came. Something profound had happened and she had no idea how to deal with it. The cautionary statement about telling no one became the one clear path of response. How could this happen, her mind told her. The sun shone brightly on this late May morning. Her daughters would be waking up soon to have breakfast and get ready for school. This was the only thought which entered her consciousness. She walked towards the circular rose bed where the new shoots sprang from the winter-weary brown branches. The dark blue iris plants also emerged from the soil. The sour cherry tree was covered with blossoms. It was a busy garden and everything was in order because it was healthy. Her son had never been.

She watched them pouring milk over their cereal and ignoring the glass of orange juice. The younger one examined her lunch bag and promptly demanded another Oreo cookie. She welcomed this touch of normalcy, it lifted the heavy blanket of thoughts threatening to suffocate her. When they dashed to the front door burdened by their school satchels, she hugged her elder daughter longer than usual.

"You are crushing me, mum."

The younger one gave her a quizzical look. Her dark eyes bored through the mother's face trying to detect what was not spoken.

"Don't run on the pavement, please walk," she bent over the girl's shoes with the loose shoelace and retied it firmly.

"Bye," they both shouted and dashed down the front driveway and raced along the pavement towards the turn for the school.

She shut the door and returned to the kitchen. Here she lifted the receiver on the red wall phone. She did not know who to speak to. Nobody in her neighbourhood knew that she had a cerebral palsy child who was cared for in a children's hospital. He had defied the odds, been reduced to a skeletal form, and survived in an oxygen tent for five years, waiting for the end of his life.

The call was to her mother, continents away.

"Yes, I know, I had a dream last night. My darling, it is over and his spirit is at rest. What are the arrangements there for his burial?"

"They are being handled and I will know more later. I am fine. I don't know what to feel. I feel nothing. Am I abnormal?" she sobbed on the phone.

"No. No. You just have the strength to deal with it. You knew that his survival all these years never meant it would continue."

"I can't talk . . . " she faltered.

"Don't cry in front of the girls."

"Never," she replied putting the phone down.

She had got dressed and pulled her car out. She had to get out of the house. The bedroom felt like an abattoir. The news that a child of hers who neither recognized her nor made any sensorial response had been put to death by his failing heart and lungs.

There was no death struggle just a deep sleep from which he did not awaken. She was reminded of Shakespeare's A *Midsummer Night's Dream* where Oberon and Titania had slept after drinking a potion. It had to be like that, she reassured herself as she parked her car near the edge of a horse farm perched on a ravine. The gentle valley housed horses belonging to a wealthy man. There was a stillness as though one were looking at a postcard. Standing under the gigantic maple tree she wondered that if she just lay underneath it and fell asleep would she wake up and find herself transformed? She did not sleep but sat under the tree. She was still devoid of feelings when she left half an hour later and drove home to make another phone call.

The family lawyer's office stated that he was out of town. They would forward the message that she had called. She was impatient, she wanted details and yet was terrified to hear them. Her husband had told her that he had instructed the lawyer to deal with this eventuality. Neither of them could ever deal with it personally. They would collapse, and she was the weaker of the two. She simply did not know what all this meant now. There was no desire to speak about it to anybody, since parting with their son was an outcome where no emotion could ever intrude. In practical terms, his breathing organism would simply collapse one day. His few precious photographs rested in a drawer in her bedroom dressing table in an envelope. It had stayed buried and unopened. Conversationally, when required, she stated that she had two beautiful daughters. The history before their birth had been obliterated. This had worked well until today.

There were years when she felt she could not remember how the rest of the day transpired. But the next day when her husband returned, she waited in her bedroom and not the front hall for him. She had asked her daughters that they were not to inquire about presents from New York. It was a family tradition when either one of them travelled without the children that sumptuous gifts were purchased for them. His footsteps on the carpeted stairs were slow. The voices of her daughters reached upstairs.

The television was on in the den and they were watching something which had been approved. Dinner was in the oven.

He opened the door and placed his small suitcase near the wall closet. She looked up at him as he advanced toward her. He sat on the edge of the bed and placed an arm on her shoulders. She found its weight heavy and she slid away from the arm. He did not seem to notice.

"Why didn't you come yesterday?" her face was contorted with a brand new emotion.

"Look, before they found this flight they even offered a seat on the corporate plane. But I didn't want to make a fuss. It's all right. He is at peace. It's been over for years." His voice was flat, devoid of emotion.

"Yes, but what arrangements are being made by Bob? I want to ask my parents how to do a funeral here." Her voice broke.

He did not reply, instead he walked to his suitcase and unzipped it before he spoke.

"He was cremated yesterday at eleven AM and this morning the ashes were scattered in a beautiful forest by the lake. Bob has been there arranging it. These are arrangements I made years ago knowing that you would not be able to handle it emotionally . . . and really neither would I."

She was speechless. The death had been handled remotely much like the plastic remote control which changed channels on the TV. This felt like a punishing body blow. Any attempt to personalize her tragedy had been ended by those whom she did not know. The faith she was raised in believed in burial as the final rite, never cremation.

"How could you do this without my permission?" she cried.

"Someone had to make a decision, and I knew you were not strong enough to make it. I did it and Bob felt it was the best way anyway. It's over, we have two beautiful healthy daughters and they will give us all the happiness we need as parents." He had returned to her and leaned over her, watching her carefully.

All she could see before her eyes were flames. A fire was lit and your boy was burned, this is what a part of her brain told her. It's scientific but just alien, the coping part told her.

"I want you to get up and go to the girls. Please, see what you have in your life and understand that you will never suffer in memory again." He pulled her up from the edge of the bed and held her in a light embrace.

She wondered if the large corporation he worked for, which led the world in computer technology, had influenced him. She had read the brochures he brought home displaying computers and systems the rest of the business world envied and emulated. One stroke of the keyboard would result in decisions, events, and brilliant innovations. The stroke could be made by anyone and remain anonymous. That was his model for handling death by remote control. She had nothing at her disposal which could duplicate it. She was not convinced that she believed in the march of technology fully, or that she had become as cold-blooded as he was. That is how she saw her husband now. Yet she knew at all times he was protecting her from emotions that could unhinge her. So no, she had to find peace in a vacuum.

That evening passed. Her scampering daughters and their appetites at dinner and questions to their father about the city where they had lived for three years and remembered less now. The ashes sprinkled in a forest became a faraway story second by second. She turned to music and played Debussy's *Afternoon of a Fawn* repeatedly on the tape deck. The music became a web in which her feelings were ensnared. It was a silken net that centered her, where the sound of the flute in the prelude teased out both memory and grief from her. After the first few days, she threw the tape in the garbage and never listened to the music again.

The following week she had to create a resume, for the monthly local magazine for which she wanted to write. She had been given the position of freelance feature writer. When she came to the section on marital status and children, her hands froze on the keys. Should she mention three or two children?

She discussed this with her husband.

"Don't be silly. This is personal. No one has a right to know your history. Don't be dramatic. It will just confuse people." He spoke in clipped cool tones.

"You had no right to make that decision without me," she still clung to the absurdity of her complaint.

"What is it? Did you want a ghastly funeral and people who know nothing of this to weep with you? Stop it. You have been doing well. I know. I watch you. But I will never discuss this subject again ever. Enough!"

First came the silence and then came the reality that the child had never left the imprint of personality on her. Try as she might, there was no physical or anecdotal reference she could draw upon. This handled memory effectively and erased whatever she wanted to cling to symbolically. It was like a bad short story. There was a beginning and then an unseen end. But history was a different matter and grief had a heft and weight to it. When this was acknowledged it heralded a condition called closure.

Two and a half decades later she divorced her husband who was no longer her friend and the family unit was reduced to three. She then took out the only large portrait of her son sitting in her lap;

his lips were parted to reveal his perfect teeth in what could be called an expression of animation, which was so startling that it became a wide-open smile. It rested in a forest green wood frame and hung in a small corner wall of her bedroom.

Her daughters never asked a question directly about him. It was as though they sensed that the subject would release something unfamiliar in their mother. The child belonged to their family was all they knew and he had died a long time ago.

It happened late one night when she watched a film on television. The film drew upon contemporary warfare. In a room, men sat at large complex computer screens displaying a war zone. This was a modern army that fought its wars by remote control. Drones were positioned in the sky above targets. The information was the product of high-level intelligence and the area was the path of vision highlighted on a screen and the person seated behind the screen was a member of the army defence corp. When he was certain the target was accurately aimed at he simply pressed a button on his keyboard. This activated and signaled the carrier drone to fire the weapon which released the bomb.

The blast or implosion lit up the entire screen. The target had been annihilated quietly, continents away, in a village. A few men, two women, and four children simply vanished. Their physical forms were reduced to fine dust. It was death by remote control. The children had only been acknowledged after the bomb had been released. They were considered collateral damage. She personalized the prophecy of this analogy. She let it occupy an unforgettable place in her memory vault. The only way to find the key to this vault was to create a narrative and it had to be written. Could she do it?

Seeing Through Green

Spirit Island, Ontario, 1994

He was unconventional and so was his island property. It was nine acres with a small pine-cabin longhouse at the end of a half-acre driveway. There was no sign or name, just a path that turned off the main road. This path had been plowed by a tractor from the town and was maintained even in the winter. When he brought her here for the first time it was summer and a riot of daisies lined the driveway. The lake was named Seeing Water and was more like an inland sea. This lake joined by others became the largest freshwater body in North America. Their island was sparsely populated, and not often visited.

"If there is an environmental disaster we have all the water we need," he chuckled.

There were six Indigenous reserves on the island and the only unceded reserve faced his property. She had flown here from Toronto. There was a stop in between and then the flight landed at the island airport about ten miles away from his home in Beaver Wood Mouth.

She had camped at Algonquin and Killarney but had never seen a place like this. There was no manicured-cottage look about the house, which was situated in the midst of an unending wild forest. His Volvo travelled easily on a path cut from forests. It felt as though they were in a park with miles of green foliage. Sometimes a deer appeared or rabbits leaped in the air and they waited until the animals cleared the path safely. She had not seen the water yet.

"I don't invite just anyone, this is my sanitorium. I recharge my batteries and treat myself here." He gave her a droll look.

He was a psychiatrist, they had married recently and he was introducing her to everything in his life. It was a state of enchantment for her and she relished most aspects of it. She had been exposed to lakefront cottages all over Ontario, but this was a special place. The name Spirit Island suited it.

The pine cabin had extensions—an indoor greenhouse and a study area. The bathroom was luxurious beyond belief, with a large tub and indoor plumbing. It had large glass windows so the effect was of bathing right in the forest under a canopy of trees. There were two wood-burning stoves and a refrigerator concealed in a wood panel. He had decorated the living space with native art from the island and his city home. Woolen blankets, dreamcatchers, drums, and a collection of books on primitive dwellings and architecture. She had brought a pile of novels he had not read. The electricity was generated by solar panels on the roof and even the water heater used the energy from the collector battery. However, being practical he also had propane backup, which was only used for the four-burner stove in the kitchen. The bedroom was a second-floor loft where a king-size mattress covered the entire floor, and conical glass windows rose from floor to ceiling. A small carved wooden staircase nailed to the wall was the way up and down. Moonlight and stars were the only illumination in the evenings and nights. They never turned on the small halogen lights in the living area. Outside, two artist friends of his from the city had created large driftwood sculptures, which completed the feel of the place.

He had brought his cheque book with him, because the builder who was also a neighbour presented his bills for ongoing work as soon as he arrived. They smoked joints together and made extensive plans for the property. She was the newcomer and although her husband wanted her involvement in everything, the builder was condescending. He was closer to her age and insolent. A hint of lechery rimmed his dull brown eyes. Although he listened to her specifications for a bookshelf and the placement of the reading lights, she had a distinct feeling that he would build precisely what he wanted. She never engaged with him without her husband present. He marched through the cabin as though it was his home and not theirs. She told her husband he could not come unannounced anymore and should call from outside first, because she often wore little clothing. He was furious and let it be known verbally. She volunteered to check the accounts book where all the bills and cheque deposits were kept. The trail of his dishonesty was evident. Her husband assured her that he would stop it.

"It is valuable to have a thief in your life. It teaches you about boundaries. I will talk to him." He did not look surprised, she thought.

The next night she could hear their voices outside. The contractor shouted and her husband's voice was measured and softer. After a while, he came in and poured himself a Scotch, swallowed it in one gulp, and laughed out loud.

"He is going to sulk for a while but then he will come back when I want him to do some work. So he is out of your hair for now. Rejoice."

She laughed but hid the relief coursing through her.

The only clearing was around the cabin. There were lookouts where the greenery had been cut back to reveal the deep blue lake. A path led to the small boxy wooden structure which housed the water pump. Its powerful motor drew water up from the lake to the kitchen and bathroom. Although this was pure fresh lake water it was never drunk. Bottled water was used. Large sheets of rock, part of the Cambrian shield, lined the edge of the water. She would lie here and gaze at the water, wondering if some sign of life would present itself, but it never did. The isolation was complete, and he taught her not to fight it but make it her friend.

It took the first three days to familiarize herself with the cabin and all its delights. She cooked stews in a little pot, throwing in whatever she found in the pantry. They ate outside and the food tasted delicious. He had a good stock of wine. There were about thirteen varieties of wildflowers, but they had to tramp through the long grass and skirt the little ponds to find them. When she did, she placed them in a round glass bottle on their pine table. Flanking it were two knobby candles she had placed in saucers. He loved to see her feminine touches and commented on them. He stocked wine, candles, music, and strange books in abundance, but could not even boil an egg. There was also a tape recorder with music. He played Mozart in the mornings, saying it was like the sun coming out. She was inclined to believe him. Her favourite music was an aria from Puccini's *Madama Butterfly*. She would take the tape recorder down to the rock ledges and play it up on high volume. She pretended she was the tragic Cho-Cho singing the incomparable "Un bel di" and imagined her lover sailing away across the sea.

Away from the water and the cabin, the world was green. The dense foliage of young and old trees and bushes continued without a break. In this colour, she saw many images. Some of them danced and others were filled with mystery. She wanted to see the real inhabitants of the island, the various Indian tribes. He gave her a book about the tribes and she rolled their names on her tongue. When old treaties were signed, benefits were intended to flow, but history did not support this. The bands even sold land to new settlers. But Spirit Island continued to be sparsely populated and in her mind, it had an incomplete feel to it. She felt an entire race of people were hidden from sight. There was never a sighting even of a canoe on the water and she felt as though her husband spoke of another era or time. There was no physical evidence of them when they drove into a tiny neighbouring hamlet.

"Don't worry, the pow-wow is next weekend and you will see them all," he said.

She wore her sarong to go around and her hair in a braid. The sun had bronzed her skin. A pair of earrings in the shape of bird feathers dangled from her ears. She even slept in them. He donned a pair of strawberry-coloured overalls which he had picked up at Guru Rajneesh's Oregon settlement.

They were both hell-bent on adopting a style of clothing that would connect them to this rural ambiance and not to their city life. They bathed in the lake and she could feel all the tension of their sophisticated city life leech out of their bodies day by day. Her make-up pouch remained closed and she was amazed how she did not even wear lipstick. She was a lipstick girl. He encouraged her to ramble and find the spot she was partial to. She did, and called it Diana's Grove. He gave her an old machete, which he had brought back from a holiday in Cuba, and told her she should clear the grove herself, which she did with great gusto. He would come by to oversee her progress and smile broadly.

"If you like, we can build a tower for you and you can write there."

"In that case, I want a moat and a drawbridge."

"Is this to keep me out or visitors?" He had his deceptive psychiatrist expression. "Well you are the doctor you can figure it out," she replied and grinned at him.

"No. I am off-duty. How did you become more beautiful here? I love the braid and how the sun bronzes your skin." He removed the machete from her hand and held her waist and made love to her on the tall grass underfoot. He had skillfully completed the invasion of Diana's Grove.

It was the night of the full moon. The lake had turned silver. He took her out wrapped in a blanket and walked her down to the edge of the water. The expression on his face was strange; he became almost unrecognizable in the moonlight.

"What is it? Am I turning into a werewolf?" his eyes crinkled in mirth.

"God! You are frightening me!" She felt overwhelmed.

"Come on let's have a dip?" he got up, shrugged the blanket off, and started removing his clothes. "No. It's cold." She knelt on the rock and dipped a hand in the water.

He dived in right near the silvery swath of water where the moon threw an arc of light. She saw his head go under and then rise after a few minutes.

"It is warm, come on."

They swam side by side in the moonlit lake. She was not cold and the water was silky and warm. Then they both saw an unusual shape rise in the distance from the water. Was it a canoe? But it vanished just as quickly as it had appeared.

"What do you think?" He held her close to him in the water. "Did you see it?" She was excited.

"It's a moonlight mirage, unless someone is fishing in the dark? Come on, time for some hot brandy," he said and swam towards the rock ledge, sleek like an otter.

Later, seated in front of the iron stove where wood chips burned merrily as they sipped warm cognac and devoured cheese and crackers, he told her that he had a native Cree friend from the city who had once asked permission to have a sweat lodge on the property. He had come with two other people, and they stayed in the sweat lodge, which was a shelter created from branches and bits of canvas, with a central pit where heated stones and wood created thick steam.

"It is a profound spiritual ritual—cleansing the toxins from the body and mind. I of course did not invade their privacy but I know how they built it."

"So you have Indigenous friends here?"

"Some of them know I am here. We leave each other alone. But then there is Carl One Feather, a fine artist and a recluse. I collect his work. We will go to visit him next week."

Toward the end of the first week, she knew that something else had entered their charming idyll. But it was a sensation that was weighted. Largely unwanted, this weight had a faintly oppressive air to it.

"Do you feel this when you are here?" she watched him gazing into the trees with a still expression.

He turned his head and looked at her but seemed to be looking through her to some horizon she was not conscious of.

"I mean is there the presence of Jung's collective stronger here than in the city?" She was determined to make him talk about it.

"Are you restless? Do you miss city life?"

"No. It's an amazing summer break, but we are both picking up something vibrationally. We have become different here. Where do you escape to?"

"You first?" He smiled at her encouragingly.

"I would say this nature and wilderness forces us to become a little pagan," she faltered.

He pounced on the word *pagan* and forced her to define it. She quickly withdrew it and said she had used it incorrectly. What she meant was more in tune with nature and less concerned with appearances.

"Everything is intense. A walk is not just a walk it's an exploration. When I cook I am choosing dishes I have never cooked before. You make love differently here. I don't feel we are as alone as we think we are."

She felt tears fill her eyes. Blinking them back furiously, she got up from the couch, but he was faster and had got up as well and simply held her.

"Is this PMS?" he murmured in her ear.

"No. Please don't patronize me. I have no such issues."

"Strange things happen here as well. Mostly on the reservations. Often a doctor is sought. Then I cannot hide and I come out and try to help, but the problems are bigger than what the eye can see." He was pensive.

Her knowledge of Indigenous culture was touristic, she knew. Suede skirts, feather headdresses, and mukluks. The lightly-tanned people even had an oriental slant to their faces. She knew that Hollywood depictions of covered wagons and ferocious Indian warriors on horses had lodged somewhere in her brain. Yet this was decades later and no tepees presented themselves in her environment. He took her to a little restaurant in the neighbouring town. One table had four people who looked different. The dark-haired men wore flannel shirts and jeans and their female companions wore cheap printed rayon dresses and plastic sandals. For some reason the two men stared at her unabashedly. They had no interest in anyone else. Plates of French fries and gravy sailed to their table. She got up after a while and headed for the toilet. She was followed by the two women.

"Hello," she said to one of the women, who was fixing her hair in the large mirror. There was no response.

"I am sorry. This is my first visit here to Spirit Island. Where do you live?" She wanted an exchange. They ignored her. She felt awkward, wanting to have an exchange but being rebuffed silently.

"Would this help?" she held out a large barrette she had in her handbag. The woman closer to her narrowed her eyes and looked at the barrette.

"No," she spat out, "I have this," she held out a thin length of leather braided with beads. The beads winked on the leather. It was beautiful.

"Oh, how beautiful. Did you make this? Can you buy it anywhere here?" she asked hurriedly.

They both laughed and then spoke in a language she did not understand so she dashed out of the toilet feeling utterly humiliated. Her husband was waiting outside.

"Everything all right?" he had an apprehensive look in his eyes.

"Why shouldn't it be? They were not very friendly and did not want to talk to me," she shrugged.

"There have been incidents of assault here. Small misunderstandings, particularly if you speak to their men. You see you look similar to them but are not. The men find that intriguing but the women find it threatening."

The drive home was in silence. Yes, she had noticed how separate the group of four was from the few other people in the simple little restaurant. It was a fish and chips place. No alcohol was ordered by anyone. Nothing inviting about the place to make you linger, chat, or order glasses of wine. For them, it was a change and a sort of outing. It was just a social occasion and he wanted her to see why he chose to stay in his forest paradise.

The pow-wow in the small town of Welcoming Path was over two days on a weekend. He told her she would enjoy it, people came from all over the island and the parade was quite spectacular. The festival began at noon and they were early. There was a hum of activity, and people dressed in Indigenous clothing manned the many craft-laden tables. Families and little children wearing decorative headdresses milled around. The food on sale consisted of hunks of bannock bread, dried fish, and jars of dark-coloured honey. There was a group of men with leather drums setting up a performing circle. He bought her a ring at a table display from a man with a large creased face and long hair flowing over his shoulders.

"Hello Doctor, I missed you last year," he greeted her husband.

"I was busy and I got married. This is my wife. She has a wedding ring, but I want her to wear a ring that you have made as well."

"A bride needs jewelry, try the bracelet also," the man suggested, reaching for her wrist.

She watched him drape a silver bracelet with mother of pearl leaves over her wrist and gently fasten the clasp. It was large and fell forward on her hand.

"I will take a few sections out," he said as he removed it.

"Please don't," she said hastily. "It is so beautiful, I can wear it loose or push it further up my arm." She smiled at him.

He returned her smile and nodded and put the bracelet in a little cloth pouch and put the money offered by her husband in a leather pouch fastened at his waist.

"Where are you from?" he asked her.

"From the city."

"And before that. Where do your people come from."

"They were Indo-Aryans from Central Asia."

"You look like one of ours," he said and guffawed.

"Doesn't she, though," her husband draped an arm around her.

Behind them, a medley of sounds arose. The beating of drums and chanting, which was full-throated and completely alien to her. The singers jumped up and down. It was an army of people advancing but keeping a circle formation intact, bringing with them a culture, language, sounds, and motion. The leader of the parade wore a full-feathered headdress that cascaded down his body. His appearance was regal and she was transfixed. This was a Canada she knew nothing about. How was this possible after living in the city for three decades? But these people were part of something mesmerizing and apart. At that moment she wanted to join their circle but knew she could not. She looked at her husband and saw the wide smile on his face.

"It is a show of colour. It is the preservation of ritual and tradition. The families are together but may not be in their daily lives." He was solemn now.

"I would love to visit all the places where they live," she said, bubbling over.

"For that, you have to contact a band office and find out which reserves allow visitors."

"Have you ever visited one here on the island?"

"Yes. Let's pick up some food." He pulled her towards the display tables. He had shared no other details and she did not press him.

She had wanted to explore his three acres of land. It was to the left of the cabin and he told her there was only one cleared-out path; when she found it she was to keep on it. The tantalizing bit of information he had included was that swamp iris grew here. A flower that grew in the water and was not a lily or a hyacinth. The tall stalks rose from a little pool of water and the dark purplish petals had designs on them.

She had walked for forty minutes before she found the swamp iris. Her footsteps halted and she felt it was a moment of triumph, as though she were standing before a panther.

She gazed at it but could not bring herself to cut the stem and gather it to take home. Dragonflies and little fish could be seen in the rainwater pool where it grew. Mosquitos also guarded it, another sort of hazard. The sun had filtered in through the canopy of tall trees and the only sounds were what could be called forest sounds. They were hushed, indistinct and one had to strain the ears to listen. She had decided not to plunder the iris and stayed content with the wild tiger lilies, which grew in abundance. A large bouquet of lilies was clutched in her right hand.

She walked further along the path and then stopped at seeing him. Or perhaps he had stopped seeing her. It seemed as though green paint had been splattered everywhere and he was camouflaged. Yet as they gazed at each other across twenty-five feet she was tongue-tied, not knowing how to greet him. He was as beautiful as the swamp iris—tall and slender with a mane of black hair surrounding a face with small fine features. The eyebrows told a different tale. They were black and slashed his forehead like the wings of a raven. His bare chest revealed black and deep green tattoos cascading across his arms. Wrapped around one hand and wrist and up the elbow was a thick rope. It was the sort of rope that could tie an animal or pull something. Perhaps he was hunting. He wore a pair of forest-green baggy shorts and his feet were encased in suede ankle boots. There was a splendidly wild air about him. He was a teenager, anywhere between sixteen and eighteen. She took a step towards him and he leaped sideways and disappeared. She ran towards the space he had left and was surrounded by thick green foliage. There was no trace of him. He had moved with great speed and she wondered if she had actually seen him or simply recalled what she had seen at the pow-wow assembly the previous day.

"Hello, hello," she cried out, parting the bushes with her hands and feeling foolish.

There was no sound. She turned around and jogged back lightly to the cabin and home. The wild tiger lilies she had collected dropped from her hand but she did not stop to collect them. Breathless, she reached the cabin, where Chopin's etudes greeted her mournfully. She opened the back door and collided with her husband.

"I was about to go and look for the trail of breadcrumbs which I was certain you would have left, but here you are." He grabbed her playfully from behind and rocked sideways.

"Oh. I need to sit," she eased out of his embrace and sank onto a kitchen chair.

"You are breathing very heavily?"

"Yes, I jogged back. Not in shape," she poured some water into a stone goblet.

"How was it? Did you find any resident magic?" His eyes were fixed on her with his physician's look.

"You won't believe me."

"Try me."

"Well, we have an intruder or a visitor. I think he was a teenager. It was a chance encounter, for a split second, and then he just disappeared."

"Where?"

"He just jumped into the bushes and did not reappear."

"Describe him. Maybe Jim has a guest who is just wandering on my property and was embarrassed?"

After she had finished describing him, for some odd reason he questioned her at length about the rope. Could she tell how long it was or how thick. She knew nothing about ropes but told him she felt it was a very strong rope. His playful banter had ended abruptly, and he decided to have a word with Jim.

"Come with me. You just sit in the car while I talk to Jim. I don't want to leave you here alone."

"Why? I am home. I think I may do something amazing and have a bath in that great big fancy tub of yours. If you are back quickly you could share it."

"Later. Not now. Come with me please."

She had seldom disagreed with him. The drive to Jim's cottage was about six minutes away. She sat in the car and wondered why he was making a fuss. The teenager was probably wandering through his secret hideouts and their property was so large he could easily have the run of it.

"Are you sure you saw him?"

Jim had walked out to the car with her husband.

"Yes," she said irately.

"That rope part is very important?" he asked on the drive home.

"Well, what do you think? He was going to catch a few rabbits and tie them up? Let's go please."

She thought about the beautiful young boy the next day. In the afternoon after a long swim, she had fallen asleep on her sun-drenched rock ledge, and he appeared in her dream. It was a bizarre dream ended by jerking her out of sleep. There was something wrong with the dream. It began in colour. The colour was green as though bands of colour encircled her and the water of the lake had also turned green. The boy had risen from the lake and the rope was now coiled around his torso. The image was terrifying and she had woken up with a dry mouth. She sat up and saw that the lake was its usual blue colour. The trees above her were green and the little boathouse was white. In some part of her brain, the colours had been rearranged. She was seeing through the green in her dream as though through 3D glasses. Her ignorance and lack of exposure to the Indigenous people had made her romanticize them, and the boy had become some sort of symbol. As though his entire race of remarkable people had laid a mantle of grace on him. Or perhaps she had just imagined him. Either way, it was all part of the unresolved mystery of this second home on Spirit Island.

She did not tell her husband about this dream, although he often offered psychological interpretations. In her family from her maternal side there was a history of prophetic dreams. She had heard about them and had been dismissive. But now she often wondered if this facility had been passed on to her. Often when she thought about people close to her, they would communicate with her with a mystical synchronicity. She had left all that unexplored, just made a few journal entries about it.

There were two days left before they headed back to the city. She had walked to her grove and cleared more bushes and even dragged out a low wooden table that leaned against the side of the cabin. On it she had placed a jug of flowers and two glasses for drinking wine. When she went back to the cabin, it was empty and thought he had gone for his long swim. She walked along the path just above the ledge of the lake where there were some very tall oak and fir trees. He often spent time examining the trees to check they had not caught disease. She knew she would find him there. They were both creatures of habit on the island. Their favourite places held the clues to their personalities.

Ducking through the foliage and heading towards the nearest tree she was confronted by a sight that froze her in her tracks. Her husband was on the ground hunched over a person lying prone. A thick cord of rope dangled down from a branch of the tree.

She heard her husband's short panting breaths before he could see her. She crashed through the underbrush to reach him and collapsed by his side.

"I was on time. I am reviving him. Almost there."

It was her native teenager with the angry mark of the rope around his neck that her husband had cut with the divers' knife he always carried with him. Another branch had collapsed under the boy's weight. She saw her husband give mouth-to-mouth resuscitation and the boy's chest rose and fell slowly. Suddenly a gurgling cry escaped from the boy's mouth. His eyes flickered open and soon after tears seeped out of them. Then he moaned and her husband massaged his chest and took his pulse at the throat.

She felt an ancient pain ripple through her. She saw the young graceful body which now twitched and heaved spasmodically. She heard her husband repeating again and again, "It's all right. I am a doctor. You are safe now. Can you stand?"

"No police. No police," he moaned.

She reached over and held his face in both her palms.

"We will take you home. And you will be safe." She held his hand with a firm grip.

He had the strength to curl his fingers around her hand. Then he moved and pulled out something from his shorts pocket and dropped it. It was a crushed swamp iris. So he had seen her observing it and decided to take it to her. She gathered the iris and smoothed the petals and tucked it into her bra. She smiled at him. For that moment they were locked in a moment of great intimacy. Now she believed that the nine acres of property her husband owned belonged to his people. He was not the intruder, they were. She also knew that she would press this flower in the pages of her favourite book. It was a book she opened every five years or so and so she knew the flower would dry perfectly and be preserved intact. It would have a home and never disintegrate or vanish.

The rest of that afternoon passed in a haze of emotions and coping devices. The boy now lay on the couch in the cabin and slept. Her husband had brought out his medical bag and conducted an examination and given him a mild sedative. Jim was summoned and searched for the boy's family. The nearest clinic that could deal with him was in the town of Healing Lodge. His family consisted of a father and a few siblings. His mother had died when he was a young boy. Jim made them collect this father on the way. Tears had rolled down the father's cheeks during the drive. At the hospital, her husband had convinced the doctors to admit him for a few days.

After two days they left the island on schedule, travelling on the ferry which would take them to Tobermory and onwards to the city. The enormity of what had happened chased speech away between them. He was a physician and could handle it, but she carried a deep trauma back with her.

Finally, it was at a fashionable and exclusive gallery that she met the great Indigenous artist. His paintings bore no resemblance to their forest and the boy. But the colours he used were spectacular and leaped out of his stylized canvasses like gems.

"This is how you see your people and your land?" she asked curiously.

"To see something very important you first have to see it through colour, then the image never leaves you and you understand its power." He was solemn.

"Yes. I saw something through colour once and the image lives in my heart." She said.

"Bring it out then. Share it, or it will be forgotten."

The Carpet

Kirman, Iran; Quetta, Karachi, and Lahore, Pakistan; Toronto, Canada; 1959–2022

Birds sang outside the large hall where it was born. Sometimes dust circled in the air, and it was beaten down with a wooden paddle so the air would remain clean and pure. It was not an easy birth, it was hung on a loom ten by fourteen feet, for a year and a half. Mostly it was made of knots and the dreams of the master weaver whose little daughters had inspired him. The daughters played in the courtyards and gathered little flowers and buds, hiding them in their head scarves. The flowers bled colour from the petals and stained the fabrics. Their mother would be angry at them and washed the scarves to remove the stains. Their father, the weaver, however, saw these colours and chose silk and wool threads to duplicate them and created a design in his head that would never change. His creation was never meant to be ordinary but Darbari, which meant fine enough to grace a palace. Its central medallion gave it the name of Darbari Kirman. Yet when it was described, another term was also used, "jaal dari." The Persian *jaal* means a web, implying that the design covered the entire surface like an unending web. It was of mixed ancestry, both wool and silk being used on the loom. Like the beautiful little girls, it was a delicate tapestry of unending flowers that curled and undulated over a red background. It was the river of life for the carpet weaver, and his labour would bring food, clothes, and shelter for his precious daughters.

I am the carpet and who else could tell my story? My existence was marked right at the beginning by an important act. I saved the happiness of a young woman. The day I was sold to a man from neighbouring Pakistan and placed carefully in a long van to be transported by road, I weighed more than the other four carpets with me. My new owner was a short rotund man who kept wiping his face with a large white handkerchief. He was nervous. The driver of the van was also nervous, and the handsome young man who had helped him lift the carpet into the van was also nervous. I knew something heavy had been placed on me right on the central medallion. Then I was rolled a couple of times and my edges folded over so I became a large oblong packet. I could feel the movement inside. I could hear the breathing and sometimes little moans. I had realized that something was meant to be hidden. I also heard three men talk in whispers when they rolled me. It was only when my owner reached the border and I was unrolled that the something was removed. I had to wait another day to hear clearly and to know what had happened.

An Iranian girl who was eighteen and loved a certain young man was going to be married off to a wealthy old man. But her father had decided her fate: she would become the third wife of a man of sixty-seven who was both cruel and ugly. Her fate would be to give birth to many children and be abused by the older wives, who would treat her like a servant. And so it was decided to smuggle her out of the province and to travel separately and unite with her lover. He pleaded with the importer, who was from Pakistan, if he would help him. The importer had three daughters whom he was educating and was aware of local customs which robbed young women of the freedom to choose whom to marry. So he agreed to assist the young man.

I had no way of knowing if the lovers united as I was travelling to Karachi. Most stories remain incomplete. All I could do was see and hear. I lay on top of other carpets in a large carpet showroom. I knew I was special as other carpets beneath me were pulled out and sold. Then destiny called. I still remember the day when a certain woman came to see me. She had a soft voice and a graceful manner. She knelt and stroked my edges and repeatedly got up to view me from different angles.

"I am in love with this carpet," she said.

"We shall bring it over tomorrow morning," the short rotund man replied.

"It's expensive but my husband never deprives me of anything," she said and tossed her head and smiled.

"I don't need the full cost tomorrow. I can ask him to clear it off in three payments."

"Oh no! He has a very senior post in the government and he would never agree to have a debt in his name," the woman said.

"You are my Kashmiri sister and it gives me great pleasure to see how much you like this carpet. I will bring the price down a little." He waved to his assistant to bring some tea.

I liked them. The elegant and pretty woman and the rotund businessman. They talked a great deal about Kashmir and its legendary workmen. He also educated her about carpets. She inquired about his family and he shared details. There was a distance between their social status. She was an educated woman, the wife of a prominent civil servant. He was a salesman, a self-educated businessman. He was not unfamiliar with how men dressed formally and the automatic respect they got for this. So he dressed in formal western suits where his belly bulged through his white shirts and he sweated profusely, but the courtesy he displayed towards her was as though she were royalty. She knew he would never be a guest at her table but she had accepted his brotherly affection. On festivals, she sent elaborate boxes of desserts and cards to his home.

For forty-seven years I had one owner and I always knew my place. It was always in the formal living room of all the homes the elegant woman occupied. There were four children and two dogs in the family. One of the little girls was the owner of the fluffy white dog.

Once in a while the dog would sneak into the living room and shed the odd strand of hair on me. The girl, never far from her dog, carefully removed the hair with her fingers, knowing her mother would be cross if it were discovered. Playing with the dogs was always outside in the garden. This rule was strictly observed. The room I occupied was treated carefully. New furniture was ordered of light-coloured wood with modern designs. The legs were placed on special glass so my pile would not be damaged in any way. Two separate sets of carpet brushes were used on me. My surface shone, I receive compliments from all visitors but I had a rival in the same room. I may have been a carpet, a material inanimate object, but I had emotions and I was consumed by jealousy of this rival, who also received attention and compliments. It was a big Geisha doll in a glass box placed on a side table next to the long sofa. Her beauty was outstanding, and the story of her journey from Tokyo was astonishing. The elegant lady had visited Japan as an international delegate to a women's conference and received the doll as a gift from the prime minister. Unlike my journey in a van over the bumpy roads of Asia, she had flown in an airplane and placed in the overhead rack in the cabin. From her elaborately styled black hair studded with delicate ornaments to her silken kimono, she was a vision of beauty. Her face was milky white, of fine porcelain, and her features were painted by fine brushes; in one of her delicate hands was a fan and the other hand rested on her sash around her waist. Her blaze of colour and delicacy could not be held prisoner by the glass box. It just hinted that her status was so precious that it had to be protected more than me. I would curse her beauty silently in the beginning, but eventually I accepted that we were beautiful companions in the room. It was the bond of beauty and not competition. It would be more dignified if I soothed the flurries in my jealous heart and also kept an eye on her.

Sometimes the gracious woman would hold a spiritual gathering, but first heavy white cotton sheets would be placed on me. Then the women would sit down and nothing was ever spilled on me.

Many secrets were revealed and events took place in the living room. Marriage proposals, gossip, and then the illness and early death of my owner's husband. When his government job ended they both retired to a country home in the mountains. I lay in the living room of that home. It was a sun-filled room where my red background would turn into a scarlet flame. In the afternoon she would draw the diaphanous white curtains across the glass doors, so protected me from the intense sunlight. She would tell her staff not to forget this chore. I was not allowed to fade. This always amused me. Organic dyes were used on my woven strands of wool and silk; they would never fade. History is a witness to that.

My favourite person in the family was the girl with the dog. She would often creep in with a book and lie on me. Here she would read her books and gently rub her bare feet on me. From the soles of her feet I could absorb all the emotions the books created inside her. Sometimes she would lock the door of the living room from inside so she would not be disturbed or discovered. Reading books was so important for her. Still, at the time I did not know how much she cared about me. Decades later found me accidentally in a sorry neglected condition, and she fought for me like a tigress. This will come later.

For two decades there were changes; my existence found different locations.

The mountain home was replaced by a magnificent home in the capital, a white city nestling in the hills. The house had been built by the couple as an investment property and rented. The rent covered the building costs. There was a small Japanese bridge which crossed a canal of water in the back garden. A wall in the living room was built of pale green onyx. In the centre was embedded a fireplace. The architect was quite fanciful. The staircase was free-standing with no banisters. It looked as though a spiral of steps had just dropped from the ceiling. Then the man, the husband of the elegant woman died. He was brought back to die here, but two of the grown-up children now lived outside the country and could not reach the funeral.

A covering of thick white sheets was draped over me and dozens of people came day after day to offer condolences. I absorbed the weight of every tear that was shed in that room and every arrangement made. Then life changed once again. Silence invaded this beautiful home. The elegant woman stayed upstairs and seldom came down to the living room. I was brushed daily and the furniture dusted but no guest arrived. There were just the two of us in the house. Meals were laid for her in the dining room but she never finished them. Her maid and the cook would talk about the sadness and the pills the lady swallowed to sleep at night. Her only son lived in another town and he would fly in once a month and stay for the weekend. He spent his time walking through the house with a scowl on his face.

He argued and quarrelled about the money being spent on the house and the domestic staff, who had no work to do and were drawing salaries for nothing. His mother was too weak to resist him when he decided to take her to his own home and sell the house.

There was desolation. I was put in a storage room wrapped in an enormous jute cover. There were many other things in the room. I could not see the Geisha doll anywhere or the elegant lady, who had loved me and owned me. I often wondered about the girl who would stroke me with her bare feet as she lay on her belly reading books, and recalled the warmth of her little stomach that made me feel safe and loved. Now I was a prisoner in solitary confinement.

I kept my faith and surprises leaped out. The elegant lady grew strong again and created her own home, and I was laid out in her living room. Unfortunately, the respite was temporary. Another experiment failed. A small annex was built for her in the compound of her son's home using money from her investments. Then the son fell ill and could not walk up to see her. His wife was a demonic creature. She was ugly not just in her features but also in her heart. Without warning she made the elegant lady leave the home. She was unceremoniously put on a plane to fly to the city where her elder daughter lived. But she did not want to live with her children ever again and insisted that a house be rented for her. Her assets were invested and an income stream was deposited in her bank monthly. Two nurses came to look after her, one at night and the other during the day. A cook and chauffeur also lived in residence, with an old and reliable family servant, whose relationship with the family was special.

The daughter who had the small dog had settled in a foreign country in the West, and she would come every two years to visit her mother. When she came, the house became happy and there would be guests. She bought bouquets of flowers from the market for her mother's bedroom and red roses for the living room to compliment my colours. She would stroke me with her bare feet again and tell her mother how much she loved me. The mother would say, "Call the staff and tell them to roll it up and send it to your home."

The girl would laugh, "No, I always want to come to see you and see your carpet in your home. Then I will know you are fine and nothing has changed."

The elegant lady would kiss forehead and cheeks and tell her, "You are so sentimental. Just like your father. Nothing will change if you take the carpet. I am here."

"No. Let's not talk about this again. Your niece is coming for tea. I think you should get dressed."

I hated hearing the word tea *because it meant that something other than bare feet would walk on me. There was a contraption that got rolled over me. It had metal shelves on a frame with wheels, and it made an appearance often. It was called a trolley. The two shelves were weighted down by plates, a tea service, and cakes and sandwiches. This weight on the wheels dug deep into my pile and caused me pain, and the aroma from the food was maddening. Tea was being served.*

Sometimes even at lunches the elegant lady had difficulty walking and would sink into the armchair closest to the entrance. Life changed and there were only small intimate gatherings. Many of the silver nut dishes on the end tables had vanished as had the Geisha doll. What remained was a pair of small black metal sculptures standing on white marble blocks. They had come from Cairo and were museum replicas of Pharaoh Akhenaten and Queen Nefertiti. Their chiselled faces and ceremonial head coverings were exquisite.

"They are bookends. But I always wanted to enjoy gazing at them alone without the books as a distraction," the elegant lady explained to her visiting daughter once.

"I used to sneak into the living room in the Karachi house and play with them," the daughter replied.

"Egypt has an ancient civilization and the history is fascinating. The Sphinx and pyramids tell us that a very refined civilization existed."

"I am enamoured by that period of history and have read so much."

"My trip to Egypt was first-rate; your father had called the ambassador, who was a friend of his, and asked that they show me all the sights . . . Just bring them to me please."

The daughter lifted the two busts, which were five inches in height, and gave them to her mother.

"Now close your eyes and hold out your hands," the mother instructed. She then placed both sculptures on her daughter's outstretched palms. "I would rather give these to you while I am alive," murmured the mother.

I was just a carpet and imagined this place called Egypt. I was in awe of the lady of the house, who had travelled to so many countries, but this gesture of the mother's love for her daughter won my approval the most. The daughter left to return to her own young family. The rhythm of the house changed with the seasons. Tragedy did not spare the elegant lady. Her son died and she was not told about it nor taken to the funeral. The day she was told, her cries reached the heavens and a flood of people came to the house. But they went straight to her large bedroom where she lay still in bed refusing to talk.

I sensed that something terrible had happened without being aware that a few years later the final tragedy would occur. My faithful mistress died. I was rolled up unceremoniously and taken to the elder daughter's home and tossed into an unfriendly space. I was cleaned badly by a male servant who did not bother brushing me twice. A machine that made a loud sound was moved over me and pulled the strands of my pile. It was a machine that was imported from the West. The young woman who lived in the upstairs portion of the house, the elegant lady's granddaughter, did not care for me.

"This red is so bright, it does not match anything. It's old-fashioned," she said to her mother.

"It's my mother's carpet. Just let it lie here," her mother told her. "We can decide later what to do with it."

I knew it was the end for me. Not only did I feel orphaned, I also felt I had become very old. But the story does not end here. This is now the story of how the other daughter will make me come alive again and she will tell you the story herself.

It lay there in a passageway spilling over onto the large recreational room. The next time when the daughter who had settled in Canada came for a visit the carpet suddenly presented itself like a long-lost friend. Three emotions flooded her. Recognition, delight, and outrage.

"My God it's a hundred-year-old Darbari Kirman carpet. The daily traffic alone will damage it." She turned to her elder sister. "Do you know, every time I came for a visit, I would admire it and she would offer it to me, but I told her that while she was alive I always wanted to see it in her home."

"Well," her sister shrugged her shoulders and hardened her face. "I can have it packed now and you can take it."

"Don't you appreciate it? It was her formal living-room carpet. It moved from one house to the next. Its glory made a room sing!"

"Well, after she died I brought it here and put it upstairs, but there was a wedding in the house so it was brought down. Not enough room for chairs so people sat on it on the floor."

The younger sister could feel a burst of rage sweep through her. The upstairs referred to was the tasteless trio of bedrooms spilling into a living room of sorts. There were no fine furnishings and guests would never see the carpet. She knelt and smoothened the section in front of her. The flowers strewn over the carpet were both irises and tulips. The Mughals revered both flowers, they carved them on the marble walls of the Taj Mahal and encrusted them with jewels. But in this hot afternoon in Lahore, in a house she no longer felt comfortable, the flowers had been trampled upon along with her own vanishing family history. Their mother, a woman who had held a clan together had died and her home and possessions had been pillaged by an uncultured, greedy lot.

The carpet had been a way of holding on to her mother. She knew it was childish to think so, but she had been prevented from attending her mother's funeral; she was informed too late. The thirteen-hour direct flight would not have got her there on time. It was the treachery of the worst order and suddenly a silence had descended in her life. She lived in this silence for a week and never shed a tear. It would be a travesty. Her mother had loved her with abandon and orchestrated many joys for her during her fleeting visits. She would count the tears she would shed even from her grave. Between them, there was always laughter and intellectual exchange. Many things tied them together; both had been partly formed by studying in the United States. Often they were not like mother and daughter but two women who adventured easily and were known for the dramatic interludes in their life journeys. She would lose her composure if she walked into the corridors of grief. It would be letting her mother down.

"Where do you want it sent?"

"I will call you tomorrow. It has to be cleaned before it is packed," she replied curtly and got up from the floor.

"Where is her German china? The dinner set?" she dreaded the answer.

"Oh, she had promised it to my daughter." The preposterous lie rolled out of her lips.

For a moment scenes from her mother's legendary dinner parties flashed before her eyes. The gleaming white table linen and the gold-rimmed dinner set with delicate purple flowers and green leaves were tastefully arranged; the serving platters and dinner plates were like a symphony. It was precious china, and apart from its commercial value it was wreathed in the brilliance of her mother's reputation as a hostess of repute. No one in her lifetime would even dare to discuss its disposition. Not even her mother herself, who had seen the dinner parties vanish along with her homes and good health. Yet in all the visits to her, the daughter knew that it rested on the pantry shelves of her kitchens. The gold rim was itself of great delicacy. It exhibited an aristocracy that flowed from her laughing passionate mother as well. The unworthy person who had usurped the China was a coarse young woman whose inhospitable home most extended family members avoided.

She collected her purse and walked towards the outside door. She was not followed and nobody said goodbye. Outside it felt like an oven. The nondescript grey sedan stood in the driveway and its driver sat idling in the shade. He jumped up when he saw her and opened the back door for her. She ignored it and opened the front passenger door and slid inside.

"You are not staying for tea? You should spend the evening here. We get to see you so seldom," he gave her a worried look.

"I was not invited." She gave him a wan smile.

"This is your home. Your home. Your mother may have died but this is your sister's home. They should be running around you and pampering you as your mother always did." His features contorted with displeasure.

"Everyone does not have your grace Allah Ditta," she said.

She was staying at a small, elegant hotel on the main promenade called the Mall. It had been part of the Hilton chain once but now was called the Avari. The clientele it drew differed from the brash and noisy one at the Intercontinental further down. A more subdued and genteel crowd stayed here, with some foreigners. There was a marvelous open-air pool which never had more than two people using it, and a restaurant that served breakfast buffets where croissants, cheese, and cold meats were offered. She stopped at the reception and asked the courteous manager if he could find her a contact for the best carpet-dealer in the city.

She was used to researching the books she wrote. Now she was here writing another book which required a fair deal of research. Mostly it was meetings, conversations, and hours of reading. She knew how to search for people. So in her room, she made countless phone calls to find the adult children of the man who had purchased the carpet for its owner, her mother, whom he had called his Kashmiri sister. The respect and love between them continued over the decades.

She discovered that he had died. There was a son, though, who had held on to the father's showroom in Karachi. The family connections had died with the owner but the history of the carpet would never die. She had to find the son. So she made dozens more phone calls.

Late at night, her telephone rang. She woke up with a start. The voice on the phone belonged to the son of the carpet-dealer. He first asked her if she was her mother's daughter. She stated she was.

"My mother purchased a carpet from your father about sixty-five years ago in Karachi."

"Was it a Kashmiri carpet?" he asked.

"No it's Persian. A Darbari Kirman."

There was silence for a while.

"I wasn't even born then. But my father kept his notebooks where he noted everything he imported from Iran. Date of purchase, price, and the route it had travelled from Iran to Pakistan."

"Do you have the notebooks?"

"Yes. Do you have the carpet?"

"Yes, I will have it cleaned first."

"Take it to Punjab Carpet House, but send me a photograph of it first. I will go through his old ledger books; his records were impeccable."

Two days later he called her.

"I have matched the photograph of the carpet to a narrative. It's quite a story."

"I can come to Karachi for a day. Can we meet?"

"Stay in Lahore, please. I will come on business for a few days and will be flying out this evening. I will bring the book with me."

They sat in the garden where he downed cups of instant coffee as she leafed through the ledger book. "You know there were many smuggling operations through the border at Baluchistan to Iran. My father used that route but he had a valid import license. Once in a while he crossed the border himself, because he loved to travel between the two countries. But he took one trip that was dangerous and your carpet saved a young girl's life. I think it was your Kirman."

She was on the page and the writing was in English. For October 1958 there were many entries noting items of silver, tiles from Ispahan, books, and carpets. It was a smuggling operation and he had bribed the border officials to look the other way. The border was in a rugged region where tribal heads exercised more power than the governments. She remembered Ghulam Ali, the rotund short man who wore silk suits and treated her mother like visiting royalty. Sometimes he brought gifts of Kashmiri food cooked by his chef. There was no socializing with his family but he was a devoted father. He sought her mother's help in getting admission for his children to the more prestigious schools. He understood the value of fine education just as he did his artifacts. Iran in his mind was the pinnacle of the carpet industry. His favourite comment was "What is old is truly gold."

"There are details of four carpets here. None of them is a Kirman," she tried to mask her disappointment.

"You are in luck. The man who was my father's driver is alive and will supply these details verbally after he sees the carpet."

"Where is he?"

"In the city. I will bring him tomorrow and we will take him to see the carpet."

"He must be quite old?"

"He is eighty years old and started working at the age of sixteen for my father."

Nothing had prepared her for the tale which spilled from the man the next day. He gazed at the carpet stretched out in the large carpet shop where it was waiting to go to the washing area. He had just removed his glasses, polished them, put them back on, and risen from the kneeling position he had taken to bend over the carpet.

A large satisfied smile stretched across his face.

"Yes. This is the Kirman. I thought I would never see it again in my lifetime. It was sold very quickly to your mother so there was no time to put it in the ledger book."

She noted his emotional response. He was a tall man with a shock of grey hair and a wiry muscular body. The outward concession to age was that he stooped a little and walked with a stiff arthritic gait.

She accompanied him outside where they walked to a small wooden bench.

"Sit here with me," he said, "and I will tell you about this carpet."

The journey had followed the usual arrangements as the van in which they travelled reached the Iranian town of Zahedan. The border crossing was uneventful. The business license was examined and the van waved through. They reached the address supplied to them, which was the courtyard of a large block-shaped brick building.

"Ghulam Ali Sahib wanted to pick up the carpets, make the payment, and head back to the border-crossing before dark."

She closed her eyes and imagined herself in the van, driving through the rough terrain of Baluchistan toward the Iran border. The dirt-baked town of Zahedan, where the mosques displayed stunning Iranian tile work, swam in her mind's eye.

"I was helped by two people to place the four carpets in the van. Then a young man came running from inside and spoke to Ghulam Ali Sahib and our trip changed."

The narrative had the flavour of a novel. The young Iranian worked for his uncle the carpet-dealer in Zahedan. Along with the sale of carpets, a forbidden love affair blossomed in this carpet emporium. The young man was in love with an eighteen-year-old beauty who had been promised to an older man whom she disliked and feared. The young man's plan was to get the girl out of Zahedan to a place where no one would find her. He would join her and they would not return to Zahedan until he had married her himself. The girl had to be smuggled out of the town and province. It had to be the border town in Pakistan.

After two days she went to the carpet shop to pay for the cleaning and its freight to her home. The carpet gleamed.

"We have polished it," said the manager.

"Polished?"

"Yes, it's magic. We have a technique for restoring the original colour." He gave her a smug smile.

I have arrived on a grey day in a cold land. The journey has been long. I have been removed from the thick vinyl cover and rolled out. Apart from the sea of flowers and the gleaming red silken pile there is also a family history woven in me.

I am the carpet and I shall end this story. I am in a strange land, but at least I have not been left behind. I am kept warm and protected. The woman seated at her desk close to me is writing on a machine. Is she writing our story and so keeping us both alive forever?

Lingering Love

Continents of the heart, 1970–2022

For five years she had not thought about romantic love. There was no time in her life for that now. Marriage based on passionate and dramatic love had been a new country until it became like the silk lining of a dress that is felt but not seen. Motherhood was joyous, a beautiful baby had appeared like a new companion in her life. Although all acts of love which flowed from her were detaching her step by step from herself, she had no idea this was happening. There was no reason to interrogate her happiness since its manifestations were so evident and pleasant. The devoted husband and the engaging child living with her in the spacious brand-new home were markers on the road which began with romantic love and led to the field of contentment.

She was visiting her parents. Overseas. Her year-old child flew across continents to be introduced to her maternal grandparents and even attend her uncle's wedding. It was a season of indulgence and a riot of cultural rituals, hospitality, and privilege. A tall woman from the northern mountain region was hired as live-in caregiver for her toddler. It was suggested that she could easily take small trips to see old friends. She was here to rest and enjoy herself.

Almost on cue an invitation for a weekend at a sumptuous home located on a highway arrived. The reason for the odd location was that a large factory was situated across the highway. Her friends, a married couple, were the heirs to a large textile consortium. Moon, the young man, was putting in a stint as a director of the factory, and so he and his artistic wife endured the boredom of the location by inviting various friends to spend the weekend with them. In her case, they bombarded her with invitations until she consented. The next day they sent her a car to pick her up.

As the car sailed in through the green wooden gate and stopped, the vivacious hostess swept her up in a welcoming embrace.

"We are so excited to see you. We miss you so. It's just us and Moon's best friend from his Oxford days. Cozy, just the four of us."

She could not tell them that she hardly ever thought of them anymore. She had accepted the invitation at her mother's insistence.

They had been affectionate friends, living in opulent homes with possessions, but they were talented artists as well. He painted and she was an actress who also designed jewelry. She found their talents to be of more interest than their wealth. They were distant cousins and a perfect complement to each other. He was slim and lean and she was petite and voluptuous. They spoke using each other's phrases and words. They were obsessed with Tarot and had a reader who often was part of their coterie. She laughed with them and was thoroughly entertained and was surprised to discover that she had a great deal of affection for them.

It was early afternoon. She was sitting on the lawn with her hostess and been served a brilliant Italian lunch. The driveway ending at a portico was visible and when the white sedan pulled in, sitting closer to the portico on the lawn, she saw Moon open the door himself for a person seated at the back. When the tall man got out Moon put his arm around his shoulder and they both sauntered towards them.

"Here he is," her hostess jumped up from her cane armchair and pulled her up.

The late fall sunshine fell softly outside. The afternoon was half spent already so the light which fell on the faces of the men was deceiving. Moon had a half smile playing on his lips as he introduced his friend. She heard his name and a whisper of familiarity echoed faintly in her mind. But she had not met him before. He stepped forward and looked at her from his great height. There was a stillness that seeped out of his near-perfect face which belonged to a Greek statue in some museum. Even the waves of his dark auburn hair appeared to be controlled by this stillness. At a shorter height, her sightline first settled on the open-collared white shirt worn under a dark navy blazer. He wore tan trousers and elegant mahogany loafers. His eyes were mesmerizing. They were hazel and the light turned them into shades of amber and green. Clean-shaven, the curve of his perfect lips and his elegant nose could not remove the one quality which she would discover momentarily. It was shyness, as though he was apologizing for his superb good looks, wanting to even shrug them away.

She was rooted to the spot where she stood on the grass. She heard herself talk to him and then moved quickly to reclaim the cane chair she had risen from. He chose the one close to her and folded his length into it. Their hosts beamed at them as though they had succeeded at some social venture. Moon poured white wine from a fresh bottle into the glasses on the table. She lifted hers and raised it to her lips and the man who had made her breath hide somewhere and still not return, leaned forward and silently lifted his own. His eyes were fixed on her and the lifted glass was a toast. Her breath filtered into her lungs again. She looked down at her wine glass and in its depth she saw her reflection. The surface of the fluid resembled a shower of sparkling confetti. Since she knew there was nothing wrong with her eyesight, she wondered if this was an out-of-body experience. Had such a surfeit of male beauty hurled her into some unfamiliar zone where she was seeing things which simply did not exist?

Then he engaged her in conversation, displaying curiosity about her and introducing himself. It was easy, as the interest in each other was mutual. He also had a sense of humour, displayed when he would take an utterance of hers and just shift it a little and create another meaning. A brand of humour that appealed to her. When she laughed, a glint of mischief shone in his eyes; he knew he was scoring many points with her.

"Look at you. You are thick as thieves," Moon smiled broadly.

"Intelligent conversations for a change. You know I am marooned in this country at my parents' summer home," she smiled back at Moon.

They had finally gone inside to relax before the evening. She headed towards her room. Her weekend bag had been unpacked by the domestic staff. An outfit was spread out on the bed. Her toiletries were unpacked and in the bathroom. She lifted the outfit and placed it on the armchair and heard a sound behind her.

"I am next to you." He leaned against her half-open door. "Oh" was all she could say.

"I have the bedroom next door. I mean if you need anything I am here." He waggled his eyebrows clownishly.

"I sleep like a log. Our hosts are impeccable and I think there is toothpaste in the bathroom," she teased him gently.

He moved away from the doorway and she shut the door firmly and collapsed on the bed. She could feel her heart race and overwhelming fatigue lazily weaved itself through her. She shut her eyes and thought that perhaps like some heroine in a Victorian novel she had swooned. Silently, she reproached herself for behaving like an adolescent. How could a stranger have such an effect on her? She opened her eyes and reached for the phone on the night table and called her husband. It was close to midnight in their hometown.

"Is it you? It's midnight you know." His voice pressed into her ears.

"Yes. I am sorry. Are you all right? I just wanted to hear your voice," she lied expertly.

"There is no time to miss both of you. It's hectic at work and I have to travel for work. A trip is coming up. Send me the details of your return flight please. Take care of yourself. I have to get back to sleep."

He casually disconnected. She felt the reality of her life slip away as the sound of her husband's voice ended. It was open season and all the emotions coursing through her returned with an intensity that told her precisely what had happened. She was in the throes of an infatuation as though she were a teenager confronted by a dazzling rock star. The infatuation had to be acknowledged. There was no other explanation. Yet the woman lying on the bed with a phone in her hand was not anyone she recognized.

Across the dinner table laden with many dishes, she watched him lift barbequed meat from a platter and serve her himself.

"This is excellent. Try this. You won't get this where you live now," he coaxed her gently.

She gazed at the grilled kebab and lamb chop. They looked perfect. The delicate strands of cilantro floating on the surface and the freshly squeezed lemon drops slid off the meat. His gaze fixed on her, willing her to eat. She forked a piece and popped it into her mouth.

"Yes," she said, "this is heavenly food."

He clapped his hands together and swayed a little. She continued eating and did not look at him again. There was no meal she had eaten on this vacation that could compare to what she was eating. Perhaps he was a Greek god who had stepped out of mythology simply to conjure a feast. He was a tidy and attentive eater himself always keeping an eye on her and noting what he could pass to her despite the serving staff. He took food seriously, she could tell. His unwavering attention fixed on her created an intimacy which excluded their hosts.

Moon, brimming with mischief and acutely perceptive, gazed at her.

"I think you have stolen my friend's heart. Ah, the allure of married women who live in other countries," he sighed theatrically.

"I don't think so," she replied sharply.

"I think they will become good friends," chimed in the hostess mounting the rescue.

"I am taking all three of you to a family wedding in Peshawar tomorrow. Great food, and traditional music." He looked only at her.

"I am sorry I have to be back by Sunday night."

"I shall get you back by Sunday night, but it will be late." He was not going to let her slip away.

It was late at night, post dinner. She walked on the lawn with him. The conversation ranged from topic to topic. He was interested in politics and serving his country. His mother was a member of parliament from his family's ancestral area. One of his brothers was a state minister.

He stopped and looked at her.

"I want to marry someone just like you."

She stepped back. As though his declaration was a weapon that could injure her. He knew she was married. A look of abject misery settled over his face. She was fascinated to note that it did nothing to mar the perfection of his face, perhaps even heightened it. In the dark night where a few garden lamp posts threw out illumination his eyes darkened.

"I think your social milieu will help you find the appropriate match with a political family like yours," she said briskly.

"I don't want that," his lips curled in scorn.

"But that is the custom here, particularly with a family like yours, isn't it? I am sure your mother is lining up candidates for you to meet. Take a chance and fall in love," she giggled.

"In love." He blocked her path and gripped both her upper arms.

The sudden contact was alarming. She used her hands to dislodge his grip. He abruptly loosened his grip and his hands fell away. She was shocked at what had happened. Physical contact was taboo, they were strangers. She stepped backward.

"I am sorry. I didn't mean to do this. But what you said felt like torture." He was breathing heavily and looming over her like a tree.

"I think I am ready to turn in." She turned away briskly and quickened her pace on the path to the house.

He followed her but she never looked at him again. He had revealed too much. She had kept her feelings hidden under light banter. He had revealed his own to her. He had intruded on her personal marital status. In her case, simply a look would reveal her own. When she reached her room she heard his movements behind her and she swung around as she opened the door.

"I think I have fallen in love with you."

"It's very late," she replied and shut the door to her room, leaving his words behind.

She was mistaken, the words had followed her in. When she changed into her nightgown they slid over her chest creating a pocket of warmth. When she brushed her teeth they collected in her mouth and settled on her tongue. Looking up at herself in the mirror she washed her face. The eyes staring back at her were his. It was too late to do anything. It was some sort of virus and they had both become infected. Whatever it was, it could never be discussed with anyone ever.

She fell into a deep sleep that lasted till morning.

Three days spent in the company of others with small pockets of time snatched greedily could not amount to anything more than holiday diversion. She believed in that strongly when they parted company. If there were words spoken she had forgotten them instantly. It was a case of out-of-sight, out-of-mind. She returned home with her daughter to the distracted embrace of her husband's welcome.

"Did you meet your old friends?" he asked.

"Actually some new people."

"Anyone interesting?"

That is when she allowed his face to float through her mind. The ultimate comedy of experiencing adolescent emotions when one had left that age a decade and a half ago. The continents and oceans which separated her from him. They would of course never meet again.

"Not really," she replied. Hers was not an open marriage.

Two years later she received an innocuous call from the consulate of a foreign mission. The caller inquired about her identity.

"Who is inquiring?"

"Please wait, I shall just connect you."

She tried to terminate the call, to put back the receiver, but a voice on the line entered her ears and froze her hand and changed the equilibrium of her life.

"Your number is unlisted and the staff here has been put through the wringer finding your phone contact and address."

"Is it you? Are you here, I mean in my town?"

"Yes," then the laugh rang out.

"Where are you?" the question was absurd but her heart hammered inside her leotard top.

"Well, your prince is here and staying at the Prince Hotel which I am told is close to where you live."

The speed with which she landed at the lobby of the hotel dressed in exercise clothes and the jacket of a track suit draped over her shoulders told her she had lied to herself. All the feelings which had lain buried for a couple of years had returned suddenly. She was no longer in control of her actions, they seemed directed from elsewhere. It was not an infatuation but love that had lingered like an unwanted guest. Her permission had not been sought, it simply coursed through her like flood waters uprooting all the structures of her life.

In that great white bed she lay entwined with him. Their marriages discarded like dirty clothes. The wonder of this coupling turning their bodies into golden wax. His deep sighs and words of gratitude for their lovemaking made her fold within the circle of his arms. A great silence made the afternoon a gift which was too precious to relinquish. After the silence he told her that he had married the daughter of a powerful politician, he had joined the Foreign Office, and this was his second posting. He had actually arranged this posting in her country so he would meet her and they would continue.

"Just like that?" she got up from the bed and walked to the window.

He followed her and stroked her naked back. But she moved quickly to the bathroom and dressed. They did not speak. He would leave in the early morning fly back to Montreal and she was expected home which was four miles away from this hotel in Toronto. "You have always been here," he tapped his chest just over his heart.

"I never thought of you. I have my life. I had it even when I met you."

"I know," he said softly.

"This is not going to be a long-distance affair. I don't have the stamina for a double life."

"It's not an affair. We are here together and this will happen again. Somewhere else?"

The comment was pensive and she sensed that perhaps his brilliant marriage lacked something, as hers did.

She had left him the delicate gold ankle bracelet given her by her husband for her birthday. It had been on her ankle for five months and never broken. But now the chain had broken symbolically in protest of her unfaithfulness.

He checked out the next day and she did not discover the loss for another day.

A decade had gone by. Her life was consumed by her two children more than her husband. Yet the unspoken and unaired condition of her heart remained within her. She claimed full ownership of this duality. There was no shame or guilt, it was simply an occurrence.

She wrote a poem called "Shooting Stars" and she let her passion for him tumble out. She was surprised at how apt the words were. She thought she had just chosen well, until she let a serious poet read it.

"This is good. Are you serious about poetry? Submit it for publication. I insist."

She had not sent it anywhere just kept it in her journal. It was for him and no one else. This love could well have been from an ancient Egyptian temple and she a high priestess who only performed rituals in secret to celebrate the beauty of love. There was never a letter that came for each of them from the other. There were no go-betweens or mutual friends who were even aware of this.

Then she heard there was trouble in his country. He had been elevated to the cabinet and the change in government meant that people from the old regime would be punished. He was singled out and tossed into jail. The news was a blow for her. She imagined scenes of jailbreaks from old cowboy films. She played with that image. Then she made a telephone call. She handled the call diplomatically.

"Yes, once again we have Martial Law thrust upon us."

"Hope no one you know is in trouble?"

"I am not in government, as you know. But the Minister for Energy was tossed into jail for using a private plane." He laughed.

"Really?" Her heart raced with anxiety.

"He was perhaps the only good minister we had. He is a good friend of your pal Moon the textile king. So now the honorable Minister is sitting in jail as we speak. He has a battery of top lawyers in court, he will get out."

"I shudder to think of jails in your country."

"So you should. But he will have some perks. Food delivered from home, air conditioning."

"No striped pajamas and latrine duties?" She kept her tone light.

"No. He comes from an important family and so does his wife."

Yet she knew she would have gone to rescue him in a heartbeat defying all the odds. The rules of this love story were never to change, neither one of them could contact the other directly. This gave birth to another poem. There was violence and grief in the poem and it was laced with mystery. In a sense it had recorded the emotions she experienced when she had heard he had been jailed.

A couple of years later she went to see her parents and was waiting at a fashionable hotel in the capital city waiting for a cousin. Suddenly he appeared wearing a cream-coloured suit. A touch of grey was sprinkled at the temples. He was sporting a mustache and looked positively rakish.

"How are you?" He loomed over her.

"Just waiting for my cousin," she said calmly, although her heart would have leapt out of her rib cage.

"How dare he make you wait. Should we sit for a while," he gestured to the seating in the lobby. "No."

"Just no? Where are you staying? How long are you in town?" He was smiling as though she had said something foolish.

There was nothing she could say to him. They stood so close together that she wanted to stroke his face, but the enormity of what could not be uttered was like the waters of a vast ocean. No horizon could be seen at this ocean's edges. Every feeling they evoked in each other hid underneath on their deceptively still faces. It was a valiant love that continued to flourish without contact. When she saw her cousin's figure moving toward them, she neatly turned away and stepped out of the poem she had recently written. She did not turn back and look at him.

Another decade rolled by. She had ended her first marriage and remarried. Different varieties of love entered her life. Then she was marooned in a foreign country where a tainted version of love assaulted her. She wrote about it. There were reviews that marked her passionate outpourings and it appeared admiration for the beating of her ardent heart. She regrouped.

He did not alter any aspect of his personal life to disrupt his marriage or the lives of his adult children. The next meeting was at a hotel where he invited her for tea and ordered platters of pastries. She sat on his lap on his insistence and he chuckled.

"You have put on weight."

"Look who is talking," she jumped off his lap like a scalded cat and flung herself into an armchair.

He roared with laughter. The laughter was so infectious that she dissolved into it herself. Their intimacy was undented by time. The way they gazed at each other, fully aware that a clock ticked away, bringing the end of yet another encounter. The strength of their acceptance that this was all that could be eternally allotted to them made them surefooted in a strange way. At the door when she was leaving, he pulled her back for another embrace. She felt he wanted to say something but he did not. Although his strong arms holding her gently for the final embrace brought suspect moisture to her eyes, it did not materialize into tears or spill out. She left without turning back. She had trained herself to do this years ago.

She landed in his country on a fleeting trip. The news reached him on its own. Then he telephoned her late at night and she told him a meeting would not take place this time. She was flying to the mountains in the morning.

"You are the woman I met fifty years ago."

He was claiming ownership of this alliance. He was telling her that he had locked it firmly as a life event. What was diplomatically left unsaid was designed to linger as it always had. It was a rare commodity this lingering love. She had always taken it out like a valuable curio from a display cabinet examined it and then returned it for safe keeping.

He stepped out of character for the first time. It was a false move and could shatter the balance which had been put into place right at the beginning.

"I will book a hotel for you," he said possessively.

"Don't," she said quickly.

"You are going to leave without seeing me?"

"Yes."

"Just like that?"

"Yes. Just like that," she disconnected the phone.

Voromar

Barcelona, Spain, 2021

The coastal town of Barcelona in Spain attracted lovers of art and cuisine. The location of one particular seafood restaurant was also its name. Voromar; was the Spanish word for "by the edge of the sea." The beach, which spread on either side of it, was called Barcelonetta and was a fishing village at one time. Pablo Picasso had painted it before it transformed into a sparkling beach location. Tonight, the two men flailing in the water, entering Spain as illegal immigrants, had never heard the name of Picasso. They were working-class men of Bangladeshi origins who had never left their countries before and had managed a perilous illegal night crossing from Morocco. Wiry Azmat, age thirty-six, and Nadeem, twenty-five, unlikely companions, could not swim. The Mediterranean had turned rough and they had clung to the sides of the raft that carried them overnight. When the raft stopped, they were already wearing life jackets and were handed two black rubber tires. They were told to jump into the water, grip the tires firmly and paddle towards the twinkling lights on the shore, which appeared very close. Hiding their immense fear they held the tires tight and slid into the sea.

Az chanted a prayer his mother had taught him as he kicked his legs in the water and heaved his chest back and forth to paddle through the water. He stayed close to Nadeem, about whose ability to move through the water he had misgivings. He was wrong, as Nadeem with his tall athletic body had actually mastered a swimming stroke and often shot ahead of him. It took them two hours to reach the shallows where their feet hit the sand. Here they removed the life jackets and let the rubber tires go. When they reached the edge of the beach they collapsed on the sand and slept in their wet clothes.

Jay, the owner of Voromar sat on a lounge chair on the beach, smoking a cigar. He had entertained two businessmen at his restaurant late into the night and now wanted to think in peace. He had decisions to make. He thought he saw two lumps in the sand and wondered what debris had floated out of the water or if giant sea turtles had swum out of the ocean to lay their eggs in the sand. They were known to lie motionless for hours when they did this. His curiosity got the better of him and he walked on the beach towards the lumps. One lump moved and rose. It was the outline of a man. He knew exactly what he confronted. The sea regularly offered these illegal immigrants, who would be arrested at daybreak when the police came to patrol the beach. Often, Jay would save them. He hired them as workers in his string of restaurants. They washed dishes and swept floors until Jay secured fake papers for them.

Jay believed that men who came from foreign countries to escape their poor circumstances were worth saving. He had cultivated a diplomat who helped him with temporary work permits in exchange for free sumptuous seafood meals and bottles of French champagne at Voromar plus the use of Jay's luxury beach apartments. Neither of them cared for their host country, Spain, regarding it as racist. The diplomat was safe hiding behind his protocol, but Jay had chosen Spain as a country to both hide in and make his wealth grow. Spain welcomed him and his wealth gave him social and business access. Also, Jay had a secret. He contributed large sums of money to the city for various charitable events. But never accepted invitations to the annual galas and fetes, and he shied away from the press.

Az growled at Nadeem to get up quickly when he noticed Jay approaching them. The tip of his glowing cigar was the first thing visible.

"Police—is it police?" Nadeem scrambled up and moved closer to Az.

"Just stay still. We may have to run very fast." Az watched the man get closer to them.

Jay did not approach them closely but stood still about twenty feet away. He knew they would come up to him. He inhaled another drag on his cigar and thought of his Cuban wife, whom he had assured daily that he never inhaled. He looked at the sea and not at the face of the man who was coming towards him.

Azmat felt as though the slim man smoking a cigar held an invisible cord reeling him in. He had told Nadeem to stay back where he was. His rubber sneakers sank with each step he took as he brushed the sand from his clothes. The man he was reaching wore a pristine cream linen suit with the shirt collar open. He was a good-looking man with dark hair greying at the temples. He looked European and Azmat instinctively knew that he could speak English.

"Sir, where is this? I am a little lost. Is it Barcelona?"

The man smiled and extended his hand. "Welcome to Barcelonetta Beach."

Jay knew he would rescue both men. He was intrigued by them and regarded them as sea shells collected on the beach. He had no idea of their value but he collected them anyway. The very fact that they did not know how to swim but had navigated the waves and reached shore safely impressed him. He marched them back to Voromar. It had closed for business but the night manager was still around.

"Feed them and let them sleep downstairs in the store room," Jay instructed. "Find them some dry clothes as well." He walked away without looking back.

Four weeks later both men were settled in a rooming house, now employees of Voromar. Nadeem often cried at night. He hated washing dishes and sweeping floors and the foreign language. He missed his young wife whom he had left behind. Azmat with his striking looks and high intelligence had instantly made plans. Even if he did not understand the intricacies of the restaurant business, confidence shone from his dark eyes. He was instinctively trusted to do the right thing. He spent his nights listening to a language tape and watching the waiters like a hawk. How dishes were placed on the tables and where the cutlery was positioned, the skill of opening wine bottles silently with a flourish became imprinted in his mind. The reality, however, was that the manager, a haughty Catalan, kept them in the kitchen doing odd chores like dicing vegetables and peeling shells from seafood. He regarded them both as unworthy of a restaurant such as Voromar, but he knew that Jay could never be contradicted.

Jay came to the restaurant one evening and asked Nadeem to bring him a glass of beer.

"But he is not a waiter," the manager protested.

"Put him in a waiter's uniform then," Jay retorted sharply.

A ripple of excitement tore through the two immigrants when they saw this exchange. They knew that if one of them made it then the other one would as well. Becoming a waiter was a leap upwards. Azmat helped Nadeem to put on the stringy tie and jacket and whispered advice to him. He watched Nadeem open a bottle of beer and pour it into a long glass. Nadeem was flushed with victory and the waiter's jacket fitted him well. He felt like a rock star. Jay never sat in the patio seating but always at a table discreetly hidden in a corner inside the main section of the restaurant. The chef always prepared a light salad for him and a bowl of lentils. Jay ate sparingly. He avoided seafood, which the area was famous for.

Nadeem walked towards him with the small tray holding a glass of beer and a serviette. He had a serious expression on his face as he placed the glass in front of Jay. Jay looked up from his telephone and smiled.

"Did you open the bottle yourself?" he asked.

"Yes sir," Nadeem stammered.

"Good. Perhaps you should learn how to manage the bar."

Nadeem's heart burst with joy. He was fascinated by all the varieties of alcohol and how the drinks were mixed at the bar and the special glasses for the drinks.

"Have you learned some Spanish?" Jay inquired.

"Yes. Yes. Azmat teaches me every night. I know some Spanish and it's not too difficult," he replied enthusiastically.

"Is Azmat happy with the work?"

"Yes, sir. Azmat is also learning how to cook. He knows how to make paella. He is very smart and watches the manager and is learning very fast." Nadeem bubbled over.

But Jay had turned his head away. He took a notebook and

started writing on a page. He was leaving instructions for the manager.

Two months later there were two new waiters serving at the outdoor patio of Voromar. Azmat and Nadeem served countless meals and learned how to chat with the tourists who frequented the restaurant. They sent half their salaries to their poor families in Bangladesh, and lived frugally on the other half. On their days off they ventured into the sea and learned how to swim. They watched the bikini-clad women discreetly and thanked their benefactor for turning their lives around. A part of this free day was also used for ironing their white waiter's shirts for the week. They had been given six each and expected to be wearing pristine washed and ironed shirts. The manager was good at finding imaginary dirt spots and wrinkled shirt collars just to humiliate them. He even shortened Azmat's name to Az.

"This country you come from is where?" he would sneer.

"Bangladesh. It is close to India," Azmat replied.

"India," the man shuddered. "Lots of poverty and people who do not bathe and go hungry?"

Azmat refused to engage, but sparks sprang from Nadeem's mutinous eyes. He kept silent as he had promised Azmat he would.

Both men also had a profound dislike for the obese diplomat friend of Jay who came once a week with a host of people to dine. As was the custom, a bill was never presented to him, but he never left a tip for the servers.

"We should put something in his food," Nadeem whispered furiously to Azmat one evening.

"He is a special guest. He is a VIP so treat him like that please," Az said sternly.

What none of them knew was that their temporary work permits gave the name of the consulate as their employer. Although they were paid salaries by the restaurant, their names never appeared in Voromar's financial record. In the disbursement records of the books their salaries came under the heading of "miscellaneous casual labour." So they hovered in a no-man's land without hope of any degree of autonomy. Azmat did independent research on the lives of other waiters in case some disaster struck. Every man had a dependent family who relied on funds sent to them. Jay made the odd appearance once a month and never spoke to them; he simply watched them discreetly. One evening he brought a Canadian tourist with him. She did not eat a meal and sipped only mineral water. Finally when Jay tempted her with various items on the menu, she ordered a seafood soup. Jay exuded charm and polished attention, and the conversation between the two was animated. The woman wore simple beach clothing and leather sandals. She appeared daily in the afternoon and brought a book with her. She would order a coffee and read for an hour. Sometimes she would sketch in a notebook using both charcoal and pencils.

Often a pair of reading glasses were perched in her mane of hair and even without any obvious makeup she managed to look attractive. Both waiters fussed around her, pleading with her to order some food.

"I have had lunch and will be cooking dinner at my apartment when I go back. Thank you, coffee is what I want."

As with the diplomat, Jay had left strict instructions that a bill was never to be presented to her. But she was smart and knew she was being treated as a special guest so she compensated by leaving a tip which was larger than the price of the coffee or mineral water itself. She insisted they keep the tips or she would not return and that would be a shame. Voromar was her favourite place on the promenade and she had dubbed the waiters the two princes of Voromar. She questioned them about the families they were separated from. They pulled out their phones and displayed the pictures of their wives and young children. Within days this relationship became personal. However, for Az the personal bordered on an intense attraction. His heart always skipped a beat when he saw her. She also spoke to him more than Nadeem. Azmat, who had had an arranged marriage at the age of nineteen was not familiar with romantic love. All he knew was that nervous sort of tension rippled through him around her. It was not something he could share with Nadeem, who was like a younger brother and looked up to him.

Azmat had a running yet silent battle with the general manager as well as the accountant, who paid them monthly. He felt both men were high-handed and insensitive, bereft of empathy for the staff. He experienced racism for the first time in his life. It was young Nadeem who was the target of the manager's assaults. Nadeem would display his hurt and frustration by getting red-eyed as he pressed back his tears. Az cautioned him never to react, or he could lose his job or wind up on the streets or be deported. However, deep in his heart Nadeem felt that with time he could learn how to beat the system. Perhaps even beat their benefactor Jay. Az did not know that the money he sent home to his wife was used by her unemployed brother who also lived in the house and drank to excess. The money he sent for his thirteen-year-old son's education in a decent school was also squandered in this fashion. The stability of the home he had left behind was in shambles.

Voromar was usually open seven days a week, but it was announced that it would close for a special day. Jay was throwing his annual party in his magnificent villa and although a catering firm would handle the food, the two princes of Voromar were given black suits with white shirts and black bow ties so they could serve as well.

The villa sat on a hill outside the central city. The architecture was classical with modern additions. The enormous swimming pool had flower bushes surrounding it. Food and drinks were served inside and outside. A four-piece band played nonstop. Fashionably dressed men and women devoured the food and drinks. But there was no sighting of their elusive host even by ten PM.

Azmat had a sense of foreboding he could not shake off. The excessively opulent environment troubled him. Azmat was a religious man and also drawn to superstition. He could not shake off a sense of doom. He was assigned to the valet parking table at the steps that led up to the main entrance of the villa. As he sat there, Nadeem suddenly appeared behind him with a large tray of champagne flutes in his hands.

"Take one. No take two. I have already drunk two," said Nadeem.

Azmat swung around and confronted his friend, noting how dashing he looked in his black suit and bow tie. His eyes sparkled but his face was flushed.

"Go away quickly," Azmat said, "You can't handle alcohol. If the manager finds out, you will be thrown out."

He turned away back to his parking valet duties of attaching number tags to car keys.

Close to midnight two things happened. The woman who came to Voromar and read books and sketched drawings appeared at the grand entrance. She wore a red dress that clung to her body. Her hair was swept up in a chignon and jewelled earrings sparkled against her cheeks.

"Oh hello, Azmat. How do you like all this?" she smiled at him.

"Beautiful. You are very lovely tonight, madam," he mumbled.

"What a lovely compliment. I am looking for our host Jay. Have you seen him? He could be hiding. His car is right here, though." She fluttered her fingers and walked away.

The second thing that happened was that Azmat went to sit in the interior of a posh car waiting to be parked. He hoped to take a few photos of himself in it, but at that moment while handling his phone he saw a WhatsApp video message that his teenage son had sent him. He was shocked. In the message, his son revealed to him the condition back home—his wretched uncle's behaviour, his mother's poverty, and his inability to go to school. Az knew his life plans had just collapsed on his head. The shock was so profound that his immediate response was to do the unthinkable. He pressed the ignition button of the car and raced it on the long driveway towards the wrought-iron gates. The car belonged to Jay, but for Az it was an angel which would fly him to heaven.

Jay watched his car moving down the long cypress-lined driveway. He was upstairs in his study smoking a cigar in front of an opened window. Even from a distance he recognized Az's dark-haired head hunched over the steering wheel. He called his chauffeur and told him to follow the Aston Martin discreetly. He informed him that the man driving it had his permission to do so. He was intensely curious about the rationale behind a model employee's irrational behaviour. He knew the man was not a thief.

Downstairs Jay's new Canadian friend was approached by a server offering champagne. But she shook her head in refusal and then stopped.

"Oh hello. Look at you. The other prince of Voromar. Just as handsome. Well, may I ask you to find someone to drop me off because Jay is missing and I am fed up with this noise and all these people."

Nadeem gave her a lopsided grin. "We don't have a car, madam but we can find Azmat, who can arrange this."

"Let's go then. A little walk will do us some good. We can always call a taxi."

Jay watched the duo walking slowly along the driveway. The woman had removed her shoes and Nadeem had gallantly stuffed the delicate high-heeled shoes in the pockets of his jacket. They looked like lovers locked in an exit plan. Nothing else mattered. A report that the sports car parked along the side of the road just outside the villa had already reached him. Any material damage or loss did not interest him; he wanted to know how this night of revelry would end. His new friend had walked out barefoot accompanied by a waiter employed by him. The Mayor of Barcelona had arrived and he would have to leave his lair and go down and spend a few minutes with him.

Azmat was resting against the trunk of a gnarled olive tree. He had abandoned the car as soon as his senses recovered. He was not a thief. He was dealing with genuine grief, and he knew he had to go back to his homeland as soon as he could. For a few minutes he toyed with gruesome fantasy of actually killing his brother-in-law when he reached home. He had no papers to travel, since there was a six-month wait before he received his Spanish resident permit. If he travelled back he could not return.

A driver racing his car towards the gates saw a glint of red on the road but missed the man in black jacket who suddenly stepped out and bent down to pick up something. He slammed down the brakes but the left fender of the car struck the head of the man.

Azmat heard the screech of car brakes and a cry and he raced towards the road. The scene that met him curdled his blood.

She was sitting in the middle of the road cradling Nadeem. His face was covered by a part of her red dress. Her shoe, which had fallen out of Nadeem's pocket and which was what he had leaned down on the road to retrieve, was the cause of his death.

Azmat slid on the asphalt as he reached her.

"I did not see him . . . only this lady . . . he just appeared and knelt on the road. I tried to stop. I stopped," cried the man who had hit him.

Twenty minutes later the Aston Martin driven by Jay with her and Azmat crushed together in the passenger seat followed the screaming ambulance. None of them spoke. Jay had draped his jacket around her shoulders, but the bloodstained dress, bare feet, and strands of dishevelled hair saddened him. Azmat's bow tie was still straight but not a single thought entered his mind. He sat silently, repeating over and over the prayer his mother had taught him.

Seated in a corridor of the Barcelona hospital, three people waited to hear the news of Nadeem's injury. A doctor with his surgical mask looped around his neck eventually approached them.

"We could not save him. We tried, but a head injury of this kind is fatal. I am very sorry. His family needs to be informed."

She cried softly. Jay and Azmat got up.

"His phone has his wife's number," Azmat said.

"You are both from the same city?" Jay asked.

"Yes. His body has to go home. He cannot be buried in a foreign country."

Jay was well known for his efficiency. Within forty-eight hours he had extracted liability payment for the accident; travel papers and a flight were arranged for Nadeem's corpse and Azmat. The two princes of Voromar would return home in a plane, flush with money. The money would be split between Azmat's and Nadeem's families. Azmat did not plan to return to Spain.

"Do you want me to come with you?" she asked.

"No. You will not like it, madam," Azmat looked away in embarrassment.

The woman's attachment to the two waiters was a true act of friendship. She insisted on returning the jacket Azmat had draped on her the night of the accident. At the final parting two days later she pressed a piece of paper in Azmat's hand.

"This has my address, email, and phone number. Please let me know how you are."

Chittagong was a sparkling city in Bangladesh by the shores of the Bay of Bengal. Among the string of restaurants along the beach was one which had a curious Spanish name. Voromar had six tables and two employees.

One employee was a female cook whose specialty was fish and shrimp curries. The other was the owner and waiter, who always wore a black suit, a white shirt, and black bow tie. The small tables were impeccably set with white china and stainless steel cutlery. In the centre of each table was a small glass bottle with a red hibiscus flower.

Azmat had used his share of the money to rent the tiny restaurant at first and within two years did well enough to buy it. He had moved his wife and son to Chittagong, and the son often came on the weekends to help him. Twice a year Azmat travelled to Nadeem's grave and said his special prayer. The money given to Nadeem's wife amounted to fifteen years of earnings that he would have sent had he settled in Spain.

Once a week he posted a special dish for a reduced price, and it was called the Nadeem Special. He had managed to photograph his restaurant and send the pictures by email to the woman. He did not get a response.

There were times when he felt that he carried her, Jay, and the Mediterranean inside him. He had left nothing behind. As an illegal immigrant, survival was not the only lesson he had learned. People like Jay, Nadeem, and the Canadian tourist inhabited his mindscape and spurred him to action. Voromar, Barcelona, was his learning ground but it was Voromar, Chittagong which became his life.

Jay received a letter one day. Five photographs rolled out of the envelope. The brief note from his Canadian friend spread a smile on his face. He lit a cigar and gazed at the sea. She was exhibiting her paintings in Rome and had sent him an invitation. A week later he stood in the gallery and found himself face to face with pen-and-ink portraits of the two princes of Voromar. He knew that all his sea shells settled in different shores were of immense value. He purchased both portraits.

Jay's attitude to people was similar to the narrator Nick in the American novel by F Scott Fitzgerald, *The Great Gatsby*. "Reserving judgements is a matter of infinite hope." His Spanish sojourn was over as he had suffered a crippling loss to all his business ventures. Jay was bankrupt.

The Last Martini

Yorkville, Toronto, 1993

Zavier ruled over his domain with inimitable style. The venue was the old bar of the Luxury Hotel Delia in a fashionable area of Toronto. This was an elaborate, carved wooden bar, set in the middle of the lounge and closed on all four sides so it looked like a cage. It served guests of the hotel and others who insisted on drinking their alcohol of choice served by an elegant man with an archival memory. A decade later when the seating area was expanded, a long, white marble bar replaced the older one. The name of the bar was also changed. For Zavier, who continued to serve, it was as though he was fused to the architecture of the hotel. Ownership was a two-way street here. He may have been an employee of the hotel for forty years but he considered himself to be a permanent resident—a tenant with a lifelong lease. The protocols and etiquettes of this hotel were imprinted in his brain. He got annual raises and a Christmas bonus. There was satisfaction on both sides.

It was not easy to lead a double life. The contrast was alarming. So he simply deleted his family history as well as the culture of the country he had come from. He believed that one life did not give him any advantage over the other one. At least that was what he mistakenly thought. With the sole exception of one person, nobody had a clue to his background, personal life, or dreams.

In the city of Kingston, Jamaica, decades ago a young man stood for hours in a passport office until he received the news he had waited for. Twenty-seven months after applying, he had acquired a landed-immigrant status in Canada. Zavier had embraced his elderly parents and two older siblings and took a three-hour flight on a shabby plane to Toronto. He never looked back.

He washed dishes in restaurants and lived in a men's hostel run by the Salvation Army. He was lean, and hungry to improve his circumstances, so he found better jobs. After two years he took a bar-tending course. Then he found two jobs and he juggled working at both. He saved enough money to move to a bachelor apartment. He now had an address, with a black-and-white secondhand TV, and made his meals in a tiny galley kitchen. He invested in clothes and purchased three pairs of black trousers and white rayon shirts that never wrinkled. He went to secondhand clothing stores and bought two suits and two ties. Both suits were black and the ties were maroon. He pounded pavements on the weekends and dropped in at all the hotels inquiring about jobs.

The personnel manager of the Luxury Delia Hotel straightened out the crumpled paper with the job advertisement and looked at the man who had slid it across his desk. There was ethnic diversity reflected in the cleaning staff, kitchen help, porters and valets of the hotel, but never at the main bar. The man in front of him was a tall well-built dark-skinned Jamaican with flashing eyes. He had close-cropped hair designed to restrain the African frizz. Dressed in a shiny black suit and equally shiny maroon tie he had a soft voice in which he spoke an unaccented English. This was the most astonishing aspect. He did not have the Caribbean lilt to his voice. For the manager this was conclusive, so he hired him promptly as a trainee at the bar. He would be helping the chief bartender by rinsing glasses and passing him ice cubes and cocktail garnishes. He would spend a lot of time observing but he would not be talking to the clients.

When his employment papers were filled, the first name Zavier was not problematic but his surname drew attention. It was Humble. Zavier Humble baptized in a Catholic church in Kingston Jamaica did not know that the priest entangling the name offered by his parents, who seemed uncertain about their own family name, had mistakenly replaced the *a* with *u*. The baby's father felt that God would be pleased with this name. The nuns at the school where Zavier learned how to speak unaccented English approved of the name, but his schoolmates did not. He was bullied mercilessly. Perhaps it was this surname that instilled a curious shyness in him. Compliments at work made him uneasy, so he kept silent. Yet this silence was like an aura around him. People who chose the bar-seating and were alone often chatted with bartenders. The head bartender Edward was chatty but Zavier considered this to be an intrusion on one's duties. He kept his own speech almost monosyllabic.

Two years later when Edward fell ill, Zavier was told to take over his job. It came unannounced and with speed. Zavier was stunned and he copied Edward's style of dress. He wore a black waistcoat and a black bow tie. He offered a pleasant smile and even laughed at weak jokes; but he kept a mysterious distance which clearly stated that he would not permit intimacy to develop. Even though he knew the familiar regular clients, he would not address them by their names. He would simply say "good evening" and "good afternoon." When they left sumptuous tips for him, he nodded in appreciation and focused on pouring the drinks, keeping a watchful eye on the levels of alcohol in the tumblers and wine glasses. The small bowls of olives and salted almonds which he placed with great precision next to the drinks along with the folded paper napkins kept him alert and focused. He had no idea that a hidden camera filmed all his movements. This was part of the hotel's security protocol and only management was aware of it. However, it became part of a personnel record as well. A client who overindulged in alcohol and could become a liability to the lounge or to himself was gently removed.

"I cannot pour you another drink, sir. I could get the front porter to arrange for a taxi," Zavier would say in a soft and apologetic tone.

Behind the soft voice and the false apology stood a man who would not hesitate to pick up the bar phone and press a special extension. Help would arrive and the person would be convinced by someone else. It always worked. The Delia was the top hotel in the city and the standards of social behaviour were observed by its sophisticated clients. Once in a while a woman from an escort service would make the mistake of sitting at the bar and slyly solicit men. Zavier would then speak to the person on that special extension on the phone and a female waitress from the lounge area would discreetly inform the woman that the hotel was not comfortable with her presence. What she had consumed was complimentary.

A decade passed and Zavier understood that he was secure in his job and management eternally pleased with him. Once in a while he was invited to a meeting where brands of alcohol were discussed. Zavier's input, written meticulously on a sheet of paper, was taken seriously.

Zavier's shift was from four PM to midnight. He was punctual and never missed a day at work. At the end of the first decade Zavier made a bold move. He purchased a tiny house in a decaying old neighbourhood of the city. The down payment was small as were the monthly mortgage payments. The only redeeming feature of the house was a medium-sized back garden. From April to October Zavier made this garden bloom and he became someone more than the head bartender at the hotel.

Late at night when Zavier walked to his house after a ride in the streetcar, he first walked to the kitchen where a door led out to the garden. Here he walked in the dark, surveying the bushes, the large maple tree that created a canopy, and his small vegetable bed. In the spring, lily-of-the valley thrust itself out of the earth followed by the lilac bush, which leaned over his neighbour's fence and the fragrance stirred memories of his childhood, but he firmly resisted indulging in them. In the fall he waited for leaves to turn red and in the winter he still walked at night in the small garden, where he had set up a bird feeder. From an immigrant to a home owner. From the confinement behind a bar for eight hours to this patch of ownership was the best life imaginable for Zavier.

Inside the tiny bungalow with its rickety porch was a single bedroom and a bathroom. The kitchen was medium size with old appliances, but the stove with its four-ring burner and oven was a joy. Zavier taught himself to cook, making stews and roasting meat and vegetables. The living room had a couch and a centre table. In front of the couch was a Formica television stand against one wall. The television stood on the top shelf and a small radio on the bottom shelf.

Further along this room was a dining table which could seat four but only had two chairs. The lighting fixture overhead was a yellowing China globe. There was a braided rug on the floor. The entire house was painted blue inside. There were two posters of

Niagara Falls on the walls. Zavier would take a day trip there by bus once a year in the summer, always enthralled by the thundering cascading water. The sight of this water also released another memory—a turquoise lagoon ringed by palm trees—but Zavier blinked the image away. He had mastered the art of changing mindscapes. He was convinced that he had left a country and a life to start a new life. He had written a brief note to his elder brother stating he was now settled and had no plans of visiting or returning. He never got a response.

One regular client at the Lounge Bar, as it was now known, always drew Zavier's attention. At precisely six PM he would arrive and occupy the same seat. He would order a classic gin martini with an olive and a twist of lemon. His attire was impeccable as was his grooming. Elegant grey hair swept back and a pencil thin mustache. He would look at Zavier and raise his index finger. This was the cue to make his martini. Like Zavier there was a restrained silence which enveloped him, yet he appeared to be known in some capacity, as he was often greeted by others. He would simply smile and nod and gaze into the depth of the martini glass. He never removed the olive from the pick and ate it as others did. He would just swirl the toothpick as though he needed to clear the alcohol in the glass. After three sips he would take out a thin gold cigarette case from the breast pocket of his suit jacket and flip it open. From the row of thin dark cigarillos he would select one. Zavier, watching, would reach just in time with a hotel matchbox and light a match in a fluid graceful manner. The man's elegant head bent and a whiff of his cologne floated into Zavier's nostrils. The top notes of this fragrance were brisk, citrus, and essentially male. Zavier carried the mystique of this fragrance to his serving counter at the bar. His own memory bank released a flash of the lemon tree which grew in the tangled foliage of his childhood home. He shook his head twice and tossed the image into the garbage heap of discarded images.

The man would then take three leisurely puffs on the cigarillo and then with a slow deliberate motion stub it out in the heavy glass ashtray and push it away from him. Zavier's ever watchful eyes made him retrieve the ash tray instantly and toss the contents into the sealed garbage bin. He saw the gold-tipped cigarillo float downwards, leaving a tantalizing odour of a specific tobacco not inhaled often. He knew it was Cuban. After five minutes the man rose and a fifty-dollar bill lay in front of the empty martini glass. When Zavier placed the change in front of him the man placed ten dollars as a tip for his twenty-one dollar martini and without eye contact with Zavier walked away. He never used a credit card, so Zavier did not know his name.

In the middle of an early spring in the fourth year of his residency at his house two things happened simultaneously at noon one day. A thin aerogramme letter written from his elder brother informing him that both his parents had died in a fire. They were buried side by side in a cemetery in Kingston. There was no inheritance. As he digested this information there was loud knocking on his front door. He walked towards the door with the thought that the contempt expressed by his brother in the brusque communication was justified. He opened the door and found himself facing an irate woman.

"Mr Humble you have to trim that lilac. It is now reaching the ground on my side and my zinnias get no sun. I am fed up!"

Zavier struggled to dislodge the image of two graves side by side across a vast ocean and stared at the woman. He felt as though a storm had battered him on all sides, he was like a tree whose roots had been pulled out. An unwelcome stirring of sorrow also flooded him.

"You . . . you don't like the perfume of lilac . . . miss?"

"No," she said stoutly.

"No?" repeated Zavier woodenly.

"Have you understood what I am saying? Maybe you don't speak English?" her eyes narrowed in suspicion.

"I understand perfectly. I will attend to it on Saturday morning." He replied softly and then shut the door in her face.

He chopped the lilac savagely on Saturday, almost reducing the bush to stumps. There would be no fragrance for him this year or the next. He did this as though life had exacted a penalty from him for abandoning his parents to a life in a wooden shack in the middle of an overgrown yard by the ocean. The Catholic church he had been exposed to as a child had often spoken of the wrath of God upon sinners. It was his personal history and it was over. His family had been replaced by the people who visited the hotel and never seemed to exact any penalty from him but instead rewarded him with generous tips.

Zavier was a frugal man who lived within his income and saved. There was every possibility that the mortgage on his house would be paid off earlier. His one weekly extravagance was to read the two main newspapers thoroughly. He read both the sports and business pages, slowly understanding how the business sector impacted all aspects of life, including the lives of the upscale clients of the hotel who charged a fortune on their expense accounts. He would also buy a new shirt every second month.

He worked six days a week and Sunday was his free day. He roamed through different parts of the city and often took the ferry to Toronto Island. Here he would bask in the sunlight, weather permitting, and even swim in the murky water. He watched families barbequing and lolling on towels. Zavier took his own home-made picnic and two bottle of beer. He eyed the women discreetly but never approached them until during one annual Caribbean picnic Jacy happened.

Lush hipped and full bosomed, Jacy with a mane of tight curls kept brushing against Zavier in the throng of people gyrating to a steel drum Jamaican band. Zavier had jostled around with the crowd until the continual bumping of hips was no longer an accident. She threw back her head and laughed. Every time Zavier would mumble "Excuse me," taking the blame for the physical contact in a gentlemanly way, she would laugh mischievously.

"Come on, man, you are Jamaican. Shake those hips," she would taunt him.

Zavier did precisely that a few hours later on the chenille bedspread covering his bed. He had invited Jacy home for some beer and within minutes desire ignited between them like a brushfire. Zavier almost wept with gratitude at this contact and coupling. Jacy, whose real name was Jacaranda, had come from Jamaica on a missionary visa. The church had used her as part of its cleaning staff. She swept floors and polished wooden pews. Then through the network of Jamaicans she found independent work as a cleaning lady, working five days a week and collecting tax-free cash payments. She considered Zavier's reserve and unabashed ardour fascinating.

"You are my boyfriend now," she announced one day.

"We will see. I am a very busy man and don't have much time for a personal life," he replied. "Yes. We will see," she promptly responded and chuckled.

This change in Zavier's life thawed him a little. He saw Jacy twice a month but did not share any details of his employment with her. The sex worked and on the odd occasion he cooked dinner for her. Her cheap and habitually tight-fitting clothing displeased him, but he never criticized her. Her laugh was too loud but infectious.

He did however tell her that she was named after a beautiful tree which in bloom was covered with cascading pale violet flowers. She scoffed at this. Like him she had left a family behind.

"I am Jacy. Just Jacy, and I am free and earn my own money and live. That's all I want. I don't want to be some silly tree," she tossed her head, rearranging the mop of curls which shot down her forehead almost to her nose.

Zavier was burying tall stemmed martini glasses in the mound of crushed ice in a steel container behind the bar. Glasses had to be chilled to give the martini its best edge. This edge meant freezing cold, which suited vodka and gin. The lemon twist he made himself with a paring knife thin as an eyelash. This was the Zavier Humble signature martini at the hotel, and it came with not one but three gigantic olives impaled on one toothpick. An elegant, anorexic woman had lifted the toothpick once and said to her companion, "Well, the olives are dinner."

The man he called his six o'clock would be arriving in ten minutes. Zavier managed to reserve his seat at the bar. He did this subtly. He had no idea that fate had something else in store for him that day. For a man who tightly controlled his entire existence and lived a modest and industrious life that even the exuberant Jacy had learned never to intrude in.

The man arrived at six and greeted Zavier. "The usual, sir?" asked Zavier.

What he got was a nod in return. He made the martini and carefully placed it on the marble surface along with a folded napkin.

"It is Jamaica? Where you come from?" the man asked.

Zavier paused. "Yes, sir."

"All settled and plan to be a Canadian then?"

"Oh yes, sir. All settled. I even got a little house." Zavier could not resist adding this detail.

"Excellent. Do you have a mortgage?"

"Twenty-five years, perhaps I can work harder and clear it off earlier."

This time instead of the cigarette box from his pocket, the man pulled out a small notebook with a fountain pen. He filled a page with writing, tore it out of the notebook, folded the paper, and handed it to Zavier.

"Call this man and perhaps you will pay the balance of the mortgage now."

Zavier, filled with curiosity, stuffed the note into his pocket and continued with his duties. He was there in time to offer a light for the cigarillo that appeared between the man's fingers. The partly drunk martini was pushed just a little aside. Zavier did not attempt to make conversation. There would be enough time he thought to read what was written on the paper when he got home. Still a thread of excitement wound itself in him.

Late at night he read what was written on the paper. He was to contact the man whose name and number were given. He did that the next morning and was asked to come to an office on King Street. He entered the elegant reception area and was led to a man in an office which had a large window that revealed an expanse of high-rise office towers. Money seemed to be the office décor. It cascaded down from the man's three-piece suit. A gleaming desk with an array of telephones and a large computer screen where numbers moved up and down. Two crystal decanters half full with whiskey and cognac, two heavy crystal tumblers, ice bucket and tongs behind him on a tray won Zavier's heart. The man knew how to serve alcohol. He was in the office of an investment broker.

"Do you have any savings Mr Humble?" he asked.

"Yes. I have seven thousand dollars," replied Zavier.

"Excellent. An investment for twenty-four hours in one of your benefactor's companies will earn a profit threefold for you. Your seven thousand dollars will become twenty-one. Where do you bank?"

Zavier was dumfounded. He had no idea that he was being exposed to insider trading and the man who came for his six o'clock martini had decided to give him the gift of a lifetime. The twenty-five-year mortgage was going to be discharged immediately. Zavier would own his little home and be the master of his destiny. In fifteen minutes he had entered his bank and withdrawn seven thousand dollars from his savings account. The bank teller was curious.

"Going on a holiday or buying a car?"

"No, this is for someone." Zavier held the large envelope of cash in both hands.

"Oh, we could have deposited this by bank draft."

"No, cash is just fine. It's real." Zavier beamed at her.

He dashed back to the financial tower office and was ushered in. The man was on the phone but waved him in and pointed to the armchair before the desk. Zavier placed the envelope stuffed with notes on the gleaming desk. The man finished the call and walked around to the alcohol stand.

"Scotch or cognac, Mr Humble?" he asked.

The bar tender in Zavier leapt up. "Let me pour, sir," he said and reached for the tray.

"I see. Yes I have heard you are quite the wonder of the Delia Hotel Bar. This is my turf, allow me."

Zavier watched how more than a single was poured into both tumblers. How the query about ice was neglected. The glass offered to him seemed to have a streak outside which meant it needed a rinse and a towel polish. However, the first sip revealed that the

Scotch was a sixteen-year-old single malt, and lived up to its price.

"Am I right in assuming you have actually brought cash?" The man's lips twitched in a smile.

"Yes, sir. It's all there, seven thousand dollars."

"Cheers. Now please write down the name and branch of your bank and your account number. Call after noon tomorrow, and you should get a good surprise. Here is my card," he dropped an engraved card in front of Zavier. Zavier noticed that the speed with which he emptied the Scotch in his tumbler meant that he liked his alcohol and probably drank often in his office. He took another three measured sips of his drink and then rose.

"May I rinse the glasses, sir? Thank you, it is a fine Glenmorangie." The man threw back his well-barbered head and laughed.

"There is staff which cleans here. A pleasure to meet you," he extended his hand.

Zavier rode the streetcar the next morning in a state of euphoria. He had brushed the halls of the elite money-makers of his city, been treated like an investor, and served a shockingly expensive Scotch in a costly crystal tumbler before noon, by a man who had treated him like an equal. His savings for the past six years would undergo some mysterious process and like a magic trick become three-fold in value. He was completely overwhelmed and in his thirty-minute break he was going to call his bank and inquire about his balance. When the gentleman who had become a benefactor arrived for his six o'clock martini, he would thank him in the best way he knew. He had to decide what that would be. He had not shared this news with Jacy, whom he would see on Sunday.

The next day, his mind raced in different directions, and he realized he had left his black bow tie at home, but there was no way he could go and be back at the hotel in time for his work shift.

The ambience at the bar was different. Stuart, his junior who rinsed and iced glasses and handed him garnishes, had a newspaper spread on top of the bar refrigerator. This had never happened before.

Zavier ignored his greeting and tersely told him to get rid of the paper. "Remove it at once."

"You better see the front page. There is a big surprise there." Stuart ignored his instructions.

"Reading the newspaper at this bar is not part of my job and neither is it yours."

"Your martini man has his picture in there, with all about his crooked money," Stuart said and whisked the paper away and dropped it on the floor next to the refrigerator.

Zavier sensed the hurricane from his safe station inside the posh hotel. Decades ago his wizened old grandfather in Jamaica had told him about the legendary Hurricane Gilbert which had wreaked havoc on Jamaica. Land under water, trees and homes uprooted, electricity and drinking water unavailable for days. As a little boy he could not understand that something made of wind could do this. It sounded like a bad fairy tale. Without looking at the paper he felt the same bewildering terror. He stooped and collected the paper and told Stuart he needed a toilet break.

Spread out on the white counter flanking the wash basin, the business section of the national paper neatly severed his dreams from reality. The article with the mesmerizing portrait of the martini man dressed in a tuxedo and leaning against a pillar told him that he had blundered and lost his entire fortune, as had many others who had trusted him. He was referred to as a rogue trader and barred from doing business in the country.

Zavier's disbelief hinged on his own faulty judgment. He had used the precise ritual of three sips of a martini and four puffs on a cigarillo plus the habitual overgenerous tip to frame his judgment.

The magnificent offer to help him financially, leading him into an office he could never aspire to enter, had been like a spiritual blessing. His well-practised restraint, interior silence, and discipline had become ashes in his mouth. He had no desire to call his bank manager—that would be like personally confronting the hurricane. He would join a lengthy list of creditors, as the newspaper suggested. The twenty-five-year mortgage would remain in place.

At five minutes to six he made a martini and five minutes later placed it on the bar at the appointed spot. He could see Stuart giving him a worried look, but Zavier had created a barrier around himself after he returned from his break. He worked all afternoon silently and faultlessly. An inane comment of Jacy's occasionally resounding in his head: "You don't get to know people if they don't show you who they are."

Every now and then he glanced at the martini glass, which was bathed in thawing moisture. It was now 6:20 and he knew with a finality that the last martini would not be drunk by anyone. His judgment of the man who had sunk fortunes had been inaccurate.

When he got home past midnight at the end of the wretched day, a black limousine was parked outside in front of his little home. There was the flash of a cigarette lighter inside, illuminating the head of a man. The automatic window rolled down.

"Zavier, please sit with me," the passenger door of the car was pushed open from inside.

Startled, Zavier climbed warily into the car.

"Here is your money." The envelope was held out to him.

"Thank you, sir. Are you all right? The newspapers say all sorts of things. There is trouble, isn't there?"

The man gave a wry smile.

"I am leaving the country and flying to the Caribbean in the morning. I own a resort in Jamaica; I shall live there. It has a beautiful bar and I wondered if you wanted to work there for me?"

This time the hurricane which coursed through Zavier was of a different flavour. It comprised of all the things he was convinced he had left behind.

"If you are interested, then this is how you do it. Rent your house and the rent will keep your mortgage payments cleared each month. It will be your security. I will give you a room at the resort and all your meals will be had there, so you can save money faster than you can do here. Give me two years and after that you can decide if you want to stay on a permanent basis."

"There is a woman," Zavier said softly.

"Bring her with you. Make a life for yourself."

"Would you like to come inside, sir. I can make a drink for you?"

"The last martini has been drunk, Zavier." He shook his head.

The Australian Woman

Rosedale, Toronto, 1964

She is stirring her coffee. The spoon makes a scraping sound in the ceramic mug, which is shaped like an owl's head. Her blonde hair cascades down her shoulders and the hem of her nightgown is half unravelled. Her feet are bare—racing up and down two flights of stairs to oversee the departure of her husband for work which is always a hectic endeavour. Flapping slippers are not part of the game. He is a lawyer and dresses meticulously in three-piece suits, with a fresh rose in his lapel. The breakfast is freshly made porridge with cinnamon and orange juice, followed by a cup of coffee. The orange juice is freshly squeezed by her. She had cut the oranges herself, placed the halves over a plastic juicer, and squeezed them. With each turn of a half orange she felt a rush of her own strength which this town has yet to sap. Although it tries daily. Yesterday it was a preposterous censure from the Toronto Lawn Club, because apparently ladies do not play squash in Toronto.

The lack of sunshine makes the three-storied house appear dark and unwelcoming, which is far from the truth. She is in fact the sun herself, glowing and full of adventure and spontaneity—a lover of daisies which she places in stone jugs all over the house in between his exuberant collection of books, art and family China. He is also full of manners, rituals, and traditions. It is a sort of charm beyond compare. He works for a top law firm in the city. Smokes a pipe, has a deep baritone voice, and drinks expensive whiskey. He lost his head over this blonde whirling dervish from Australia, skied with her in Europe, and brought her home to Toronto to marry and deposit her in Rosedale, where his parents still lived. It was a done deal. She fell in line, or so everyone thought.

She left behind a vast group of people in Australia. Her jeweller mother, her dentist brother, and various aunts, great aunts, and cousins. Friends. She did not speak with the Australian intonation but with a sort of upper-class British accent. The boarding school her mother sent her to had something to do with that. She studied nursing and worked in London for a few years and travelled through Europe, where she fell in love with Greece. So her canvas was large; she believed that any place had the potential for magic. She knew how to find it and invite it into her life. So the Greek taxi driver in Toronto who brought her home one day was invited in for tea. Instead, it was not tea but her husband's good whiskey. Her surprised husband informed her that Toronto was not ready for this. She redeemed the situation by saying that he could do the Zorba dance and would teach them. Within seconds Greek music from the film *Zorba* resounded in the living room. Later she played Leonard Cohen's songs and served tea and oranges.

Then came her first pregnancy, during which she wore denim smocks with a mass of pendants around her neck. Her beauty turned ethereal. Her blue eyes blazed from the high cheek-boned planes of her face as she raced through the city daily, finding her adventures. She gave birth to a daughter who was a replica of her father. Within two months of her birth a wall of darkness descended on her. A mystery-riddled black curtain which silenced her laughter and speech and made even the act of getting out of bed impossible. Her husband consulted doctors and it was declared that this was more than postpartum depression. The condition was unmentionable. It became a secret from everyone including herself. A dossier of behaviour and diagnosis prepared by the venerable old psychiatrist who zealously followed a book.

It was as though sunlight had vanished from the lives of a brilliant married couple. The international romance and the first-born child all tarnished by a black ailment. She fed her child but the bathing and dressing was done by family caregivers. Silence was the language spoken and the bonny baby cooed and gurgled, gaining weight and even a small personality, but the mother sometimes found it difficult even to lift her head from the pillow.

"We can do something about this," the solemn husband told her one day.

He sat on the edge of their bed by her side. She looked at him with unseeing eyes, simply twisted her wedding band round her finger.

"He is a very senior doctor. One of the best psychiatrists in town. He has examined you and is confident you will get better."

She spoke after days.

"I don't want a psychiatrist. As nurses we were not keen on them. They will make you sick even if you are not."

"He is not like that. He is brilliant," he retorted and got up from the bed.

A palpable fear entered her life. She often felt like a condemned prisoner waiting for the hangman's noose. Something was being planned and it was to do with her, but nothing was spoken out aloud. So one day she forced herself to rise and dress her child and pull out the high black pram and took the girl outside. The winter light cast a grey pall over the bare trees in the early afternoon. The only colour visible was that of the baby's pink cheeks framed by the hood of a padded snowsuit. The pram resembled a hearse, she thought—its large wheels and sturdy undercarriage defied any obstruction. She leaned on the handles for support and wheeled it along the pavement. She had no destination but halted at the potted plants outside a store, the display almost straddling the pavement.

Inside was a grocery store. She avoided going in, but lingered outside, looking for flowers that bloomed through the winters. She found only a cactus displaying a coral-coloured bud. For a moment she felt a glimmer of hope. It was a hope that skimmed the surface of the sea of dark waters in which she felt she drowned daily. She lifted the pot of cactus and held it to her chest. Her sudden movement dislodged the tiny bloom and it dropped inside the pot.

When she looked down again it was no longer visible and the glimmer of hope vanished abruptly. A young man came out of the store and looked at her curiously.

"You have to pay inside for this, miss," he pointed to the pot in her hand.

"No. No, thank you. I was just looking," she said and placed the pot back on the shelf and turned back to the pram.

She returned back to the house. It was a small street with homes on either side. They knew three families. Her close friend Paulie's husband Dick was a close friend of her husband's. Paulie gave lovely dinner parties and her three toddlers were well behaved. She was slender and competent. She wondered if she should drop in for a visit, but it had been about two months since she had seen anyone from outside. There would be questions. As she had not deciphered what had happened to her, it would be difficult to make conversation.

Later that evening, even before any talk of dinner, her husband, who had come home earlier than usual, brought a little bag down to the front hall and made a statement.

"Dr Harold has made the arrangements and you will be admitted for treatment this evening. I have packed a bag for you. They will take you safely."

He fiddled with his pipe as he said this and she knew that the hangman's noose she had feared had just dropped around her neck. The kitchen where she stood holding a casserole to put into the oven became the site of betrayal. The man she loved, had married and borne a child with, giving up her own country, had consulted someone other than herself about her feelings. She whirled around and dashed past him down the front hall and through the unlocked door outside. Her mouth was dry and her heart pounded as she raced towards safety. She ran to Paulie's house.

There was a sound of dishes and cutlery in the dining room. Paulie and Dick were at the table with their youngest child, who was in the highchair.

"Please stop them," she shouted hoarsely. "Gerald is letting a doctor do this. Take me somewhere? Please tell him I will be fine at home."

Tears rolled down her face. Her friends were shocked. Paulie lifted the baby from the high chair and left the room. Dick rose and draped an arm around her shoulder and made her sit down.

"Sit. Sit please and calm down. I will call Gerald. Does he know where you are?"

"He is wrong. He is so wrong, and that doctor has misled him," she panted, trying to fight her way through the tide of anxiety overwhelming her.

"Drink some water, please, I will just be back," Dick poured a glass of water for her and also left the room.

The kitchen was close enough that she could hear Dick's voice.

"She is here. No, she is not hurt. What? Shoes? I haven't noticed. Well bring them anyway."

The water did not slake her thirst. She looked around the room and its inherited furniture that reflected comfort and a quiet charm. A small painting of a lake on the wall and a sculpted head of Dick's famous father. But now she did not feel entirely safe. The walk from her house to theirs was merely crossing the street. Gerald would arrive immediately. A sharp pain invaded her right heel. She looked down at her feet and realized she was not wearing shoes. Her instant flight had taken her barefoot out of her kitchen down the four steps of the front and across the street to Paulie's house opposite. She lifted up a foot and saw that a small wood splinter had pierced it. There was a pinprick of blood.

Her nurses' training kicked in.

"Dick I need some paper towel, water, and a band-aid," she said in a quavering voice directed towards the kitchen entrance.

"Oh for goodness sake!"

Gerald had entered the room followed by Dick. He immediately knelt by her chair and examined the foot.

"You can't be trusted. You can't be trusted," he mumbled as he pulled out a large white handkerchief from his jacket pocket.

"It doesn't hurt. I can do it myself." She wept openly now.

"Hold still!" thundered Gerald.

Dick appeared with a bottle of disinfectant and Paulie's eyebrow tweezer. The man who had orchestrated a terrible outcome for her then proceeded to remove the splinter carefully with the tweezers dabbed the area with disinfectant and stemmed the small trickle of blood with a band-aid. It was done gently. He then pulled out her soft ballet slippers from his pockets and placed then on her feet. She closed her eyes and saw Gerald making love to her in the cabin of a ski chalet in Austria. She could feel the velvet of his cashmere sweater and the smell of his fragrant pipe tobacco. The wild palpitations of her heart slowed down. She smiled at him with love spilling out from her eyes. He straightened up and took a few steps backwards away from her.

Paulie and Dick shepherded them to their front door. She clutched Gerald's elbow when she saw the two men waiting outside. Her nostrils flared like those of an animal catching the scent of danger. She moved ahead of him, dodged the man closer to her and bolted across the street to her own house. She could hear the flurry of steps but she made it to the front door, which was open. She was home. She was safe, she thought, and wanted to charge up the steps to the nursery and her child.

This remained a dream. The bodies of the white-coated men closed in on her. She lost her balance fighting them off and they put a straightjacket on her. Gerald had vanished, and her inert upper body told her what was being done to her. She tried to kick her legs at them but they lifted her easily and placed her in the small white van standing outside the house. Here she was pressed back on a narrow bed. The straightjacket was loosened to release an arm. The sting of the hypodermic in her vein was surprising and fleeting.

Five weeks later she was lying in bed. Her eyes opened slowly. Someone appeared at the foot of her bed with a tray. "Lunch, my dear, and then a quick shower. You are going home. Isn't this wonderful, dear."

She sat up slowly hating the cheerful women with the merciless brown eyes. She had no appetite but she took a few forkfuls of meat loaf with a murky gravy. There were rules which had to be followed. She lanced peas with the fork one at a time. The purple jelly quivered in the small bowl; she tapped it with the knife and it shuddered more. It was an elaborate game. She had to be seen to be eating. The small paper cup of capsules also had to be swallowed at the end of the meal. She had mastered the art of taking the sips of water and hiding one pill at a time under her tongue. When the tray was removed and the nurse left, she hurriedly slipped the pills under her pillow. Later she flushed them in the toilet.

Her days, most of which she could not focus on, were grey and monotonous, except when they took her to the room. Here she was strapped down on a narrow bed. Dr Harold loomed over her and then withdrew. A current of electricity was passed on the sides of her head and her body convulsed. She never remembered how long this lasted or what actually happened, but a portion of her brain went numb. It took hours for her to come back to consciousness and her own room. Something infinitely precious had been taken away from her she thought. Her vitality and even bits of her memory and most important of all her desire to do or feel any emotion.

Often she would see her husband placing flowers and magazines by her bed. She longed to talk and see her child but could not utter a word. A month had gone by and then another, and she felt old thoughts and feelings returning to her. She read the letters her mother had written on thin blue aerogrammes which her husband had brought her. She also learned how to deceive Dr Harold by giving intelligent responses and adopting a humble air. She knew the game at this hospital wing was to make him into a living god because he decided when you could go home.

She dressed in the clothes which had been brought for her. It was a green linen dress with pockets and a row of pearl buttons in the front. She brushed her hair and fastened it into a sleek ponytail. Her fingers shook when she applied the lipstick. She held up the perfume bottle for a while trying to decipher where the spray would come out from. Strangely, she had forgotten. But she remembered the ad on the back of the bottle which said "Promise her anything but give her Arpège."

The nurse helped her, smiling mischievously.

"It's French. You look beautiful." She gently sprayed the fragrance near her ears.

"My husband chose it for me," she replied, memory and betrayal returning like a bolt of lightning that severed her thoughts with contradictions.

He brought her home, and her child crawled towards her and rocked with joy. She lay on the carpet and played with her, singing old nursery rhymes. Gerald joined her as he leaned against the door. He held his pipe in one hand and a glass of Scotch in the other. Her child was intact and rubbed her face with her little hands and she knew life was now restored.

"Dinner. I want to cook dinner," she got up from the floor.

"It's all done. I have made chicken divine. It's in the oven," he smiled at her.

"Let's have some wine to celebrate please?" She wanted to prolong the sense that normal life had returned.

She wished Dr Harold could see this. He was the one to inform her that she had a mental ailment which required treatment that had been administered and the medication that she was to take daily. She could consult him anytime by making an appointment. She did not believe a word he uttered and knew she would never contact him. The dark sensation and lifelessness of the time before would simply not return. It was spring and like the pots of sleeping hyacinth she was ready to rise and push her way out of a mistaken diagnosis. As a nurse she had never worked in the psychiatric wings of hospitals. She telephoned her mother in the small town of Mudgee in New South Wales, Australia. It was known for its wineries and wool.

"Mum. Mum. It's me. How are you?" Her voice caught in her throat.

"I am fine, girl. How are you and how is that bonny girl Melly and that handsome husband of yours?"

"We are good. Spring is coming soon and maybe even sunshine," she replied.

"Well come down, all three of you. Peter has a lovely house in Sydney with a swimming pool."

"As soon as we can." She felt the fertile wealth and breadth of her country, Australia, filled with streams and a long river, press on her Canadian life like a warm forgotten blanket.

She invited Paulie over for coffee who hugged her warmly. "All better now?"

"Yes, of course," she replied briskly.

"Do you want to talk about it? I was very worried," Paulie said softly.

"Not really. Gerald overreacted and the doctor is a fool," she said.

"But how are you feeling? Do you remember we had planned to go to the ballet?"

She could not remember. It was as though there were images and words which had simply disappeared. A ribbon of anger unfurled within her. Secrecy, a trait she loathed, had entered her personality. The arrogance with which she had been declared the victim of a chemical imbalance requiring treatment still amazed her. She was the trained nurse who had taken care of scads of people in her ten-year nursing career. Never once had she seen or heard of the concept of electrocuting the brain. It was a type of barbarism she now associated with this staid city where a grey sky ruled the heavens nine months of the year. Her passionate image of her husband had also altered; an authoritarian patina had glided over his innate charm. She felt she had failed him somehow. The lack of interest in her native home and her own customs were hurtful and her vivaciousness was often dubbed as being clownish. She found his two pallid sisters standoffish. His younger brother, who was a doctor, evoked feelings of tenderness for her husband, who drank more whisky than he should as an antidote for a colourless upbringing. His formal parents whom she met sparingly she saw as the epitome of Canadian frigidity. It was as though the climate had dictated their personalities. They did not travel overseas but congregated at a large cottage enclave on a lake in the summer.

The person who seemed to understand and parcel out doses of affection to her was his cousin's wife, always referred to as Godmother Margaret. Her husband Douglas had committed suicide. Gifts flowed from Margaret in a steady stream, and at her home steaming owl-shaped ceramic mugs brimming with Spanish coffee were presented as libations of the moment. In her own right Margaret was an enchantress and she intuitively understood that "the Australian woman" her cousin-in-law had married was like a giant sunbeam imprisoned in a bell jar. She orchestrated charming escapes for her as often as she could.

She is sitting in Dr Harold's office and her husband is outside in the waiting room. She has been coerced to keep this follow-up appointment, and she does it just to maintain marital accord. No matter how often she told him I am just fine now, he's still cajoled her into this. It was easier giving in to him than to refuse. He had also come home with tickets for the Broadway musical *My Fair*

Lady showing in Toronto and a stunning lavender dress for her. It was a big date night so she felt this was how she could thank him in advance.

The door opened and the doctor walked in. She felt a shiver through her body although she kept calm. He sat in the armchair which was opposite hers and settled into it.

Nobody spoke as they examined each other. She found his wiry frame, poker-straight longish hair, and pinched lips unpleasant. He resembled a policeman in a comic she had read as a young child.

"How is your mood these days?" he spoke softly.

She almost jumped in her chair. He had managed to startle her. He acted as though they were known to each other and meeting for tea.

"I am just fine, Dr Harold. Really there was no need for this appointment, but my husband insisted." She burst out defensively.

"I see," he replied and then gazed at her silently.

The two words filled the space between them, spilling into the rest of the room. She knew what was happening in the seemingly innocuous comment. The two words "I see" were a trap designed to make her spew out wild utterances that he would immediately jot down in the notebook which seemed to sprout from his fingers. Hazard, in neon lights, flashed above the seated figure of the doctor. She fixed a smile on her face and quietened down her pulse and decided to follow his cue and say nothing.

He outwaited her, though. His capacity to sit silently, only fixing a gaze on her, was infinitely more superior than hers.

"Can I stop taking the medication now?"

"Your condition does not vanish spontaneously. I think we discussed that in the hospital at length." He said that mildly as though he was discussing the weather.

"I was sad and it overwhelmed me. This city is a big change

from London and Greece. I suppose I miss my family as well. It is too far for them to even visit me." She could feel moisture pressing against her eyelids but did not allow tears to wash over her eyes.

"So you feel it is cultural dislocation and not a bipolar disorder then?" He started scribbling in the notebook with great speed.

"Is it possible?" she tossed the challenge lightly at him.

His head snapped back as though she had hurled a boulder at him, which would shred his professional reputation.

"Please be compliant with the medication. It is a mood stabilizer and I can see the benefits just in your body language," he said, shutting the notebook.

She clenched the handle of her handbag tightly and knew she could get up from the chair and leave the room. She could halt the montage of images flitting through her mind that the presence of the doctor had evoked. Yet she waited with a show of obedience which seemed to satisfy him.

"You can always call my office if you feel that a particular feeling overcomes you. Please send your husband in, so I can just have a brief word with him." He rose and walked to his desk and sat on the chair behind it.

She wanted to do a polka right there and then. Polka right out of his office and home to make preparations for the stew she would make for dinner. She had already decided she would never return to his office or consult him. She had not taken the medication since she had returned home. Plans had to be made for the summer. Godmother Margaret had promised to take care of baby Melly, while Gerald took her for a weekend to Montreal. She had to have her dress fitted. There was a flower bed she wanted to dig out in the front of the house. Also half a dozen letters she meant to write. Gerald had given her his bicycle, but she wanted a funny horn and had to look for that. Every day would be filled with action and fun. No one would ever catch her on the wrong foot. That was her private expression for the entire hospitalization episode. The memory she seemed to have lost for a brief spell returned. She could deal with everything and had lots of energy. She had made a new friend who was a sculptress. The sculptress wanted to use her head for a coin she was designing. She would invite her home for dinner and introduce her to Gerald and then ask her to do two coins for their anniversary. She kept this a secret from Gerald. She had also discovered a long street which had three Greek restaurants and a few grocery stores where Macedonian feta cheese and gigantic olives were sold.

She played with her baby Melly who was now eight months old and already crawling. She called her Melly Moon and sang songs to her at bed time. The rhythm and mood of the house bloomed in the summer. Her outings with Melly were on the bicycle, the child strapped into a seat at the back. She rode the ferry at the bottom of the lake and headed to the islands. Here, despite rumours of polluted water, she waded in, with Melly on one hip, and scanned the horizon. She had boundless energy and never got tired.

The next day Melly fussed and howled. As a nurse she felt it was teething issues and rubbed glycerine on the baby's gums, but she felt a heaviness descend on her. It descended on her with relentless speed. She recognized it was the same mood that had broken her equanimity two months after Melly's birth. It was as though a known beast had leapt on her. She watched the rain pelt the windows, thunder roar, and lightning crackle; an ancient sorrow pressed on her. She placed Melly in her crib and raced to her bedroom. Here, she opened the large armoire. She knelt down and crept into it. She shut the door behind her and hid in the forest of clothes. Lying on the floor of the armoire she sensed that she had no desire to ever leave it.

Gerald discovered her an hour later he helped her out of the armoire, holding her so she would not lose her balance.

"What is it? For God's sake are you taking the pills? Is it happening again?"

"Nothing is happening. I am just being an Australian woman."

The Actress

Ontario, 1988

Her career began when she was two years old, and had started mimicking her mother. This was her theatre, and she grasped the art quickly. As the only child, she was her mother's companion. The bonding was both physical and emotional. The physical resemblance to each other grew stronger by the day. The sense of order and occasional chaos that ruled the family life was adopted by her as well.

Mother and child were intimate companions for five years until the next child arrived. Later, she would say she felt she lived in the set of a play with numerous acts, elaborate sets, nonstop applause, and always two leading ladies.

When she was three she realized that there were three prized accessories her mother never moved without. These three items made her as magical as the queens in the fairy tales. There was a handbag which contained a set of keys and a lipstick. When the mother picked up the handbag and held her hand she knew movement was imminent. The keys started the car, where she was placed in a car seat in the back. But the minute the car started moving, she wiggled out of the child seat and sat on the car seat with her toys and books spread out next to her. She was reminded mildly by her mother to climb back into the child seat, but she ignored this, knowing that she was a front-seat girl. Then the mother took out the lipstick and applied it to her lips. She used the rear-view mirror and the little girl was mesmerized by the sight of her mother's lush lips shaded in red and cyclamen, transforming her. Her mother's beauty acquired a high sheen. She longed for a handbag and the power of car keys and lipstick.

Once she was left with one of her grandmothers for a week when her parents went on a vacation. The grandmother noted her interest in her mother's handbags, so she created one for the girl. She found a small white soft-sided purse with a handle. There were a set of plastic keys and a plastic lipstick as well as a mirror in it, so it resembled the mother's. The girl picked up the handbag one day and walked out of the house, determined to find her own adventures. When she was found five minutes later she had managed to walk down half the block on the pavement. On the way back she kicked the tires of the car parked in the driveway with her little shoes and decided not to forgive her rescuers for putting an end to her role of mother.

Both her parents had a great love of the theatre. The mother had acted in high school and varsity productions. Later she acted in the local community theatre group when the girl was about three. The mother gave her the first public-speaking lesson when the girl was in junior school. A speech had to be written and then delivered extemporaneously. The mother taught her how to enunciate, use dramatic pauses, and memorize her speech entirely. The girl won this competition three years in a row. She mimicked her mother's enunciations, and she did not shy away from the countless rehearsals her mother insisted on.

"When you are on stage, you have to be perfect, so you hold the attention of the listeners," the mother had told her. The girl held this advice close to her heart. Winning her mother's admiration mattered more to her than the prize.

When she was thirteen she told her mother she would be a baby doctor when she grew up. Her mother enrolled her one summer as a voluntary "candy-striper" at the local hospital so she could experience a hospital environment and see what the doctors did. She completed the stint but came out not at all enthusiastic. Her one caustic comment shocked the mother. "While I was taking the gift cart to the old people, there was an old woman who was very sly. She said she couldn't lift, but she was just pretending. I know it, I watched her when she thought I wasn't looking." Then she screwed her face and mimicked the elderly woman. The mother's soft heart froze.

"That's not nice. You never make fun of old people," she rebuked the girl.

"You better not get old, Mum," she said cheekily and darted away.

She had already taken dance classes followed by gymnastics so the next summer the mother enrolled her in a drama course. The man who ran it was a seasoned director; at the end of the course he would mount a play with his students. The girl would return from the classes with a different shine in her eyes but did not comment much. The mother was pleased and looked forward to the play, which would be staged outdoors. On the evening of the play the mother got two surprises. The play was based on Antoine de Saint-Exupéry's *The Little Prince*. Her daughter played the biggest supporting role, that of the snake, who spoke in riddles.

The director was enthralled by the girl, who could undulate and actually coil like a snake. Her features and hair were also perfect and all he did was enhance the drama she carried within. The play was dazzling and the girl received more applause than the lead character and executed perfect bows again and again. The mother was moved, and when she clapped, tears of joy came to her eyes. She congratulated her daughter as though she were an adult. A year later the girl bagged the lead role of the high school annual play. When she commanded the stage alone she thought she was ready and so did the audience.

A year later a number of university applications and brochures lay on the desk in the girl's room. The mother read them with her.

"I have decided I am going to be an actress," the girl announced solemnly.

"What happened about medicine and baby doctor?" the mother demanded.

"My mind is made up. I want to be an actress."

"In that case I want you to be an educated actress. So let's choose the best undergraduate degree in fine arts majoring in drama."

The father was less enthusiastic but the mother convinced him: "It's her life and her passion."

"How is she going to earn a living?" he grumbled.

"Let's not worry about that part now," the mother muted his displeasure.

At that point in her life the girl had told no one about the force which guided her decision. She had not shared the lure of the stage and its transformative force acting on her. The mother was unaware that the stature which admiration gave the girl in fact masked a feeling of inadequacy that she often experienced. She had close friendships with girls who always seemed to have more flash and social attention. They had boyfriends, and wore lip gloss and torn jeans. They belonged to families with few social niceties. And more freedom. In her case both her parents were involved in aspects of her education and her extracurricular activities. She remained shy around boys and one of her friends even orchestrated a first date for her. The boy was ordinary and a little dull. The girl refused the second date.

She had great difficulty expressing her personal feelings, which the mother knew was a handicap and made her unduly secretive; being emotional on a stage freely was a liberating experience. She inserted herself into the characters she played with the precision of a cosmetic surgeon removing a layer of scarred skin to reveal a new one. The process was undetectable. The moment, after a brilliant performance that was rewarded by praise, was most precious.

The quiet, petite girl, short in stature with a beautiful face took to power like a duck to water. The stage makeup enhanced her appeal. When she boarded her flight to another province to head for university her mother wept. This empty nest syndrome was a new experience for the mother. The telephone calls between them went back and forth.

The mother flew up for a week's visit to see her daughter. The girl proudly showed her around the beautiful campus. The mother took her out for dinner in the city each evening. Walking through a famous park together on the weekend the mother saw an artist drawing. She was impressed by his skill and asked him if he would do a sketch of the daughter which she could take home with her when she left. The girl was sullen and did not want to sit still for a portrait. The mother cajoled her and she gave in reluctantly. He did a portrait in ink and crayons. The likeness was faultless but he had caught something else that was the hidden aspect of the girl's nature. The mother took the portrait back and had it framed and hung. Yet every time she gazed at her daughter's familiar face, a cold and forbidding expression presented itself. The artist had caught what was hidden.

She enjoyed the courses of her drama degree but what she

loved more was performance. Her talent gave her leading roles in Shakespearean plays as well as contemporary theatre. She also fell madly in love with the leading actor in her course. They acted together and became the reigning sweethearts of the campus. She thought she had found a soulmate whose talent matched her own. Six months later, the love affair ended. Although she could command the stage and dazzle her audience, she could not stop the heartbreak or prevent the coldness growing inside her. She called her mother and said she wanted to come home, and although the father wanted her to wait till summer the mother compelled him to send a ticket immediately. The girl had wept and said she wanted to come home.

The girl returned to her home but refused to share any details of the love that had soured.

"He abused me emotionally, so I ended it," she said in a clipped voice and refused to go further.

She graduated with distinction and announced she was not returning home but staying in the city where she had spent four years.

"Why don't you pick up a graduate degree then. It may come in handy later."

"Directors are lined up offering me leading roles in plays. I am sick of studying. I just want to act now."

The reviews of her performances were generally laudatory and her photographs appeared in newspapers. She flew home sporadically for vacations, and a boyfriend soon appeared on the horizon, who became a fiancé in time and finally a wedding was planned. He was also an actor, though not as recognized as her. He did small roles in television and film. She clung to the stage, but her agent made sure she also auditioned for film and television. The young couple became financially independent.

The young actress learned something. Competition made her colleagues in the industry untrustworthy. She also had a vengeful nature which she had to conceal. Any slight evoked an excess of emotion. So she guarded herself zealously and often turned down roles which she felt were inferior. When daily life became stressful, it was the stage that restored her. Waiting in the wings for her cues, although she peeked at the audience they were of no great importance to her. She was another person, lingering in the world of the character she portrayed. The curtain calls and applause were to her an out-of-body experience. Later when she sat before a mirror in the change room and cleaned the makeup, her pale face became nondescript and defenceless. She then left the theatre quietly and alone.

One day she was flying on a long flight and a deep-vein thrombosis suddenly appeared in one leg. The trip halted in a city where she was hospitalized and treated. When the mother got the news she immediately booked a flight and dashed out to pick up accessories for the trip; but when she returned home her husband led her to the phone.

"There is a message for you. It is quite disturbing."

The mother pressed the button, and the rage in her daughter's voice stunned her.

"Mother. I don't want you to come. Do you understand me? It is not about you. It's about me. Me!"

The receiver fell from the mother's hands. Her maternal response to her own child in trouble had been snubbed. And so she stayed back and did not call again. She waited anxiously. She thought the girl's husband would give her some update, but he did not. She wondered if the daughter was aware that she had behaved as though her mother were a rival. The thought was troubling but she rightfully assumed that the medical care her daughter had received was good and a subsequent inquiry revealed that she had been discharged.

In the next two years the actress auditioned twice for a role which she held in great esteem—that of a mother. Outside of the stage she tried to have a child twice and failed. A miscarriage and then a tragic stillbirth at five months. The culprit was the blood thinner she had to have for the thrombosis. Her world of wishes exploded and she mourned silently, deeply and alone. She was advised that she should not contemplate pregnancy again. On the stage she gave one riveting performance after another. She kept her distance from her mother. She did see her as a rival, who was in a role that she herself was denied.

The mother decided. It was time to meet her daughter and boarded a long flight armed with many gifts from a recent European trip. The actress had a leading role in a provocative new play. The mother informed her daughter by message that she would be present for the final performance and then spend a week in her city to spend time with her. She booked room in a hotel since there was no invitation to stay with her daughter. Neither was there an offer to collect her from the airport. She did not make a fuss and pressed ahead.

The play was disturbing. It was set in a brothel and her daughter's performance as a caged sex worker was brilliant. During the intermission her son-in-law came to greet her and say that the daughter had planned to have dinner with her the next day. At the end of the play she met the director, who invited her to the cast party that night. Other people noticed the family resemblance and greeted her as she waited for her daughter. When she arrived, the mother leapt forward and pulled her into an embrace. But the slender column of ice which the mother held in both arms neither reciprocated the gesture nor exchanged a familial glance.

"Great performance. Difficult play, though," the mother said to cover the shock of this encounter.

The daughter leaned back, eased out of the embrace, and rapidly walked away.

The mother's hotel room was a stage set itself. She was dressed elegantly, having spread out all the gifts for the daughter on the bed and made a reservation for a dinner. She dismissed the cold reception from the daughter the previous night, thinking that the performance could have drained her from her natural emotions. When the knock came on the door she opened it with excitement. The actress stood there wearing a pair of faded baggy obviously male shorts, a stained grey t-shirt and worn sneakers on her feet. Her hair was swept back and fastened with a rubber band and her face was scrubbed and devoid of makeup.

"Darling. I had mentioned I am taking you out to this fabulous place and you haven't dressed?"

"You can order something from room service," the daughter responded brusquely, moving away.

Her eye flickered briefly over the gifts. The mother felt as though she had stepped on a land mine, there would be an explosion and there would be damage. The actress let the mother express her love and desire to share the trauma she had undergone. She watched her own timing and prepared for the exact moment she would mount a hideous verbal assault. She was a seasoned actress and gauged her cue. When the moment arrived, she delivered the sole obscenity in a silken wondering tone. As if stung by a scorpion, the mother cried out in pain and disbelief.

The actress having got the desired result from her verbal obscenity, then turned for the exit but the mother was just as fast and caught her at the door. The actress gave her a push and as the mother stumbled and fell, she raced to the elevator. She was gone.

Often deep at night the actress replayed the one comment the mother had hurled at her before the elevator doors closed. "You don't deserve to be a mother." She regarded it as a challenge and so it became a game of war and rivalry. The biggest role which she now actively contemplated would give her the power to eradicate another. She would now become a mother herself and adoption was the only route. It would not be a prescribed procedure with cumbersome applications and waiting games. She chose a faster and more economical route. She publicly adopted a racially mixed baby headed for foster care. Triumphantly she brought the baby home, believing that her gesture added a heroic lustre to her status. But she was genuinely in love with her child. She could now play a role unchallenged.

The child was raised more by the father, who lacked steady employment as an actor. The actress eagerly accepted more challenging and even commercial projects. Her voice was used for an animated feature film that won an Oscar and took her to Los Angeles, where she stood beside a Hollywood star to hear her nomination announced. It was a golden period for her, and she was bringing home eighty percent of the family income.

The husband dedicated his free time playing hockey and dabbling in carpentry. His own father had not provided the opportunity for these pastimes and he was righting a wrong. But he loved his daughter immeasurably. And he always disconnected any call from her mother, allowing his emotionally lacerated wife to assume that her own mother did not care enough to call her.

She raised her daughter exactly as her mother had raised her. The vivacious little girl was lively and intelligent, and her racial difference from her parents gave her the cachet of becoming an exotic accessory. When the mother eventually heard about the adopted child, all her attempts to communicate or send gifts were repelled by the daughter and her husband. Parcels with gifts for the child were mailed back. The sorrow grew unbearable as she saw her living history being erased year by year. As she was no longer treated as a mother, she could not be a grandmother as well. Her concern for her adult daughter grew day by day. As a mother she knew, this false premise would damage her daughter and even handicap her as a mother. Old family friends and her own sibling tried to contact the daughter and remind her that this behaviour was hurtful and disrespectful but she ignored them.

Time rolled by and then a playwright whom the actress knew offered her a role in a new play she had written about women suffering from emotional traumas residing in mental health clinics. The actress was drawn to it, since the part she was offered carried the same name as that of her own mother. She took the role and injected an almost serpentine element in it. She debased the character of the woman by inserting unscripted mental ailments and won excellent reviews. She was committing matricide.

The actress now viewed her life as an open canvas on which she could hurl any colour with creative impunity. Then heartbreak set in as her marriage folded and co-parenting of the daughter began. The actress put steel in her spine and shared her child with the father. She became interested in bees and became a part-time beekeeper. Bee-keeping, with all its protective gear, became an analogy. Protection could guarantee safety, it mistakenly suggested. But sometimes a hurricane gives no warning of its arrival and that is what fate had in store for the actress. This particular hurricane only measured nine inches by five inches. It was a book, its title, *Daughter of the Lie: a Tale of Matricide.*

Narrating a story that was a poignant love letter and a psychological analysis, it told a cautionary tale. The mother had written a novel about the actress. Only the two of them would know this. The world at large would take a while to realize this. A distinguished young female film director optioned the book for film. The mother-author was encouraged to write the script, which she did. She was stepping out of the prison of silence created for her by her daughter. Motherhood did not define her entire life. She was like a treasure chest rescued from the ocean. Thousands of women whose adult daughters remain estranged from their mothers could identify their own pain lurking in the pages of the book.

The actress reading the laudatory review in the Saturday newspaper felt as though a hurricane had plucked her from her kitchen table and pulled her upwards through the ceiling of her apartment and suspended her in a cradle of clouds. It made her light-headed. She was to stay suspended, and largely it was due to disbelief. The mother sought the help of an analyst and saw him regularly. Together they pieced all the events of the daughter's life. The parental alienation of adult children was a syndrome and happened everywhere. It hinted at a personality disfunction. Many letters were sent to the daughter to even meet with older family friends and offer some explanation. The daughter rejected them all.

Then one day a telephone call came from the daughter's agent to audition for a film. The agent was convinced she would be selected. The only role being offered to her was of an older woman's provocative lament for her estranged daughter. The actress did the unthinkable and accepted the role.

The mother had no idea the play had been cast or that her daughter would be playing the role of the mother. She landed in the theatre on the opening night.

Solitaire

Toronto, Ontario, 2020–2022

She thought some thief had stolen her life. A new life was thrust upon her. It came with no warning and it was alien and heartless. Was it that she had not recognized the thief or was this some form of biblical punishment? Perhaps she had turned into a pillar of salt like Lot's wife. This was a woman whose only crime was to look back at a life she had been forced to leave. She found the Bible to be full of drama and terrifying parables. Her imagination fixated around a woman who had perished in a unique way, but her own spirit was bold and she did not see this as her own fate. A great resistance surged within her. She would continue reflecting on what seemed to be lost and would not turn into a pillar of salt.

She instantly locked a regimen in place without giving it a name. Life had been like a railway station, companions and destinations giving texture and meaning to it. She had lived alone for about sixteen years. She embraced the world holding herself wide open to experiences. She travelled and entertained avidly after her husband died. It took her a year to weather this particular storm, functioning without a partner. Then she moved with speed to fly solo. She seized new creative projects professionally and stored his photographs in a cabinet. She loved entertaining and prepared delicious food with joy, always refusing offers of contributions to her table. The flowers on her table complimented the china she used. There was a prevailing mood to her home, which was filled with books and art carefully preserved. From time to time she needed to see her friends push the front door open and bring their personalities and personal histories along with them. The ambience created by their chatter and familiar faces added a rhythm to her high-octane life where she worked and played hard. More importantly, they witnessed her life and in their reflections she was able to see who she truly was.

Foolishly, she believed this would continue unhampered. When the great disruption called the pandemic came, she lost her bearings and realized that she could only rely on herself. There were survival themes discussed in the press and media and she found them to be a nuisance as they cast a pall on her innate optimism. Her friends had turned like lemmings in midair to talk on Zoom. She found this abhorrent. Instead she spread her yoga mat on her living room carpet and did a complete workout daily. Hand held weights were sold out at all the sporting stores by the fitness-obsessed residents of her city, but she found some on a personal ad site. Her gym was closed and her morning activity ceased, and she knew that if she did not move her body she would go mad. She hated walking, but chose a walk down an incline and up again. It took twenty minutes and she considered it a daily penance. More like a necessary evil where her challenger was in fact her own self.

She made telephone calls to friends who neither picked up their phones or called her back. The silence was deafening so she played music nonstop. Partial to instrumental music she now chose lyrics.

The voices of the singers made her feel there was someone else in the house other than herself. To her shock she realized a few days had gone by without her uttering a word. Paranoia wrapped itself around her throat—she became convinced that her unused vocal cords were already shrivelling up. She went to the corner drugstore just to make conversation with a salesperson. Pointedly she greeted everyone in the elevator. She sang old songs with incomplete lines loudly at home. She was a Gemini, an arch communicator and the very thought that this pulse of life within her had been halted made her angry. The anger was a new emotion and it clung to her with a tenacity that was unsettling. It appeared in small spurts and she wondered about the causes for it. Life, she decided, had to have an order that should be pleasing and vanquish those spurts of angry thoughts. Her universe became the open spaces of her penthouse apartment and a large balcony that offered a vista of a locked-down city. There was no escape, except for trips to the grocery store or the drugstore. She lingered in them as though she were window-shopping in a favourite boutique. Rows of unfamiliar shampoos and piles of polished fruit and vegetables confronted her with a crippling banality. It had come to this. She knew she was overshopping. The whole nation was cooking and experimenting. All restaurants were closed. The packed refrigerator was a reassuring touch. She was convinced she was not hoarding as she never purchased any canned food items or pasta. However, when she regularly tossed out uneaten salad greens a new guilt assailed her. No one is ever coming for dinner, she had to remind herself. You are now cooking, not for one but half. Eating became a health drill. It was an activity which marked the passage of the day. The small bookstore nearby did not permit more than three people inside, and was so fear-laden that it became unwelcome. She did not pick up a single book. It was confinement which she intended to tackle and she would make hers an aesthetic exercise.

She placed a heavy white linen table mat on her dining table and started using her formal fine China daily. Instead of a mug she used her fine teacups one by one. It made her solo meals more delicious. It finally gave her the opportunity to enjoy in peace the dishes which were a luxurious buy and used for guests or special occasions at home. Beauty, as she well knew, always centred her. She was in fact a contemplator of beauty. She learned this when she first grew roses. She never tired of gazing at a rose or the patterns on her family silver stored in a cabinet. She prowled through her apartment, opening shelves, examining items. It was a perpetual spring-cleaning mode but nothing was discarded. This ritual was ultimately dissatisfying but the minutes on the clock ticked by.

The chess set sat closer to her now. She had been taught by her father to play leisurely games. Chess, he had told her, was a game of Life. Strategy, strengths, weaknesses, and triumph. Now she played both sides walking around the board and actually changing her seating position. Her games would last for days, as she was in no rush. A small marker would be placed near the black or white side to remind her when she resumed. She tried new moves and never consulted books. There was a change, a recklessness to her now. Decisions were made faster. She experimented with playing parallel games and boxed herself into defeat. The chess set was small, made from the scented thuya wood of Morocco. Soon she cleaned it and used wood oil to make it gleam. But a pawn dropped from her fingers and rolled under the heavy leather couch near her desk. She tried for days to retrieve it, moving the couch a few inches away in both directions, but was unable to find it. She asked the property manager for help. He was kind enough to assist, but the chess piece would not reveal its presence. She took tin foil and sculpted a replica. It stood in the row of black pieces like a ruffian.

She hated it with a passion and deliberately compromised it so it could be removed from the board speedily. But it was a game of strategy and not whims. The tinfoil pawn became a symbol of defeat. A life had been lost.

The isolation carried an oppressive weight which descended on her entire body but more so on her mind. She thought of convicts who were in isolation in prisons. The words "solitary confinement" became the theme of a mournful Bach fugue. Even the gay music she played was a mockery.

Her personal grooming habits changed. The quick showers at the gym followed by a lie down in the steam room gone. She had a daily bath. Floating in her bathtub, where a pool of water made silky by almond oil and rose-scented foaming bath gel comforted her. She dressed for the day in velvet leggings and a top. She never wore her gym shoes outside and wore ballet flats. She gave herself bimonthly manicures and pedicures and wore her favourite rings.

Her work regimen remained unchanged. She spent four hours at her desk. Then headed to the garage and pulled out her car. The drive had one purpose, and that was to change what she saw daily. It was mandatory. It was for her health. Like unused vocal cords, she felt the cornea and pupil had to be stimulated. It was a home-doctor game she played daily. In any weather the drive was on and as unfamiliar streets, homes and shores of the lake flew by, she sang her old Leonard Cohen songs in the car.

I am off my mind, a little voice whispered in her head. Mad, mad as a mad hatter, she made a rhyme and sang that with gusto. But she never laughed. She remembered laughter, though. It almost became a faded memory of an infinitely precious aspect of life. Instead, it had been taken over by the sinister spurts of anger.

She had majored in philosophy at university decades ago. It became necessary to examine her life and see what aspects of popular thought marked her. This resolve lasted a few minutes, as there was no one she could bounce her thoughts off. So she reread Neruda's poems and Durrell's *Alexandria Quartet*, which led her to Egypt and kept her there. Still the nagging thought that an unwitnessed life could alter her personality continued like the tongue fingering a new filling all the time. The meditative aspects of Vinyasa Yoga had placed her weekly in a gym class. Here she learned how to breathe and hold stretches and still her mind. She chose shavasna, the death pose and held it for four minutes.

Truthfully, it did all the yoga teacher had said it would. One came out of position floating in the air without any thought and weightless limbs. She wanted to do this right in the middle of the drugstore and the grocery store. It involved lying flat on the back with arms and legs extended as far as possible. She imagined she would cause a stir and be asked to leave.

The national news became an obscenity. It was all doom and gloom and statistics of people dying. The faces of the lively anchors were sullen, and figures were hurled around the globe. The virus demanded masks be worn. So people became invisible. She pulled out a garnet-coloured strip of chiffon purchased in Paris. It was a scarf. She draped it around the lower half of her face, tucking the ends behind her ears. She could breathe through it. It halted most people in their tracks, but soon dozens of varieties of home-made masks were sported everywhere. Mask-making and baking sourdough bread became the national pastime. She kept away from both. Carb-loading and lack of movement were a lethal combination.

The solution presented itself accidently one night. She was always interested in films and never in serials but she had signed up on Netflix. The television for her was for news and special documentaries. A film meant the big screen of a movie house and surround sound. She watched a European serial on television one night set in Holland. It ensnared her with its interlocking stories stretched over episodes. The story lines were inventive and clever. This took her into European cities which were off limits for travel now. The characters no longer occupied the dimensions of the screen; they stepped into her home and she could not let them go. The dark isolation of the nights vanished as she watched for about three to four hours, shocking herself as she glanced at the clock before collapsing to sleep at night. She raced through the activities of her day knowing that her real life would start at around nine PM when she switched the television on. She was not just a voyeur but in her mind a participant. She did not lie on the couch to do this. She sat on a chair and sometimes just stood and swung her arms and legs about. The health-conscious part of her brain warned her about the couch-potato syndrome associated with overweight people who watched television and snacked their way into an obese oblivion.

There seemed to be a buzz of activity pouring out from the screen into her living space. The image ignited invisible activity. She raced on railway platforms and sailed in boats and even trudged up the slopes of snowy mountains. All she had done was join the narrative as a secret agent. It was the best game and she had no time for self-reflection anymore. Miraculously the spurts of anger vanished. She knew that she clung to the characters as though she were related to them. She converted them into a sign of life.

The great hunger she had for physical contact with others abated curiously. It felt as though she had changed her social circle. She was in a new country where continents and cultures invited her just by viewing to partake sensorially and play a vital role, that of the listener and observer of stories that had no end. She twinned this sensation to that of the fictional sultan who heard 1001 tales from his courtesan Scheherezade. The stories could not stop or Scheherezade would lose her head. In her own case she would be condemned to a crippling isolation which would alter her personality. When the various male characters appeared during sleep through dreams she would wake up sexually aroused. Mistakenly having thought this pictorial arousal was either the male or bisexual preserve, laughter flooded her body, so she orchestrated her own physical pleasure easily and this also became part of her pre-sleep ritual a couple of times a week.

Outside her apartment seasons flew by and the lifeless face of a town gripped by fear stamped the shut doors of clubs, restaurants, and shops. She ventured into the only opened department store close by, searching for a quilted long walking coat. The aisles were stocked and sales staff virtually nonexistent. When she made her selection, the search for a sales person exhausted her and she contemplated leaving. Then she saw her. Masked and bundled in an ugly black suit. The eyes above the mask red-rimmed pools of misery. The distance between them about twelve feet.

"You want to pay for this. Only one cash register is operating. It's at the other end," and she started walking briskly in the opposite direction.

She wanted to throw the coat at her like a hunter's net and bring her crashing down to her feet. Hold her there until she could ask her questions about size, colour, and durability. These were her rights as a customer making a purchase for an item not on sale. But she was treated like a leper about to infect a multitude. The buy was a necessity for the daily cold walk regimen. Her shorter jackets needed to be layered and she was sick of that. It appeared that during the unseasonably cold winter every woman she saw queueing up to enter the drugstore wore one. The appearance ranged from bathrobe shabby to arctic explorer. She would walk in blizzards, she thought, intending to check it out. The encounter made her accept the blind buy, so she roamed the empty floor until a cash register at lingerie presented itself. The young man at the register extended a rubber-gloved hand for her debit card.

"Do you want to apply for the store's credit card. You will get a temporary one and ten percent off. I will do it online, it will just take a minute."

"Would you tell me if the coat comes in any other colour?" she deliberately ignored the hustle. "Do you have two pieces if identification with your photograph?" his head bent over the computer screen, oblivious to her request.

"This," she plonked the puffy coat over the tip of his console where it slid downwards covering his screen, "is the coat and is there any other colour in the store?" She pasted a fake smile on her face.

He drew back as though the coat was an invading army spilling over his work counter. It seemed to have also given him some indecipherable offence. His mission to engage her for the store's profit had failed and now she had the gall to make him work.

"We hardly have any staff. You need to go back to the rack and check. If you did not see it when you selected this, then there isn't any," he flicked the coat away as though he was shooing an animal.

"Ring it up please." She knew he was probably right. She held out her debit card and he narrowed his eyes.

"It would have been cheaper on the credit card today."

"I need to go, please. Trust there is a coat hanger and a garment bag for this." She said punching her numbers on the card.

"I don't know about a garment bag. We have the large bags," he held out her receipt leaning backwards.

"It's a four-hundred-dollar coat. I think it deserves a garment bag."

Out came the small spurt of anger. The lack of civility, the rubber-gloved hands, and the inability to produce the cheap plastic garment bags which the coat department must have had a thousand. The obnoxious salesman with his eyes narrowing above the mask. The vast empty second floor and the parking metre ticket on her car expiring.

"I will wear it, just cut off the tags please." She almost cried out.

"Well you have to have the tags if you bring it back." He frowned and reluctantly pulled out a pair of scissors.

"I never bring anything back," she said definitively. "Could you hurry this up, I may get a parking ticket."

He snipped the tags and held them out with the receipt as though he was holding a dead rat. She simply lifted the coat off the counter and eased into it. It was light as a feather and reached her ankles. She raced to the elevator and took the escalator down to the main floor on the street level. The mirrors on the walls caught her reflection and she looked like nobody she knew. The colour was a sophisticated bluish grey. It had a French feel to it. Her first shopping expedition in a year and she allowed herself to feel happy.

A policeman stood by her car and was pulling out his ticket book.

"Officer, officer. Please don't. How do you like my coat," she landed breathlessly at her car door. "Well I was about to write a ticket." He looked at her sternly. "Coat's not bad."

"I have not shopped for a year. I am actually happy, please don't spoil it," she pleaded.

"Yes, but apart from the expired ticket, it is a no-parking zone with a highway sign," he scolded her.

"I cannot understand this sign. Oh please just don't do it, I am leaving right now." She felt like a balloon which had been punctured.

He paused, the tip of his pen just hovering over the yellow ticket but not descending. “I could have had your car towed,” he said caustically.

“Well then I would have just walked home in my new coat,” she could not stifle her laughter. He could not either. He chuckled, nodding his head.

“Don’t let me see your car here again,” he raised an eyebrow. “Think the coat is expensive, and with a ticket on top you may not be able to stay happy.”

“Officer you are the best,” she opened the car door and flung herself inside.

She received an email from a friend. “Connie is in intensive care. It’s serious and I have been looking at coffins.”

“Pick up the phone,” she replied in uppercase. When she dialed his business line he picked it up.

When Connie’s husband gave the shocking details, with all the details of the viral assault, she cried for him silently. The virus had ravaged her body and her entire respiratory system had folded. She was on a respirator in an ICU. It was her third week there and Andy was not allowed inside, he could only watch her through a glass wall. She berated him for not sharing this with her before, as she would have driven over to him and lent him courage. Connie, a fragile diminutive academic and Andy’s devoted wife of forty years had other plans. Within weeks she displayed a resilience coated in steel to recover and even walk, hooked up to a rolling oxygen cylinder. Andy monitored her progress daily with the two doctors who attended to her.

They hinted that she would in time be discharged barring any further complications. At present she was just being taught how to breathe. She called Andy every morning, whom she knew to be a pampered Eastern European bonds trader. He made a fortune and spent it as well. A concert years ago had made their paths cross and a solid three-decade friendship had emerged. He was also a man who could not boil an egg. She noted his grateful response to her attention.

"Where are your friends? Are they preparing meals for you?" she inquired belligerently. "There are no friends my dear," his voice was sombre.

"Well stop coffin-shopping, she will get better. What are you having for lunch?"

"I think I will have a glass of good Chablis with some yogurt!"

She called after a day and said, "Let's do an outdoor lunch tomorrow. We have both had our double vaccinations. A snow picnic. I will prepare it. Just show up at noon."

He pulled up in his Jaguar wearing a tweed coat and a plush felt hunting cap with velvet flaps. His mask was draped across his chin. Laughter bubbled up from her chest as she climbed into the back seat. Her solitary existence ended temporarily. She was giddy with excitement. She was wearing a deep garnet lipstick and used fragrance. The chiffon scarf not masking her face but draped around her neck. When he got out and settled her in the back seat his eyes sparkled playfully. He blew her a kiss from a distance and made her feel intensely female.

"No kisses alas . . . this wretched plague. Shall we head to the Castle my lady." He broadened his vowels comically.

He had placed delicate hand towels on the teak-lined arm rests at the back. The dashboard of the car was panelled in gleaming tortoiseshell lacquer. He drove to the Casa Loma grounds, which were closed but the old riding stables had a patch of grass and a picnic table. It was the spot for lunch. She wore her new coat and carried her package of sandwiches, salad, and bottle of wine. He pulled out a picnic basket, a bottle of sparkling wine, biscuits, cheese, and chocolates. It was an ornate picnic. Here in the wintry afternoon, the sun hidden as always, eating became the activity. She thought he looked leaner, a new fragility marking his face. He nibbled on the sandwiches and lifted one and said, "You. You have made these? Delicious."

He poured the champagne into two enamelled mugs which he pulled out of the picnic basket. They emptied the mugs in record speed. The bottle was placed under the picnic bench. They also kept an eye out for a patrolling police car. No one came, as the only thing guaranteed on this February afternoon was the bitter chill, silence, and the complete absence of people and cars.

"I have had the test and I am fine. But poor Connie is not like her former self," he said, looking into the distance.

Between them the space was deliberately planned. They sat at opposite ends of the bench and were conscious of what the year-long lockdown had done to them. She was starved for physical contact but knew that his vivacious personality was subdued as though an actual death had brushed his life.

"You are so normal. I am pleased that your spirit is intact." He smiled thinly.

"It's not, really. You have brought a bit of life back, Andy. Some of us feel as though we are disappearing. Hanging on to sanity is a struggle," she blurted out.

"No. Stay the course. Eventually everyone will be cured. Time for chocolate, I think," he chuckled like his old self, displaying his three-decade-old knowledge of her.

He was the only person in the entire city who had consented to meet outdoors. When they parted, she debated whether she should tell him about the TV serials. But he had in a great moment of intuition shared his own coping mechanisms.

"I will send you a list of documentaries. They function as a first-rate history lesson I watch them every day and am pillaging the local library."

"Keep the music on," she replied watching him drive away. They exchanged their lists the next day.

It happened late one night when after the delights of a thoroughly absorbing Chinese serial she wondered if she was honest enough to accept that a particular element was making a permanent home in her consciousness. To continue to fight this daily and actively is what demoralized her. There were many spiritualities that embraced the concept of acceptance, but she had shied away from them. So she thought in an act of daring courage she would try for a few days to embrace it.

Alone and bereft of regular social contact was no longer to be viewed as a deplorable condition. After all, she was living a life and the days on the calendar rolled by one by one. Solitaire was to be added to her life. The word loneliness had to be removed from her vocabulary. There had to be legions of people like her. If she would ever be asked to identify herself she would add this word like a university degree. With acceptance, a peculiar consolation flooded her. This was not a mental disorder, it was simply what was happening for over a year. So she made friends with herself all over again. To do this she had to split herself into two. Half pronounced and the other half recorded. When she woke up in the morning she greeted the world by sipping green tea in her balcony and whispering, "Hello loneliness. Are you OK? Stay by my side, everything will work out."

Seemingly it did, yet Fate had another plan. It was a reminder that even the best laid plans can be toppled like a row of dominoes, separating the losers from the winners. A particular physical discomfort swooped upon her. Her physician required tests that she took in a disinterested fashion. The real hazard was the virus that claimed lives and she was free of that. Every other ailment would be minor. But a new companion had entered her life and it was physical pain. It came without warning, knocking the breath out of her and for moments she lost her bearings. Disbelief, as the removal from a hitherto normal life free from pain had now been altered.

She was seated in the small office. Her youthful family physician had lowered her voice and she began with an apology.

"We can manage these unsettling symptoms with medication up to a point, but I am afraid the condition is a permanent one and it will deteriorate. I am so sorry."

She walked out of the office with prescriptions stuffed in her hand bag. Picking up a coffee she drove to her favourite spot by the lake. It was a secluded gravel path that ended at the water's edge; a small strip of pebbles lent it the appearance of a beach. She often came here to read and was left undisturbed. It was an accidental place that she had always thought had been forgotten by a city clamouring for the more popular island and boardwalks. All of a sudden the prevailing thought in her mind was like a cacophony of sound. She no longer felt alone as the sound of this thought roared like a mighty body of water obliterating everything else. This sound became a conversation. It was one she had with herself. She could have been a criminal under interrogation, being asked the same question again and again and only one reply came to her mind.

The night was dark largely through the absence of stars. The only light in her home was the table lamp on her desk. Lying on top of her computer was an unsealed envelope. A single sheet of French note paper lay inside. The ink used to write was a dark prune colour and was also French. This was the signature of her personal aesthetician. The four written lines inside had a misleading frivolity. "It is better to leave a party at the top, always, and not when it is ending."

She drove carefully through the silent city streets with the impatience to be done with it all. Solitaire was an existence she had just learned to accept, but the future spelled to her in the confines of her doctor's office and confirmed by her copious reading brought only one decision to her mind.

She wore cotton trousers and her handbag was at home. She reached her spot and parked at the beginning of the small incline which led down to the water. Turning off the car lights. Waiting for a few minutes to make certain there was no movement around her. Confident that she was alone. She started the car pressed down on the accelerator hard and shot down the incline with an engine roaring and skimmed the edges, like a hydroplane, landing into the lake further where the depth was substantial. The small car descended rapidly. Within seconds her lungs were flooded with water and her breath ended. She had left the party.

Up on a crest behind this edge of the lake a couple stood on a third floor terrace. They were escaping their own party spread over the lower two floors of their home. The few stragglers who were not ready to leave had made them look for some respite.

"Did you see it?" he turned to his wife.

She was lighting a cigarette, head bent over the lighter in her hand. "What?" she looked at him exhaling smoke.

"Something just shot out over the water and disappeared."

"There is nothing. How much Scotch have you had?"

The Inheritance

Pakistan, 1949–2019

A fading copy of a land deed lay in a paper file which Said had not opened for years. It had come from a country which he had left decades ago. He had arrived as an eighteen-year-old to study at Berkeley and when he qualified as an architect, he decided he wanted to go on living in California. His parents did not object even when he told them he was trading in the citizenship of one country for another. His life in his adopted land was like a perfect chemistry experiment, elements combining harmoniously to produce a desired synthesis. He changed his horizon permanently and became a brand-new person. He was a successful architect in a small firm. Now a telephone call was threatening to change his life. A piece of paper which he had stored years ago as a curiosity had transformed into a declaration of war. A large parcel of land had been gifted to eight siblings from their mother's estate. The two male siblings rejected the gift outright, but five of the six sisters claimed their share and sold the land. The remaining female sibling, his mother, had held on. What the phone call told him was that a series of maneuvers orchestrated by people he had never met would make his inheritance disappear. He knew immediately that he was not going to let this happen. In his beloved mother's memory he would put up a fight. It meant he would have to return to a land he had truly left behind. Sixteen years had passed since his mother's death. He had then entered the country, placed flowers on her grave, and left in twenty-four hours.

Now, a week later he was seated in a plane crossing the Atlantic. He had told his employees that he would be missing for a couple of weeks but available on the telephone. He had booked accommodation in a rest house used by tourists in the capital city. He had only one remaining sibling, who was much older than him, and their contact had frayed over the years. So although he shared the inheritance with her, she had not bothered to claim it. Even as a child they had not been close. With her indolent life in a large mansion, with domestic staff and doting children, she had never extended any hospitality over the years. He was aware that she had scorned his decision to immigrate and troubled their parents for decades by calling him an irresponsible son. He did not inform her that he was arriving. He had made a plan and would execute it and contact her only when necessary.

He arrived late at night and wheeled his luggage out of an airport which had been given a farcical facelift. The luggage retrieval carousal moved in fits and starts, taking almost an hour. The baggage carts squeaked, the signs were confusing, and the airport officials were slow and mostly stupid. He disliked the environment and his knowledge of the local language was rusty. He could feel jet lag threatening to drop his eyelids. Outside, a row of slack-jawed and some outright thievish cabdrivers jostled each other to reach him. With his fair complexion, and light eyes, and American clothing it was assumed he was a foreign tourist. He chose the first person who reached him out of impatience. The airport taxi circled around a residential district trying to locate the double-storied villa masquerading as a guest house; finally he found his phone and called them and they gave instructions to the taxi driver. He knew he was being hustled but had no choice but to sit it out. Eventually the white house nestling amongst trees and flowering bushes appeared. The gate was opened and he jumped out when the car stopped. The night air was redolent with the fragrance of jasmine and a breeze lifted the leaves of trees overhead. The fragrance and the sound of rustling leaves bludgeoned him with an uncharacteristic nostalgia and for a moment he felt he saw his mother, but it was the front desk manager who appeared, he spoke softly and looked pained as the guest paid the taxi driver in US currency.

"Welcome sir, you must be tired," the manager said and placed the guest's bag on a trolley and led the way towards the entrance.

He had automatically spoken in English assuming that the guest was a foreigner. The name itself, Said, could have hailed from anywhere. The luggage, clothing, and passport he handed over for check-in seemed to perplex the man.

"You were born here and are just returning home, sir. I have the best suite for you upstairs. It is very peaceful," he smiled.

"Home is California and I have some local business here," Said ended further engagement.

"If you dial 1 on the phone in your room I can have anything sent up to you. You must be tired."

After sleeping for nine hours, Said woke up at noon. The room was spacious and the bed enormous. The bathroom a glitter of marble and shiny faucets. He showered and dressed and headed down to have the breakfast which was included in the room rate. He took the short flight of the curving staircase and landed in the vestibule. Beyond this was a large sitting room and a dining area. The manager rose behind his desk.

"Breakfast can be ordered. I am here and please tell me if you need any service." He offered a shy smile.

He was a slender man formally dressed in dark trousers, white shirt, and a blue tie. He wore a blazer with shiny buttons. His well-groomed hair settled into neat waves. His eyes were dark and expressive and he had the appearance of a poet.

"I am sorry, I was very tired last night and just wanted to sleep. The room is wonderful. Thank you." Said had a momentary pang of regret for his brusque attitude at check-in. He liked the manager.

Breakfast was sumptuous but the instant coffee vile. The rest house WiFi was slow but functioning. His mobile phone got charged. He converted money at the front desk. He knew he needed a lawyer to get the ball rolling and secured an appointment with a female lawyer whose specialty was land inheritance.

She was an associate with a well-known law firm. The website was elaborate. He made the mistake of thinking law firms all over the world would operate on the same principles. She sounded very pleasant and confident on the phone when she gave him the address and the name of a reputable taxi company he could use.

He confided in the manager, who muttered, "You have to be careful of the big lawyers here, they charge a lot."

"It's all right. I shall discuss this up front," he reassured the man.

"Would you like to order your dinner now? The cook can prepare continental food."

"No. I Think I will go out instead. Of course I shall take any recommendation you make."

A shadow moved across the man's face.

"Sir, if I may. You don't want to get sick, so please eat in the rest house for two days and then try the food outside. Here it is clean, home cooking. Outside there could be germs. Many foreigners get sick. Stomach trouble."

Said was touched by the man's solicitous attitude.

"Even barbeques? Isn't that safe?"

The manager relented. It was as though permission was being granted to a naughty child reluctantly.

"Only the barbeque and no salad."

Said laughed. It was the first time in forty-eight hours that he felt cossetted and he realized it was the manager who had achieved this.

He was not familiar with the city, which seemed to comprise of residential areas with lush greenery. The cab drove by a large outdoor shopping enclave. He noted how zoning requirements had been violated by add-on structures. The address of the law firm was with the driver, who appeared to be using a GPS. The route led to a large double-story home and not an office building. When the cab halted he asked,

"Are you sure this is it? It's a lawyer's office. A big law firm."

"Sir. Here big homes are used as offices. This is the capital and not much land for commercial areas. Mostly for homes of government officers." He laughed, revealing a set of yellow teeth.

Said removed a large bill in local currency and handed it to the driver.

"I cannot wait for you, sir. City Taxi is very busy all the time. So when you finish, call and a taxi will reach you in five minutes." He was collecting change from his various pockets.

"It's all right, keep the change. That's the tip," said Said.

"You foreigners are the best, sir. Nobody here tips a taxi. When you call, ask for me and I can take you anywhere else, even sightseeing." His manner cloying and ingratiating.

Said walked through a set of ornately carved walnut wood doors and walked up to a man seated behind a reception counter.

"I have an appointment with Ms Sanniya Gul."

Seated at a large gleaming table in a room which resembled a sumptuous dining room, he noted the velvet drapes and a Persian rug on the floor and wondered why he had not been taken to the lawyer's office. Soon, however, a young woman walked in and sat next to him.

"This is our board room and we see all new clients here," she said after greeting him. She flashed a wide smile at him as she placed a legal pad and a pen in front of her on the table.

He was instantly drawn to her hands. There were two diamond rings on the fingers of one hand and two more on the other. The small hoops in her ears were also encrusted with diamonds. She was expertly made up and wore an outfit made of a gauzy printed fabric. His heart sank as he thought lawyers did not dress like this anywhere. He wanted to get up and walk away, but she was fast.

"Have you brought the 'fard' with you? Let me see it, please."

He picked up his bag and placed it in front of him. Unzipping it, he searched for the envelope which contained the land deed.

She opened the envelope and removed the flimsy paper.

"It's a copy of the original." She sighed. "Don't worry, I shall send my clerk down and he will find the original in the land registry office. It will take a day. Let me have all your personal information now."

He put his passport and his driver's license on the table. She opened the passport and said, "But you were born here. Where is your identity card?"

"I have no local identity card. I am an American citizen and we don't carry identity cards. I have my professional cards, though. Here is one."

"It's all right. It's all right. I can handle this."

"What is the retainer that you require?"

She rattled off a sum which was absurdly low. It amounted to about six hundred dollars. He was worried. "Thank you. I can give you that right now if US dollars are acceptable."

"They are. The office will prepare a receipt for you before you leave."

"Will I get to meet your senior partner?"

"He is not in town."

"I am not being rude, but there is so much written about him in the website."

She tossed her head back and laughed.

"I am an associate in this firm and have already pleaded cases in the Supreme Court."

It was faster than he imagined. There was a process, he was informed. Fake diamond rings notwithstanding, she could handle it all. Her office was upstairs she informed him and too cluttered to see anyone.

"This is a much nicer room, don't you think?" She got up and stuck the hundred dollar notes in her pad.

"Don't forget to collect your receipt at the front desk. Don't worry, it will be settled." She flashed another smile and walked away, leaving a trail of some fragrance behind her.

He collected his receipt and asked for a taxi to be called, but did not give the name of the taxi driver. There was an Alice in Wonderland feel to this experience. He had handed over his sole copy of the deed to a most unlawyerly lawyer. He felt he should have at least explored the office. There was no sign of activity downstairs. But he trudged out and waited for the taxi at the door. Then it was jet lag all over again. This time his quest was a decent cup of coffee and some exercise. The cabdriver took him to a tiny strip mall with two patio restaurants and a tiny bookstore. There was also a butcher shop, a general store or mini market, and a fruit seller.

"It is Kohsar Market and very famous," the cabdriver told him.

"For what?" he asked.

"A federal minister was shot right here in front of everyone."

Said eyed the tiny restaurant, which spilled over into the courtyard. Next to it was the bookstore. He sat at a table, ordered coffee, and told the waiter he would pick up some newspapers from the bookshop and return to his table. He collected three local newspapers and a copy of the *Economist.*

The coffee arrived.

"American," the waiter said proudly, setting the cup down.

"No. I said Americano. That is a drip filter coffee," Said told him.

"Yes, sir. It is American. You trust. You trust. I am very responsible."

Said wanted to placate him now. So the words that came out of his mouth were in the local language. They were like water rumbling out through a rusty pipe at first and then flowing freely. The waiter froze in his tracks. Said kept his face still and then could not control the laughter bubbling out of him. He laughed as he added milk and sugar in the coffee. The waiter chuckled and then whispered.

"You fooled me. I thought you were an American tourist. You are coming home after many years?"

Said was in no mood to tell him he had traded this country and culture for another. There seemed to be a new light in the waiter's dark eyes. He thought it was relief. He took a sip of the coffee and realized it was good. The waiter had waited for his response.

"This is your land. You are welcome here no matter how many years you live in another place. It is part of your spirit."

Said opened one of the newspapers to indicate that the conversation was over. The waiter was clever though, he held his tray close to his stomach and cast one last lingering look and walked away. The newspaper was like a tabloid, full of scandal. It was the national daily and the newsprint ink smeared his fingers. He turned to the classified section and saw jobs and real estate listings. There was no business section, just blocks of news about government and development projects. He could not get a sense of either the country or the city he was in.

He pulled out his phone and dialed his sister's number. He wondered if it had remained the same. The phone rang for a while and just when he was about to hang up it was picked up.

"Hello," spoke the sister he had not spoken to since his mother's death almost two decades ago. "This is Said." They exchanged greetings, then he told her, "I have come to settle our inheritance. I have engaged a lawyer."

"Oh my God! You come back without telling me. Which lawyer? What is it going to cost?"

"I will take care of it. And I will keep you informed."

"Well, will you come here to see me?"

"No." The old hostility flooded in him. "I shall be busy here. I will call when there are developments."

"You should go and see Aunt Khush, who is dying. She still lives in her house." She rattled off the address.

He wrote the address down quickly on the newspaper in front of him. Out of the five aunts, four had died and she was the remaining one. He remembered her house with the large mulberry tree in the back garden. He had found her censorious as a child and recalled a particular dish she made. White radishes cooked in ground dried mango powder. The memory spread like a fine cobweb. The family history had perished for him at the death of his parents, so the recollection shocked him a little. What would he say to an elderly woman, his mother's sister? Yet the thought nagged him as he drank another cup, rifled through the newspapers, and spied on the people who sat like props on a stage around him. Trays of food sailed out from the interior of the restaurant and the largely male patrons ate and spoke loudly. Many stares came his way. A group of young women occupied a table close to his. They ordered coffee and smoked. They laughed and one of them smiled at him. She was so beautiful that he thought his breath had caught a little. He simply nodded at her and buried his face in the magazine. After a while when he looked up she had turned away and all he saw was a sheet of gleaming dark hair cascading down her back. He thought of his girlfriend Sharon, who was a curly-haired platinum blonde. Sharon was slender and tall, and this dark-haired beauty was petite and swaddled in a printed outfit, which his design-conscious mind said was all wrong.

He counted the money for his bill and summoned his waiter and held out the page on which the aunt's address was written.

"How far is this?"

"Oh, very close, about ten minutes. You need a taxi?"

"Can I not walk?" He needed the exercise.

The waiter drew back in horror.

"No, no. You would get lost and houses are numbered in a strange way here."

Said sat in the front with the cabdriver, who had also consented to take him back to the guest house later. Said felt he had gone a little mad for embarking on a visit to a relative who was in her late eighties and would not even remember him. Yet as with the inherited land, he felt his mother had nudged him from her grave to visit a dying sister. He wondered if both were a mistake, but the taxi had already reached a green metal gate.

"I will park here by the side and wait till you come out," the cabdriver said and went to open the gate, which he did just enough for a person to walk through.

Said slid through the space and confronted the ugly concrete home with a portico, where a car was parked. He walked further along and confronted the gnarled old mulberry tree which had crept along the roof of the garage as well. Suddenly an image came to mind. He saw pockets of his long shorts crammed with maroon mulberries. He remembered vividly the stain of the mulberries. He was five years old. It had to be a visit to this house. Now he was forty-five and the tree still lived. He walked up to the screened front door and rang the bell.

After a while a woman appeared. A scarf covered her head and her clothing was shabby. He just repeated the name of the aunt and she opened the door wider and let him in. The interior also looked shabby and they passed through several doors.

"She just stays in bed and whispers. My family lives here too, and we take care of her," she told him. "She had a son."

"Where is he?"

"He works in Saudi Arabia and sends money and telephones us every week."

They had reached an open doorway. A midsized bed, a large wood armoire, and an armchair were the furnishings inside. His aunt lay on the bed under sheets, and her head was propped up on pillows. He had nothing to remember her by. She whispered something and her eyes flashed behind black-rimmed glasses. The woman bent over her and said loudly, "Your nephew has come from America to visit you."

Said moved closer to the bed and said, "Salam aliekum, I am Said your sister Mubarik's son. Can you talk?"

She lifted a hand and motioned him to sit. Then she whispered something to the woman, who left the room. Said noted the pristine white bed linen, the night table on which lay a watch and a glass of water. Her aquiline features bore a marked resemblance to his mother's. Her blue-veined hands were delicate, ending in long tapered fingers.

"Please talk, so I can understand. You need to sit up. Let me help you."

She raised both hands in a gesture of refusal. The woman returned to the room with a tray that she placed on the night table close to him. It had a cup of tea and a plate filled with large maroon mulberries. He became five years old again. He was now certain she knew who he was. When he popped a mulberry in his mouth, the tiniest smile hovered around her lips.

"Rascal," she said softly and turned her face away from him so as not to look back at him again.

The lawyer called him the next day. Her clerk had secured a copy of the title deed.

"All the sisters had equal shares, but your mother's has shrunk to a third of theirs. Did she sell a portion of it?"

He checked with his sister, who was quite shocked and said that was not the case. Their mother had been incapacitated in her last five years and would not have transacted a sale without his sister knowing about it. He informed the lawyer, who sighed.

"Illegal sales. Land grab. But all sales are registered at the local registry office. I will have to examine those books. I will need more payment from you."

"A bigger retainer for expenses?" he asked.

"No. For bribes."

He was incensed. He would clear all her fees but not bribes. His loathing for the country he had left rose afresh. He had to strategize. He took a cab and went to an upscale hotel. He thought lunch and a drink in a different environment would help. The rest house manager threw him a worried look when he walked out to the waiting cab.

The restaurant was ornate and overstaffed. He ordered fish and a salad and asked if he could get a drink before lunch was served.

"Yes, sir. What would you like?"

"Scotch on the rocks. If you have a decent single malt I would prefer that."

The waiter stiffened and drew back a little.

"Alcohol is not served in public here. We can send a bottle to your room, if you are a foreigner and have your passport with you."

"I am not a guest at your hotel. I don't run around with my passport in my pocket. Cancel the lunch please. I am not staying."

He got up and threaded his way between tables, not turning to look at the waiter, who kept up a running dialogue behind him. He reached the reception desk and asked for a taxi.

"Taxis are not allowed inside the property due to security. If you just take a seat in the lounge we will inform you when it arrives."

"What about outside, can I not flag a cab?" Said asked.

"This hotel is a little outside the busy area. Perhaps a drink while you wait?"

"Which department of the local administration deals with land reclamation here?" he took a gamble.

"That would be the DC sir. The District Commissioner's office."

"Could you find me a telephone number for his office?"

"Yes. If you wait a minute." His turned his head towards his computer console. "Here it is, sir," he handed Said a paper with the name and number. "He has just been appointed and is a very nice officer."

Said did not wait. He dialed the number immediately and in a stroke of luck was connected to the commissioner. He introduced himself and told him what had transpired.

"Fire the lawyer and come and see me immediately. This is the address. Do you have a car?"

"Give me half an hour and I shall be there."

What transpired over the next two days reaffirmed Said's choice made twenty years ago not to return to the place of his birth. The young man who sat in a large government office had a plaster-wrapped ankle propped up on a foot stool. He was the Assistant District Commissioner and had the authority not only to see the handwritten ledgers of transactions but summon the local functionary called Tehsildar who controlled them.

"I am the boss of all these Tehsildars. People wait years to see them and they are corrupt beyond belief. Just watch the fun."

When the burly man entered the office with a leather-bound ledger book, he threw a contemptuous look at Said.

"They come from London and New York and have no idea about the procedures for land sales. What is the fuss? Portions of this land have been sold years ago."

The ledger book revealed sales for chunks of lands all in his mother's name.

"They are fake. I suspect that. Land litigation takes an average of ten years. The buyers are summoned to court, but their lawyers will delay and one can do nothing. Plus, you don't live here, so your legal costs will accumulate, because these sales will have to be challenged in court," said the Commissioner over the pages.

"This is outrageous," Said said and walked out.

He returned to the rest house feeling that the practices of open corruption within the private and government sectors were an obscenity. He felt overwhelmed. He should just return home and let his sister deal with the matter. A surprise waited for him in his room. On a console table stood a bottle of sealed Black Label whiskey. Next to it was an ice bucket, tongs, and a heavy cut-crystal tumbler. He walked to the phone and called the manager.

"Thank you for arranging this. What does it cost?"

"The rest house has a source and it's not cheap, sir, but at least you can enjoy a drink."

"Your timing is perfect. Don't worry about the price."

He would never know if it was the alcohol that released a different mood in him. He was a moderate drinker. But the double Scotch seemed to take the sting out of the events of the day. Then his sister called. She suggested they take the reduced portion and sell it and gave the name of a man who had hounded her for the land. Said called the man, and suggested that he wanted to see the property before making any decision. The man was delighted and told him he would pick him up in the morning.

The man who appeared the next day had the looks of a thug. He wore native clothes and a flashy gold watch and ring. His shock of black hair gleamed and a handlebar mustache sat over a set of large teeth. Said greeted him politely and sat in the passenger seat of his midsized sedan. The man rearranged his tunic and then flashed an apologetic smile.

"I am always armed so I have to turn my revolver a little when I am seated."

Despite his unease Said did not comment.

"I have a lot of enemies. With land this is always the case. I bought most of the land from your aunts years ago, but your portion is stopping me from building further."

The drive went just outside the city border. From the main highway a paved country road forked off into a pastoral scene which reminded Said of Italy. Gentle rolling hills and lush green shrubbery. Said was transfixed; the architect in him saw the designs of a home filled with picture windows and solar panels to harness the sun which shone in this region daily. His mother's face swam before his eyes. His complete alienation from this country wobbled as though on shaky ground. The man driving the car gestured towards the hillocks.

"It starts from here. I have grown some fruit on my land but you can grow anything here. Your family should have built a home here years ago but the land has been left vacant."

"Do you know good contractors here?" asked Said.

"Yes I know the best one. He is completing a big house I am building."

"Is your architect local as well?"

"Architect!" the man snorted and then laughed. "They have a title but are useless. You don't need them. I decide myself about how many rooms I want and then just tell the contractors."

Part of the land-viewing jaunt included lunch in his prospective buyer's new home, which he said bordered Said and his sister's land. Despite Said's reluctance, the man insisted and turned his car into a tree-lined path that ended in front of a grey concrete monstrosity. A huge double-story home with a row of badly positioned windows, giving it an institutional look, was where the lunch would be served.

Entering the house, Said had a moment of revulsion in the cavernous room which had a couch, two ugly wooden armchairs with garish cushions, and a long table. The table was laden with barbequed meats and stacks of leavened circular discs of bread. A domestic server pointed to a faucet and sink mounted in the wall for washing hands. However erroneous his thoughts, instinctively he felt the land on which this house was built had been stolen from his mother's portion. He could not stomach the food as a silent fury raged inside him. He knew at that point that he would never sell the land to this man. He would buy out his sister as well.

The following week was spent with the excellent Assistant Commissioner to get the certificates of inheritance for the land. He offered his sister to buy her portion.

"Don't cheat me, send me the certificate of appraisal as well. When are you coming to see me?"

"Soon," he lied expertly.

"What are you going to do with the land? It's in the middle of nowhere!"

"When you build a home, that nowhere becomes somewhere."

He knew he would not build his vacation home in Italy after all.

The Photograph (1889)

It had been discovered under a dying man's pillow. After his death, when the bedding was removed; the small black-and-white photo lay on the mattress; it would challenge the history of an entire family. In pencil, "my mother" had been written on the back of the photograph.

The dead man's eldest son pocketed the photograph and did not share it with his siblings. It took another twenty years before he revealed it, but only to his son. The son worked in advertising and was a gifted photographer given to retouching. In his hands the face of the woman in the photo remained untouched, but her clothing, hands, ornamentation, and poise gave her a different persona, and he made copies for the various relatives.

Now, more than a century later, a woman would daily pass by that photo which hung on a wall in her home. The silver frame, thirteen by sixteen inches, was an impressive example of Italian Renaissance design. Its beauty complemented that of the photo's subject. The combination made viewers halt and linger gazing at it.

The family itself was scattered all over the world. The original photograph had been taken from one country to another along with a cache of secret documents. The sons and daughters of the photographer put their copies in albums and forgot about it. It never generated a dialogue among their children. In the following generation now, the woman, a sentimental aesthete, retrieved the photograph and spent months searching for the right frame to display it as a piece of art. She embarked on research, but unsuccessfully. The subject was her maternal great grandmother. All her other descendants had died, but an octogenarian relative finally released some information. The woman clung to the information like treasure and placed it in the vault of her memory bank.

She felt a sense of reassurance from her history. This framed photograph of a young woman who could not be more than nineteen exerted a hypnotic effect on her, and of late she was feeling that this was not a one-way street. It felt like a case of the watcher being watched. The bold expression on the face of the young woman of the picture was striking. The apple-cheeked beauty with jet eyebrows, which slashed her forehead, creating a border for eyes that blazed with an unspoken fury, made her stare back resolute with emotion. She wanted to get inside this face and touch its real history. She realized that to accomplish that she had to step inside the frame.

One day when her great grandfather, who was a lawyer and enjoyed a good fortune from his land holdings, visited a home ten miles away from the city he was led to a formal sitting room. As a choice of refreshments was brought before him, he was intrigued by the sound of a female voice in the adjoining room. This voice and the language wafted into the room and wrapped around his senses as though he was submerged in a pool of refreshingly cool water. Only a gauze curtain separated the two rooms and he was mesmerized both by the unseen proximity of the speaker and her voice. He was already married and the father of five children, yet he left that home obsessed by the experience. Within days he indicated to his family that he wished to marry the owner of that voice. He was a man of substance and so his offer was accepted and he married the woman secretly, making her his second wife. When the family of the first wife came unexpectedly to visit, this second wife was hidden in a teak armoire.

It was late one night when a sound awoke her. The near silent hum of central air conditioning always prevented sound from entering her darkened bedroom. She awoke with a start and knew immediately that she had not been dreaming. It was a song. She walked into the large open living space, wondering if her music system had just begun on its own. Yet no sound emerged from that area. In this late summer night moonlight flooded through the glass enclosing wall of the balcony. She walked slowly, coming closer to the wall where the portrait hung. She bent to switch on the lamp on the ornamental table. Having done so, she looked up out of habit. The frame was empty.

Every year for three months her favourite uncle came for a visit. He had fought for her education and taught her everything about Persian poetry. She was bright and grasped sufficient vocabulary of the refined yet foreign language. She was then encouraged to recite for her father, who would smile with pride. When she reached fifteen, proposals for marriage started coming for her, but her two elder sisters had to be married first. She didn't care, as she climbed the trees in the big garden and draped herself in her mother's shawls and created little pageants with her speech and poetry. In the summer, her fair complexion reddened with the sun and her dark long hair framed her face; vivacity sparkled from her eyes. She had thick jet-black straight eyebrows, which forced attention to her face. Two years later when she was informed that a proposal had been accepted and the prospective husband was an educated lawyer, she was disappointed. She was eighteen and she wanted her life to continue as it was. There appeared to be something disturbing about living with a stranger in a different home. But she had to keep these thoughts to herself.

The man, who had an attractive Kashmiri face and light hazel eyes, had sent ropes of pearls fashioned as necklaces and delicate long earrings of pearls studded with tiny rubies, along with a set of ivory-brocaded clothes for the wedding. Her mother was appalled at the restraint in colour and made her wear a deep crimson outfit instead. When she signed her marriage contract her fingers trembled and he leaned forward and steadied her grip on the pen. She had not looked up at him from under her ornate head covering but was grateful for this gesture. He had saved her from embarrassing herself and her family. A fragrance floated from him which intrigued her. She was only familiar with essence of rose, which she was wearing, and his was sandalwood. The strange-looking conveyance which was a motor car was festooned with strands of jasmine and he settled her in the back seat. The sound of the engine starting surprised her and she clenched her hands with sudden tension. Seated beside her he chuckled softly and forced her hands to unclench and she was shocked by the intimacy.

The house he took her to was in the inner city. It had a large central courtyard but no garden. Two other floors spiraled upward from here. The room on the second floor he took her to had a large bed decorated with garlands of flowers and a magnificent carpet. Covering almost the length of one wall was a gleaming teak armoire for clothes. She had never seen anything like it. There was a shelf with books in a corner. There was an ornate dressing table where a set of hairbrushes lay flanking a bottle of fragrance. A double set of windows opened out and all that could be seen was the central courtyard below.

She was then led up to a rooftop terrace where pigeons sat on the ledges. There was a large bird cage which held two parrots and another a pair of nightingales. There were three large clay containers with flowering plants. Her spirits lifted a little when she saw the jasmine bush and a miniature blooming wild rose.

When he had brought her back from the terrace to their room, he moved closer and playfully slid her head covering off.

"I wanted to see your hair, Inam. How long is it?"

She thought someone else was in the room, not recognizing the name he had used.

"I have changed your name. It will now be Inam. A prize. Because that is what I feel about you."

She promptly burst into tears. Her name was gone as was the garden she had grown up playing in. She hated birds in cages. And she felt that he was making fun of her. She knew there would be physical intimacy in the big bed and was frightened about what would happen. Perhaps the tears would repulse him and he would leave her alone. Instead he pulled out a large white handkerchief from the pocket of his tunic and made her sit on the edge of the bed and gently wiped her tears. So she continued to weep and he continued to smile as he dabbed her tears.

The woman in the penthouse was aghast at the empty frame. She blinked her eyes furiously and felt a chill invade her body on this summer night. Was it a mind game? The minute she saw the empty frame she had looked at the floor hoping that when she looked up again the frame would be filled. She sought refuge in humour and thought the young girl had gone for a walk and would return. Perhaps people in photographs were imprisoned and found a way to simply walk away. Yet nothing could make her look at the frame again, because she loved the girl in the photograph. Was it to be a sudden isolation thrust upon her without her permission?

The woman had recently taken up the practice of Vinyasa Yoga. It was a slow-paced easy flow of postures and meditative breathing techniques. One particular posture always made her relax to the point of feeling that she felt she was having an out-of-body experience, drifting to an altered state where her own physical dimensions dissolved. She lay on the carpet on the floor and held the posture and began a breathing exercise. From the forehead to the soles of her feet all body tension vanished. Her outstretched arms and legs were wide open and weightless. Then she thought she felt a drop of moisture fall on the palm of her right hand. She raised the palm to her lips and her tongue told her it was salty. A tear had been shed, she was convinced of it.

Inam sat at the dressing table trying to coil a large chignon at the nape of her neck. It was a tedious exercise, but her husband Jaffer had requested that she do this. It suited her better than the tight braid which dangled along her spine like the tail of an animal. When he boldly tucked a sprig of jasmine or a tiny rose in the chignon, the reflection in the mirror did not displease her. She thought she looked like the women in Persian miniature paintings that her uncle had shown her. But she fought each new ritual which this odd man who was her husband eased her into. He had a gentle authority and graceful manners that confused her. When she had released the pair of nightingales in the cage, he had simply sighed.

"Now you will have to sing twice a day just as the birds sang twice a day."

Her face turned red with embarrassment, but he laughed uproariously. He had asked her if she could cook and she told him she had never been interested. He suggested that she visit the ground floor kitchen and observe the cooking. She was expected to cook on special occasions.

"I want to eat what is cooked by your hands."

She found his ardour flattering and yet unsettling. He often took small trips which she assumed were for his work, but when he returned she could not stop the quiver of excitement that rippled through her.

Then she would immediately cook a special dish for him. Often it was a dessert. He would create a little ritual. He would make her have the first spoonful. He did this as though he were a parent feeding a child. As though all the fuss was for her and not him. There would be gifts which he would produce like a magician. A fountain pen with a bottle of ink and sheets of loose cream paper just appeared on her side of the dressing table.

"I have had a small table and chair placed on the terrace. You can write poetry there in peace."

The day she learned her status from an elderly maid in the house, she was so shocked that she could not utter a word. Her thirty-eight-year old husband had been married for fifteen years, had five children and maintained two homes. She was his second wife. She never recited a single poem for him after that day. His gifts to her lay unused in the teak armoire. Silently, she gave birth to two sons, repressing the fury that raged within her. She was afraid it would poison the milk in her breasts. Her contact with her own family became minimal and strained as she felt they had also concealed the fact from her. Despite the prevailing customs of her culture, she was gripped by two emotions: betrayal and injustice.

The woman had fallen asleep on the carpet. The bizarre night and her refuge in a yoga posture and falling asleep confounded her as she opened her eyes. She looked up at the wall and the young woman with dramatic eyebrows gazed back at her from the frame. So it was a dream and her imagination could no longer be trusted, she thought. There was no one she could share this experience with, except a psychiatrist she consulted from time to time. She felt this was crazy enough to have an informal chat with him. He had always encouraged her to communicate with him.

Later that day she pulled out a file folder from her papers. Inside was a hand-written family tree she had created under the supervision of the octogenarian cousin. It started with Jaffer, the great grandfather who had married twice and fashioned the tradition of changing a wife's name to suit the husband's fancies. Her own grandfather had done this to her grandmother and in an act of great arrogance chosen her name and her sister's name before they were born, before he died. Her own mother had bowed to this tradition and kept the two Persian names for her daughters. Then the young woman rifled through an album of vintage photographs of the women of her family. In the array of fashionable and traditional clothes and postures no one mirrored the clothing or ornamentation of Inam, the second wife of Jaffer. There was something wrong with that amazing portrait.

Women at the end of the eighteenth century did not pose in this bold fashion. Inam's cascading earrings made of jasmine and the profusion of rings and bracelets which she wore as well as the barbaric splendour of the necklace flowing down her chest was excessive. The pose itself, with one ankle crossing the other, as she stood leaning against a chair would have been by a contemporary model of the present era. The jewelry she wore was associated with dancers and not the wife of a lawyer.

The lawyer's son, the photographer, who had enlarged and circulated the photograph was dead, and when she questioned his wife whether the photograph had been retouched, the wife vehemently denied it. An entire extended family treasured this sole memory of the great grandmother. So she backed off in acceptance but remained conflicted.

She had a session with the psychiatrist.

"It was late at night. Was the frame truly empty? Had you had any alcohol or a sleeping pill that night?"

"No. I was wide awake. I was stunned and then frightened."

"Frightened? Why?"

"It was outside the limits of reality. Perhaps even supernatural."

His head jerked up and he gazed at her silently.

"You mean a hallucination? Or did you just imagine this. What is your relationship with this photograph?"

"I think we both watch each other," she blurted out.

He put the notepad away and faced her.

"Photographs are inanimate material not known to have physical movement. But you know that." A thin smile appeared on his face.

She was silently gathering her thoughts. He waited silently as well, superior in his knowledge that she would soon make an utterance which would drive the session along.

"I have a close link with her through my grandfather. She was his mother. So it's there. I think the photograph has been retouched, today we would call it photoshopped. I think it is fake. She is not fake, though."

"What do you think guided the person who did this?"

"I don't know, he was a photographer and quite feminine himself. He is no longer alive. It's a dead end, but I can't let go."

She was desperate she wanted him to unravel her mind and her behaviour.

When the session ended he seemed to have stimulated some

introspection. She had no idea where it would lead her. When she got home she stood in front of the framed photograph and did not move for a while.

"Is this a fake photograph?" she asked the impossibly beautiful face, gazing into the eyes. "I think you are dressed like a courtesan. Were you really his wife and the family records incorrect?"

The face just gazed back at her without revealing anything.

Inam was heavy with her second pregnancy and the antics of her older son who was three exhausted her. Jaffer had brought a special pair of baby shoes for Siraj. He told her they were replicas of shoes made by English shoemakers. They would keep the ankle firm and had excellent support. It was her duty to ensure that Siraj wore them daily despite his penchant for crying and kicking in protest. Jaffer was absent from the home more often now. When he returned he would bring back fine gifts. Inam wondered if this was due to his guilt or genuine affection. She did not have the courage to confront him outright and he never shared any details of his other family. It was half a life for her but a full one for him. These troubling thoughts crystallized into a knot of pain which had invaded her normally sunny disposition. She was growing older and bitter. Yet in front of Jaffer she behaved in the prescribed fashion. She was the model wife and now mother. In place of the birds a small hutch was built for a pair of rabbits that her toddlers played with. Instead of reading poetry she wrote a story and kept this a secret. When Jaffer was home she worked on embroidering a large tablecloth. If he was disappointed he did not reveal it, and instead he made the time to read to her from a large, heavily illustrated book containing the work of the Persian poet Rumi. She was taken by the reach of his stanzas. They appeared to have messages for life. She did not know that the Diwan e Shams, a book of quatrains, was inspired by Rumi's love and longing for Shams, who had died suddenly and mysteriously. Jaffer had chosen wisely, as the wife he had considered to be a prize had vanished. He thought perhaps she would listen to the quatrains of longing and return to him.

After her second child, another son, was born she avoided physical contact with Jaffer. The boy was named Miraj. At night, she would linger in Miraj's room. On the occasion that Jaffer reached for her she turned limp and unresponsive, and Jaffer was puzzled. For Inam, her husband had also become someone else. Yet the bonds of this marriage were traditions which were older than both of them. She had given him two sons and maintained a comfortable home, so she had not shirked her duties. There was no rule that stipulated she had to share what was in her heart with him or anyone else.

The woman in the apartment decided to embark on a trip to the city where Jaffer had brought Inam as his bride. The old section of the city still existed and Jaffer's central courtyard home had an intact ground floor, though the upper two floors were in ruins. An elderly family member consented to escort her, amused by her great interest. He told her she was at least a hundred years too late. The family no longer owned the property and some very poor relatives lived as squatters in the two rooms on the main floor. They did not mind visitors. She walked through a laneway that would permit space for only two people to walk side by side or a bicycle. The houses on either sides had walls and doors facing the lane, and the sun hardly filtered inside.

In front of her stood a dark wooden door with some embellishments of brass turned dark with age. Crude plaster covered the walls on either side of the door. On the right side a chunk of plaster had parted and through it a sliver of red brick was visible. The sight of this three-inch section of brick stunned her. The home had withstood time, and Inam's history had not perished. She felt her heart race with excitement so she pulled the door to open it and stepped in.

In the darkened vestibule a man greeted her and tried to lead her further inside, but she resisted and went on to reach the courtyard. Only windows remained on the ruined two upper floors and they were more like arches. The roof was missing. She wanted to see the ghosts of her ancestors reciting poetry in this courtyard. She wanted to hear Inam's bracelets and anklets tinkling and nightingales singing. The man walked behind her and kept repeating,

"There is nothing here. The municipality sends notices to demolish it, but we manage in the two rooms. We don't let them inside. But we will have to go soon."

"There was a woman, my great grandmother, she came to this house." She could feel tears gather in her eyes.

His face turned blank. It was obvious he had no inkling about the history of the family who had owned this house.

"My wife has made some tea for you. Come inside please," he tugged at her arm.

Inam knew Jaffer had something in his mind. He told her he was expecting his nephew, who had returned from studying in Europe for many years. Preparations had to be made. She was to be dressed formally. Then he went to his side of the armoire and brought out two velvet boxes. He placed them on the bed and asked her to open them. The old maid was to take both the boys to the rooftop and keep them there. Inam knew her older son Siraj would be happy playing with the rabbits but the younger one, Miraj, clung to her and disliked the maid. Jaffer had his stern authoritarian air. The one he used in court as a lawyer. Inam knew she could not disobey him. She heard her younger son's wail pierce the house as he was carried upstairs, and she hated Jaffer at that moment. There had been no time to give the maid an extra lump of brown sugar with nuts which both her sons loved. It was called gurh and was a popular confectionary of the region.

Jaffer told her to open the boxes. She opened one and was stunned to see an ornate gold necklace with medallions of pure gold fashioned like leaves. The second box had heavy ankle bracelets and bracelets with rings. The gold jewelry blazed like a king's treasure in the bedroom.

"I want you to select clothes over which this jewelry will sit well. Wear white, please." He walked out of the room.

Inam was curious about the jewelry, particularly the heavy anklets. She put them on and stepped on the carpet by the bed. She was dying to see her reflection, but the oval-shaped mirror above the dressing table only revealed her head and shoulders. Was he taking her to a wedding somewhere? It was clear that there was a purpose to this. Why was the nephew so important that she had to be dressed in such a fashion.

She did not change her clothes but draped a diaphanous length of white fabric over half her hair and shoulders. The necklace was partly concealed but the lower medallions were visible. She slipped the rings and bracelets on but there were no earrings. She knew she could remedy that and lifted the strands of jasmine lying in a saucer of water on the dressing table and threaded them around her ear lobes. The effect was dramatic as they cascaded down, brushing her cheeks. She had turned away from the mirror and had no idea of the effect. The brocade shoes with turned-up toes were big for her feet but she slipped them on anyway.

Ten minutes later, Jaffer's nephew entered behind Jaffer. Both men were transfixed. The nephew held a camera in his hand.

"Please let her stand. Maybe against the chair," he pointed to the narrow chair with a cane seat and a simple curved frame.

"Inam," said Jaffer, "let's make you immortal. You will never be forgotten."

The woman had spent only twenty minutes in the ruins of the house. Although she longed to go to the second floor, the stairs had disintegrated. The rooftop terrace had vanished.

She left the home and the city and returned to her own home. Her project had collapsed, and along with it, her obsession. She changed the position of the framed portrait and placed it in an alcove like an afterthought.

Then the call came from a visiting academic in New York. He wondered if she had any copies of her grandfather Siraj's poetry. They met for coffee.

"He held a literary salon in Sialkot. Poets recited their work and he presided. He was quite instrumental in promoting poetry in the region and always thanked his mother for that."

He chuckled. "His father was a lawyer and quite notorious."

"Notorious? Why?"

"There was some scandal about a courtesan he married whom he kept hidden."

"She is not hidden anymore," the woman spoke, choosing her words carefully. "Come for lunch tomorrow and I shall introduce you to her."

Acknowledgements

I did not bake sourdough bread, learn to make masks, or watch videos on how to wash hands during Covid. I experimented with the short-story format in fiction and wrote this book. My agent Anne Confuron, who is French, diplomatically stated that although there was praise for content and style from publishers, somehow the book did not fit their lists. Short stories did not sell in France. Canada, however, thought otherwise.

I thank the literary savvy of my long-time pal Margaret Atwood who asked a year ago that I send her my best story and she would bring it to the attention of the editor of *Walrus* magazine. I sent her two and the one she chose brought an instant response. The editorial team at the magazine said "Wow" and announced they would publish it in their upcoming issue. The lovely payment was forwarded instantly. My confidence shot up and I knew the stories would find a home.

I thank the brave publisher Nurjehan Aziz of Mawenzi House for offering a contract and the services of her mystery star editor. The editorial process was cause for hilarity and accompanied by some ferocious teeth gnashing. The polish of the manuscript relies on the talent of my multiple award-winning author/editor. The only people I take orders are from my editors.

There are a host of usual suspects who hand-held and managed some of my life crises well. For this I wish to thank Jonathan Bashinsky for his "life line," Dr Alexis Arlis Harlan Martin of California, Rollin Bredenberg of Texas for keeping trains and people on track, Dr Steven

Connell "Merlin" who takes care of my soul, Jon Slan for being his fabulous self, and Khalid Usman and Anwar Saifullah Khan for their enthusiasm for my work and timely e-transfers for emergencies. Many thanks to my technical wizard, Kia Nader of Rosedale Computers for rescuing me from glitches.

I also appreciate the Toronto Arts Council, the Toronto Arts Awards, and the Ontario Arts Council for their writing grants.

Finally, I wish to thank my sister Mahjabin for enduring the slings and arrows of sibling angst with fortitude and grace.